Fateful Revenge

JANE BLYTHE

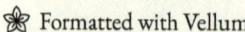 Formatted with Vellum

Acknowledgments

I'd like to thank everyone who played a part in bringing this story to life. Particularly my mom who is always there to share her thoughts and opinions with me. My wonderful cover designer Letitia who did an amazing job with this stunning cover. My fabulous editor Lisa for all the hard work she puts into polishing my work. My awesome team, Sophie, Robyn, and Clayr, without your help I'd never be able to run my street team. And my fantastic street team members who help share my books with every share, comment, and like!

And of course a big thank you to all of you, my readers! Without you I wouldn't be living my dreams of sharing the stories in my head with the world!

CHAPTER One

January 3rd
    5:11 P.M.

The list of crimes he was guilty of was growing.

All the things he'd feared for so many years had come to fruition. All the reasons it was best for him to stay away from people, to shove them out of his life with a ruthlessness his cold-hearted parents would have been proud of, had turned out to be true.

All the reasons he'd given up on Cassandra Charleston proved true.

Dragon stared at the tablet he clutched in his hands as he watched footage from a CCTV camera. It was almost impossible to drag his eyes away from the woman on the screen. Not only was she drop-dead gorgeous, but she was one of the strongest people he had ever met in his life. Given that he'd gone through rigorous special ops training, that was saying something.

Even after all the revelations of who she was and what had happened to her parents, in part because of her very existence, Cassandra still stood tall and proud. She hadn't crumpled and fallen apart after learning she'd been conceived when her mother had been gang raped. Or when she learned that the man she considered her father had been targeted and killed along with his SEAL team to set up her mother as a traitor. Or when she learned that her mom and stepdad had been arrested and killed to shut them up, so the truth could never come out.

Her entire life had been upended, and yet she kept moving forward, putting one foot in front of the other, as she figured out what she wanted the rest of her life to look like.

With the maturity and grace with which she'd handled finding out the horrific truth, Cassandra seemed so much older than her twenty-four years.

But he'd smelled the tears she shed in the middle of the night when she thought no one was paying attention.

"I hear you, Cassandra, I see you," he murmured as he watched her cross the street.

As though she somehow heard his words, she suddenly looked up, checking all around her to see who had spoken. It wasn't possible that she'd heard him speak, several states were between them, and even if he'd been close by, he wouldn't have let on that he'd intruded in her quiet moments of weakness by standing outside her bedroom door.

Those months that Cassandra had stayed with them had changed something inside him.

Something he had fought tooth and nail against.

"Keep moving, little rabbit," he urged when he saw that Cassandra was still standing in the middle of the street. "Don't want you to get hurt." She needed to finish crossing the street before the traffic started moving.

Thankfully, the universe somehow pushed those words into her mind because she shook her head as though to clear it, then quickly crossed to the other side of the street just as the lights turned green and traffic began to roll.

Since he was watching her through a camera, he couldn't get a clear shot of her face, couldn't stare into her light green eyes, couldn't see her long chestnut locks that were tucked beneath a beanie. With her bulky winter coat, he couldn't get a clear view of her soft curves and slim legs. Cassandra was a vision, and he'd been hooked the moment he first laid eyes on her.

"Why couldn't you have been more like Steel?" Dragon asked himself, but the too-silent room offered no answer as he watched Cassandra disappear inside a store.

There was another woman with green eyes he was forced to offer begrudging respect to. Rose Gardner was the younger sister of the man who had played God with their lives. Ridge Gardner had turned them into monsters and cost him the future he could have had with Cassandra if he didn't sicken and terrify her.

Using Rose was supposed to be easy. Abduct her, terrify her into breaking, video it all, and send it to her brother to lure the cowardly scientist into a trap.

It all would have worked if Rose hadn't turned out to be a little bit psycho, too.

The crazy woman had turned their plans on their heads, and in doing so, she'd bought herself a reprieve when their team leader fell for her. Despite Steel's attachment to the woman, Dragon still would have been prepared to follow through with their plans, but he'd been outvoted and threatened that if he laid a single hand on Rose, he'd not only lose it but his life as well.

Taking out his anger on Rose for losing Cassandra because of their plan to use Rose wouldn't have been fair, but it hardly seemed fair either that Steel and his little ladybug had gotten their happy ending while he sat in his room alone. Right now, the couple was downstairs getting tattoos to mark each other as theirs.

The thing was, even with the jealousy coursing through his veins, he was happy that Steel had found love. Happy even for Rose, who had suffered more at the hands of her deranged brother than any one of them. She'd put her life on the line to help them get revenge and almost lost it.

Her brother might be on the run again, slithering back under whatever rock he had been hiding under, but they were going to find him. When they did, the man's screams would soothe that fury that raged inside him every second of the day.

Most days, Dragon could barely keep it under control.

The only reprieve he'd had in the last decade was the months when

Cassandra's warm spirit filled the cold, dark rooms of the Gothic mansion where he and his team lived.

Even after the threat against the Charleston Holloway family had been eliminated, Cassandra had chosen to stay. He knew it was because of him and the attraction that hummed between them. There had been no more than a single kiss shared between them, but it had been all it took for him to know that she was his.

His, and yet he'd allowed her to walk away without a fight.

She'd known that he and his team were planning something that would turn them into the monsters they'd always feared they were. She just hadn't known it was abducting Dr. Gardner's innocent little sister.

Without even knowing the details, she'd looked at him with disgust and betrayal, like he wasn't the man she'd thought he was.

"Tried to warn you I was a monster and not good enough for you, little rabbit," he said as Cassandra appeared on the screen again. "You saw something in me that doesn't exist, and once you realized that, you left."

Not just left, but left with an ultimatum.

Trust Prey to help them get their revenge and not give into the darkness that wanted to claim him, or she'd leave and never see him again.

What did it say about him that he'd chosen vengeance over redemption?

Steel hadn't. He'd chosen Rose over her psychopath brother. Instead of focusing on finding Ridge Gardner when he'd taken Rose and run, ensuring that the doctor would now be locked up in their basement, enjoying Delta Team's special brand of hospitality, he'd put Rose's life first.

Why hadn't he been strong enough to do the same with Cassandra?

Already she hated him, thought he was a twisted monster. How much more would she hate him if she knew he'd kidnapped an innocent woman, participated in torturing her, and continued to threaten her life even when it was clear one of the men he considered a brother had caught feelings for her?

Even though Cassandra was hiding it from everyone she loved, he knew she was struggling. And since he spent hours a day watching her,

Dragon knew she would be heading home now, ready to change into running clothes and head to the local park for her daily run.

He hated that she was alone, so vulnerable, an easy target.

It was winter, and it was already dark by the time she got to the park. Knowing she was so exposed out there, and he couldn't properly watch over her because there weren't any cameras inside the park was hell.

Didn't she know how many evil people lived in the world?

If anyone should know that, it was Cassandra. Her own biological father was the reason behind all the hell her family had lived through. He wished she would take her safety more seriously. If she needed to go running, she had a new half-sister, or five new almost sisters-in-law who would go with her.

"Why do you have to be so stubborn?" he asked the screen as he switched to a different camera to follow her journey home.

Watching over her like this wasn't any real protection. If something happened to her, he couldn't get to her in time to save her. Even calling one of her six brothers who all lived close to her wouldn't get her help in time.

Minutes ticked by as he watched her get home, disappear inside for a short time, then come back out. She drove to the park, and when he watched her climb out of the car, he felt that familiar ball of tension tighten in his gut.

So damn vulnerable.

Like he did whenever he could, he sat there, watching the camera by her car and waited until she was safely back inside it. Then he followed her journey home. Dragon was so deep in stalker territory he had no hope of digging himself back out.

Nor did he want to.

As he watched Cassandra park and climb out of her car, he noticed a shadowy figure in black approach her, and the bottom dropped out of his world as his worst fears sprang to life in front of him, while he was powerless to do anything about it.

~

January 3rd

7:19 P.M.

All day, she'd felt like she was being watched.

Not just all day, Cassandra Charleston thought with a shiver as she parked her car in the small parking lot of the local park. Ever since she'd walked away from Dragon and the rest of Prey Security's Delta Team, she would have sworn that someone was monitoring her every move.

Well, not really *someone*. Cassandra knew exactly who was watching her.

Dragon.

The man had caught her attention the very first time she'd met him. Something in his unusual violet eyes called to her. That was years ago, before she'd gone to stay with the team while someone was targeting her family. As soon as she was permanently in his orbit, there had been no hope.

Bit by bit, she felt herself getting pulled into his larger-than-life presence.

There was no charm, Dragon wouldn't know charm if it came up to bite him on his deliciously toned butt. But she didn't need charm. All she wanted was someone who could see her.

Not the baby of the Charleston Holloway family.

Not the young woman who had been conceived via rape.

Not the girl who was the cause of all her family's suffering.

Not the person others tiptoed around because they were worried about upsetting.

And definitely not someone who had shot and killed her own father.

Somehow, Dragon saw beneath all of that. He was as gruff and grumpy with her as he was with everybody else, but she caught the little looks he sent her way when he thought she wasn't looking. He looked at her like he'd spent the last year in a desert, and she was a glass of cold water.

Like she could give him something no one else could, and it was a heady feeling for someone who had always been seen as the helpless baby to six overprotective big brothers. There had definitely been a time when she had played up to that role in the family, but that was when she was younger. Now that she was all grown up, twenty-four years old, she wanted to stand on her own two feet, wanted to find what she had of value to offer to the world and find her place in it.

For a while there ... she'd been sure there could be something real building between her and Dragon.

It certainly felt real.

But then he'd chosen a path that she couldn't in good conscience support, so she'd had no choice but to leave.

And now here she was, drifting through life with nothing to anchor her, feeling like one strong gust of wind could send her flying off into space. Each day felt more pointless than the one before. What was she doing? What did she want out of life?

Who was Cassandra Charleston?

With a sigh, she shoved her hands into a pair of gloves, tugged on a beanie, and wrapped a scarf around her neck, tucking it into her sweater. These nightly runs were her way of clearing her mind or at least trying to.

In reality, it usually wound up more clogged than when she'd begun.

It felt like she was never going to find her way out of the maze life had dumped her in the middle of. How was one supposed to learn at twenty-four that your father wasn't really your father, that your mom had been gang raped, and once her assailants found out about the pregnancy, targeted her husband and his team, then had her locked up and faked her suicide, and know who you were?

The fact that she'd killed her biological father didn't even bother her.

He'd deserved to die, and she didn't regret what she'd done.

Pushing open her car door, she climbed out, enjoying the sting of the icy air against the exposed skin of her face. Maybe it wasn't really the fact that she could pretend she was clearing her mind with her runs that she enjoyed them so much, maybe it was really because the cold air was the only thing she felt all day that she knew without a shadow of a doubt was real.

While well-meaning, her six brothers and their girlfriends and fiancées hovered around her constantly. They were always checking in to make sure she was okay, which she appreciated because she knew it came from love, but it was utterly exhausting. Between pretending she was handling everything better than she was, and the doubts about her own emotions, she struggled to read herself accurately.

Should she be more upset about shooting a man? Did her paternity really change who she was as a person? Should she have been so tough on Dragon?

Cassandra didn't know all the details because Dragon and the guys were pretty tight-lipped about their pasts, but she knew enough to know the revenge those six men craved was well deserved.

"I get that," she whispered, looking around, still feeling eyes on her and assuming it was Dragon somehow hacked into CCTV cameras watching her. "But you did it the wrong way. I couldn't stand by and be part of that. I don't need any other black marks on my soul. Why couldn't you have listened? Why couldn't you have chosen a different path?"

Knowing she was never going to get answers to those questions, she took off for the entrance to the park. Even if she went back to the Gothic mansion where Delta Team lived, she wasn't going to get any real answers. Dragon wouldn't discuss anything with her, even though at times it felt like he truly saw her—maybe even better than she saw herself—at other times, he still fell into that same hole as everyone else and wanted to protect her.

"I don't need protecting."

No sooner had she muttered the words than a figure came rushing up toward her.

Startled, Cassandra let out a shriek that her brothers would never let her forget if they'd heard her, and stumbled back a step as a woman dressed all in black stood close by.

Blue eyes watched her warily, flaring with fear, and a lock of blonde hair escaped from a black beanie pulled low on the woman's head. The stranger looked to be about her age, and Cassandra wondered if something had happened to her. Had the woman been attacked?

"Are you Cassandra?" the woman whispered.

Ice flooded her veins. This wasn't random. This woman hadn't been hurt. She was there specifically looking for her. "Who are you?" she asked, taking another step back.

The woman's hand darted out, grabbing her wrist. "Wait! Please." Gaze darting around nervously, like she expected the bogeyman to come jumping out at any second, the woman dragged in a few breaths. "I need to tell you about Dr. Gardner."

"Who?" She didn't know a Dr. Gardner. She didn't know any doctors well enough that someone would accost her in a park to talk about them.

Faltering slightly, doubt crept into the woman's eyes. "You're Cassandra Charleston, right? Your brothers work for Prey?"

"Y-yes." Maybe agreeing wasn't the best move, but she didn't think the woman was there to hurt her. If the stranger had wanted her dead, she would have just killed her, not come up to her to talk.

"You know them, right? Steel and the others?"

Was this about Dragon and his team? Why was someone approaching her about those guys? How did someone even know she knew them? "I know them," she whispered.

A breath whooshed out of the woman. "Good. They need to know that Dr. Gardner won't ever stop coming for them. He needs them. He's kept working on his experiments, but they never turn out the same way. The drugs destroy them mentally and they devolve quickly. No matter what he tries, he can't get another team of men to survive. They also need to know that he has an antidote. Something he thinks will undo what he did. He wants to get them so he can give them the reversal drugs and then inject them all over again to see if he can figure out why they're different. But ... I don't think they can survive that. They can't let themselves get caught. Please, tell them. Tell them they have to be careful. Their lives depend on it. They won't just be held captive again, have tests run on them, they'll lose their lives."

It was dark out, the woman illuminated only in the glow of a street-lamp, but Cassandra would have sworn she saw tears shimmer in the other woman's eyes before she turned and hurried away.

"Wait!" Cassandra yelled, hurrying after her, a million questions running through her mind along with fear for the man who had wriggled his way underneath her skin.

Picking up her pace instead of slowing, the other woman jumped into the driver's seat of a vehicle parked nearby. Right where she would have gotten a good view of the parking lot, waiting for Cassandra to arrive. Somehow, this woman knew more about what had happened to Dragon and his team than she did. She knew they worked for Prey and about Cassandra's connection to Prey and the team.

How on earth did she know all of that?

Who was this mysterious woman?

Answers disappeared along with her as the blonde's car tore off down the street.

CHAPTER Two

January 3rd
9:57 P.M.

For hours, he'd been pacing his room.

Trying to figure out what he should do.

What the hell had he seen?

Dragon's gaze slid to the discarded tablet that lay on his bed. At first, he'd thought Cassandra was about to be attacked or abducted. His heart had raced so fast he wouldn't have been surprised to see it beat its way right out of his chest, and his pulse had pounded in his ears until it was almost deafening.

All he'd been able to smell was his own fear.

But no one had laid a hand on Cassandra.

When he calmed himself enough to look carefully at what he was seeing, he'd realized that the person dressed all in black was a woman.

A friend?

No, Cassandra's body language said she didn't know the woman, and while it was tense, it wasn't radiating terror.

Scenarios began to tick through his mind, and he wondered if perhaps Cassandra was buying drugs. It could account for her being tense but not afraid when she was approached in the empty parking lot.

But that was just his anxiety talking. He knew she wasn't handling everything that had happened last year as well as she wanted others to believe, but she wouldn't take drugs to cope. She kept her sunny disposition firmly in place, she acted like she wasn't sobbing inside, and pretended that she wasn't as deeply affected by the revelations about her paternity as she was.

If it wasn't for his ability to smell emotions in people, much like a dog was capable of knowing when you were sad and needed their love and attention, then he probably would have believed her lies.

"I see you, little rabbit," he murmured, still watching the tablet as though it would give him the answers he craved.

But it wouldn't.

After their brief exchange, the woman in black had run off. Cassandra had briefly followed but then turned and headed into the park. He'd watched her complete her run and then climb back into her car and return to her home.

Should he contact one of her brothers and let them know she was up to something?

It would be a massive violation of her trust. While they hadn't talked about him knowing she wasn't as okay as she wanted everyone to believe she was, they both knew that he knew it. Talking wasn't his thing, never had been. Of all of the six Delta Team guys, he was the most sullen, had the worst temper, and was the least likely to be of any help to anyone if they didn't need saving from something.

What Cassandra needed saving from wasn't something he could destroy. It was something inside her, something only she could battle.

Yet she seemed to find comfort in his presence, and if he called one of her brothers and told them he was worried about her, it would ruin the tentative trust they'd built.

Shatter whatever was left of it after she confronted him with Delta Team's plans and told him that if he went down that path, she couldn't be part of it and asked to be flown back home to join her family.

Still, if she was doing drugs, and he didn't do something to try to stop her, he would be partially responsible for whatever happened to her next. What if she spiraled? What if she got addicted? If she wasn't already that was. What if she wound up losing her job and her home, living on the streets, a junkie whose only focus was their next hit?

What if she wound up dead?

What if *he* was the one spiraling? That probably made more sense.

But if she was in trouble and he didn't do something, he'd never forgive himself. After all it wasn't like he could really ruin her trust in him more than it already had been. She'd already walked away from him. And he'd let her.

Knowing he didn't have a choice, Dragon went to pick up his phone. Cassandra already hated him, and if this could help her, he'd take whatever anger she wanted to throw at him. If he was wrong and he hadn't witnessed a drug buy, then it wasn't like she could loathe him more than she already did. She might be embarrassed and annoyed that her family would then be on to the fact that she was struggling, but at least she'd be safe.

And maybe she needed the people in her life to know she wasn't okay.

Just because her brothers had all been through hell this last year as they followed revelation after revelation to find the people behind what had happened to their parents didn't mean they wouldn't want to be there for her. Cassandra seemed to have it in her head that her brothers and their new girlfriends and fiancées shouldn't need to be bothered by her struggles, so she kept them bottled up tight.

Only Dragon didn't think her family would see being there for her as a bother.

Scooping up his phone, he scrolled through the contacts until he found Cade Charleston's number. Cade was the oldest of the four Charleston and two Holloway brothers, and while the man was busy with his five-year-old daughter, and pregnant fiancée, Dragon knew he wouldn't hesitate to go straight to Cassandra and ensure she was okay. Even if that meant forcing her to take a drug test and putting her in rehab against her wishes.

Right as he was about to touch his finger to Cade's name, his phone began to ring.

Cassandra.

Talk about a coincidence.

Maybe this was her first drug buy, and she realized once she got home that she didn't want to go down this path and decided to reach out to someone. But why would that someone be him? She hated him, and she knew that he and his team had gone ahead with their plans, she just didn't know that things had changed, and their hostage had turned into an ally who was now getting Steel's teeth marks tattooed onto her breast.

Nerves hit him as he accepted the call. What Dr. Gardner had done to them with his experimental drugs hadn't just given him and his team-mates enhanced skills, it had also messed with their ability to feel and process emotions. The crazed scientist's goal had been to strip them of a conscience so they would become his perfect team of killing machines.

For the last decade, Dragon and the others had believed it to have worked.

Only Lion couldn't let go of the woman from his past he'd been forced to leave behind, Steel had fallen for the woman they'd abducted to use as bait, and he himself had become attached to Cassandra.

"Dragon," Cassandra said the second she must have heard the call connect.

Something in her voice scared him. She sounded worse than he'd been expecting, but she didn't sound high. Hopefully, that meant she'd called him before she took the drugs.

"Are you there?" she asked when he didn't say anything.

"I'm here." Should he tell her he'd been watching her this evening when she met with someone at the park or wait for her to bring it up?

"I met this woman today," she said in a rush, like she couldn't get the words out quickly enough.

He also wanted her to get them out so he could tell her that taking drugs wasn't the answer. Admitting she had a problem was the first step in figuring things out.

"She came up to me at the park. I'd been feeling all day like someone was watching me—"

"That was me," he inserted, not wanting to add to any paranoia she might be feeling.

"I know you've been watching me, Dragon, or at least I suspected.

This was different. It felt different. When I feel eyes on me and I think it's you, I usually feel ... safe. Today I didn't. I can't explain it, it just felt ... wrong."

Anxiety hummed inside him. There was no denying that he'd gotten a buzz when she told him that she knew he'd been watching her and it made her feel safe, but the rest ... he had no way to tell if it was drug-induced paranoia or real unless he was there to smell the pheromones she was giving off. Even then, it would be partially up to his judgment as to how to read them.

"She said that someone called Dr. Gardner is angry that all the other people he tested his drugs on died. That you and your team are the only ones left."

Those words had him straightening.

There was no way that Cassandra should know the name Dr. Gardner.

They'd only learned the name of the scientist who had played God with their lives a couple of months ago. As far as he knew, the only people who were aware of the man's name were Eagle, his wife Olivia, who had managed to find the name after years of searching for it, and the members of his team.

Paranoia, drug-induced or otherwise, couldn't supply Cassandra with that intel.

"She said you guys are the only survivors, and that Dr. Gardner wants you back so he can figure out what makes you different," Cassandra continued.

That was something they already knew. The insane scientist would do anything he could to get his hands on them again. It was why he and his team had been in hiding these last seven years after they managed to escape the facility where they'd been held captive for three hellishly long years.

"Dragon, that's not all she said." Cassandra's voice was brimming with fear now. "She said you need to know he has an antidote, something that is supposed to undo everything he did to you."

For a second, it felt like the earth stopped spinning.

An antidote?

A way to take it all back, go back to who he'd been before?

The key to living a normal life, maybe even getting a chance at making things right with Cassandra.

"She said that Dr. Gardner plans on giving you the antidote, studying you, then doing whatever he did to you the first time around all over again." Cassandra's voice had dropped to the mere hint of a whisper. "Dragon, this woman doesn't think you'll survive if he does that. She said you can't let him get you because if he does, then you'll all lose your lives."

∾

January 3rd
    10:10 P.M.

Her hands were shaking as she set her phone down.

So badly, Cassandra almost dropped it on the floor of her room.

Why couldn't she be as strong on the inside as she pretended to be on the outside?

It took a lot of energy pretending to be strong all the time, to have it all together, to act like she wasn't absolutely shattered inside after learning how she'd been conceived and the chain of events it had set off.

If she didn't exist, would her mom still be alive?

The fact that she existed, living, breathing proof of the gang rape, that the people involved decided to use their connections to target the man she'd thought of as her father and had his SEAL team killed. That allowed them to frame her mom and stepdad, the only man who had survived the ambush that killed the rest of the SEAL team. The two had been arrested and then suicides staged, designed to put an end to the whole issue.

Only it wasn't the end.

Because her brothers wouldn't let it go. They'd dedicated their entire lives to searching for the truth, and while she was glad they'd found it and got justice for their parents, it had stolen so much of their lives from them.

Sure, they were happy now, all paired up, dating the women who had captured their hearts, planning out the rest of their lives, but still, Cassandra couldn't help but feel like her existence had made so many people's lives worse.

There had to be a way to undo some of the bad her existence had caused, and calling Dragon to warn him about what the woman in black had told her might edge her a little closer to that goal.

Calling him hadn't been easy, though.

Cassandra had been falling in love with that man. Drawn in by the pain in his eyes, the way he held himself apart, even from his team, like he didn't deserve to have any comfort, any connection. She'd noticed it those first few days she stayed with the guys, and she'd decided that while she was there hiding out as her brothers risked their lives to save hers, she could try her best to help him however she could.

Not that she'd ever expected it to grow into anything more.

But it had.

If he had just listened to her, understood that he wasn't a monster and never had been, no matter what had been done to him, then maybe those sparks she felt could have grown into something more.

There had been nothing else to do each day but spend time with the guys. Founder and CEO of Prey Security, Eagle Oswald, hadn't sent out Delta Team on any ops while she was staying there, their job had been to protect her, and while all the guys were polite and nice to her, she'd been drawn into Dragon's orbit and couldn't seem to get out of it.

Hadn't wanted to.

Not until she figured out they were planning something she feared would turn them into the monsters she knew they saw themselves to be.

"Why couldn't you have just listened to me?" she whispered, staring at the phone sitting beside her on her bed. Her feelings for the mysterious man with the unusual dark blue eyes that appeared violet couldn't just be turned off like a switch. They existed despite the fact that he'd chosen to try to get revenge for what had been done to his team, over seeing if there could be something real and beautiful between them.

Still, what was done was done.

There was no going back.

She'd left, come back home, was trying to rebuild her life while keeping her sunny disposition, something that felt more and more like a mask with each passing day, and trying to figure out how to not feel like she was drowning in emotion she couldn't express.

That her family loved her was never in doubt, they'd do anything for her. They *had* done anything for her. They'd put their very lives on the line to find out who was behind the threats to their family and protect her. She loved every one of them with her entire being, so why couldn't she let them know how badly she was struggling?

Every time she opened her mouth, determined that she had to let someone in before she drowned, she couldn't seem to get the words out. It was like they got clogged in her throat, stuck there, and her mind conjured up a million reasons why telling anyone that she felt lost, adrift, and uncertain of who she was anymore was the wrong move.

When the phone beside her began to ring, Cassandra gave a weary sigh as she looked down at it.

Half expecting to see Dragon's name on the screen, she was disappointed when she saw it was Monique instead. Not that she didn't love her recently discovered half-sister, because she absolutely adored the woman, but she'd thought Dragon might have reached out, even if it was just for more information on her encounter with the woman. Not that she had anything else to give him, but she was desperate for a little more time with the only person who she felt understood that she wasn't as okay as she pretended to be.

Which annoyed her.

Dragon wasn't in her life anymore. Reaching out to him had been the right thing to do, even if she'd debated that with herself during her run. He'd hardly said two words to her on the phone call, barked out a few questions, then hung up once she'd answered them without even a thank you.

"What did you ever see in him?" she asked herself as she picked up her phone, knowing that if she didn't answer, Monique would just come over to check on her.

That particular question didn't have an answer anyway. Who you developed feelings for rarely did. It was the craziest thing, one day you were just going about your life, and the next, you couldn't stop thinking about a huge man with dark hair, the most stunning pair of eyes, a body you couldn't not drool over, and a damaged soul he hid from the world like it was his purpose for existing.

"Hey," she said, injecting sunshine into her tone even though it felt like she was drowning in a storm of rain, hail, and sleet.

"Hey, yourself," Monique's breezy voice came down the line.

Even though they were half-sisters, sharing a father but different mothers, they were a lot alike. They both had sunny personalities, both looked for the best in others, and both took their circumstances and made them into something good, even when it was hard. They had more in common than that, their father was responsible for the deaths of their mothers, and they'd both been in the room when he died. Although she was the one to pull the trigger, she knew her sister would have if given half a chance after learning her mom hadn't abandoned her, but instead, had been killed when she tried to leave with Monique.

Finding her half-sister had been the best thing to come out of the whole ordeal of finding the truth of what happened to her parents, even if she had wanted to shake Monique when they'd first met, and beg her to hand over DNA so they had proof they were sisters and her father was involved. It had taken her sister a little while to accept the truth, which was no wonder since Cassandra's stepbrother Jax had set out to use her to get to her dad. The two had worked through it, and they were now together and deeply in love.

She was surrounded by happy couples, and that made being alone so much worse.

"You there?" Monique's voice asked, a thread of concern in it, and Cassandra realized she was zoning out.

"Yeah, I'm here, sorry, it's just been a crazy evening," she admitted. While Monique knew that she had caught feelings for one of the enigmatic Delta Team men, she hadn't let on that the reason she'd decided to walk away was because of Dragon's choice to do something he couldn't come back from. Her sister just thought things hadn't worked out, and she wanted to keep it that way, no need to make the Delta guys look bad in front of the rest of the Prey family. She truly understood they had good reason to want revenge, even more so after what she'd learned tonight.

"Ooh, that sounds juicy," Monique said, and she could practically see the warm smile on her sister's pretty face, the interest in her gray eyes. "Want to share? Did you meet someone?"

Since she knew that it wouldn't take long for the intel to spread through Prey, the guys could be the worst gossips she'd ever met, she decided there was no harm in answering. "No, not the way you mean anyway. Someone came up to me because they somehow knew that I was connected to Dragon and the guys. They wanted to warn the guys that someone is after them."

"Oh no," Monique said quickly, and she knew that her sister had grown close to Dragon's teammate, Lion. Well, as close as you could get to these guys anyway. "I should call Lion when I finish talking to you, make sure he's okay. Are you okay? This person didn't hurt you, did they?"

"I'm fine," Cassandra rushed to assure her sister. The last thing she wanted was anyone worrying about her. "I called Dragon to tell him what she said, and I guess the guys will handle it. I didn't really understand much of what she was talking about, but Dragon did."

"You were okay talking to him?"

"Totally. Sure, I had some feelings for him, but sometimes things just don't work out. It's no big deal, I'm just glad this woman came to me so I could warn him, but it didn't bother me talking to him," she lied.

What was another lie between family?

They already didn't know she felt like she was dying inside, so they certainly didn't need to know that it felt like sticking a knife through her chest to know that while she was grieving a relationship that never even got off the ground, Dragon didn't miss her at all.

CHAPTER
Three

January 3rd
   10:19 P.M.

So many things were running through his head that Dragon didn't even remember ending the call to Cassandra. The next thing he knew, he was barreling into the living room where the others were all strewn about, watching Rose get her tattoo.

"It's Cassandra," he blurted out. "She just called me. Something's wrong."

That immediately captured everyone's attention, and all eyes turned on him.

"What happened?" Steel asked as he sat up from where he'd been lying tucked against the back of the couch, his head resting on Rose's bare stomach as Lion worked on the tattoo.

Worried as he was about Cassandra and someone knowing of her connection to them, he still had a moment of surprise that possessive, obsessive Steel was allowing everyone in the room to see Rose half-naked. They'd seen the woman completely naked already when they first abducted her and locked her in one of the cells in the basement. To try to torture her into cracking so they could send a video of her to her brother, Dr. Ridge Gardner, they'd pumped hot air into the room, unprepared to see their captive just strip and suck it up without complaint.

Even back then, it had been obvious that Steel was affected by his little ladybug, but the man had always been a good team leader. Always tried to put them first, even if he blamed himself for not figuring out sooner that Dr. Gardner wasn't being completely honest with them about the experimental program they'd signed up for.

But none of them had seen it.

They'd all been too excited about the prospect of getting enhanced skills that would make them better than everybody else. They'd been cocky young men only seeing the small picture, not the big one. Because if they'd been looking closer, they would have seen that Dr. Gardner was nothing more than a crazed scientist with delusions of grandeur.

"Someone approached Cassandra when she was going out on her nightly run." There was no point in pretending that he hadn't been stalking the hell out of the woman he'd been drawn to when she was staying with them.

"Approached her?" Blade asked.

"Because of us. About us," he explained, hardly able to put anything into words because emotion was throbbing inside him. More emotion than he'd felt in the last ten years combined. Anger had been a constant companion, a result of the drugs they'd been given that were meant to erase their consciences, but that was about the extent of what he'd felt.

Now fear, worry, and regret, all tangled together, making it hard to think.

"About us?" Thunder asked, confusion marring his features was echoed in the others' expressions.

"How would anybody even know that we were connected to Cassandra? To Prey?" Voodoo asked.

"Oh no!" Rose suddenly gasped, shoving to her feet, looking at him with horror and a tiny hint of trepidation. She knew he'd been the one campaigning to continue torturing her to try to get her to break, and then to kill her once they knew she was of no use, so she couldn't go to the cops or her brother, but he never really would have killed her even if

Steel hadn't threatened him. He'd just been working out his anger at turning his back on Cassandra, taking it out on an innocent woman instead of aiming at himself, where it should have gone.

"What's wrong, little ladybug?" Steel asked, immediately turning his attention to his girl as he drew Rose into his arms.

"It's my fault," she said, guilt heavy in her tone.

"How is someone connecting Cassandra to us, your fault?" Steel asked her.

"Because I told my brother that you work for Prey," she said, her voice shaking, and given that this woman was all but impervious to torture, given the abuse she'd suffered at her brother's hands while she was growing up, seeing her distressed hit hard.

"You told him what?" Dragon growled, but he wasn't really angry, just afraid for Cassandra, who now had a massive target on her back.

Sensing his rage, Steel shot him a warning glare before returning his attention to Rose. "It's okay, you couldn't have known that he'd get away."

"But you didn't want him to know that because now he has a way to find you. I'm so sorry, Dragon. I wasn't thinking. I believed you guys were coming after him, and we were going to bring him back here so you could torture him and then kill him. If I'd known, I never would have said anything, but that wasn't my intel to share, and I should have kept my mouth shut. I just wanted to not silently take his abuse anymore like I did when I was a kid. I'm really sorry," she said, turning imploring green eyes on him.

Rose's eyes were a darker shade of green than Cassandra's, but still, staring into them reminded him of the woman he'd just spoken to on the phone. The little rabbit's fear for him had come through loud and clear. She hadn't been upset that she was accosted by a stranger while alone after dark at the park, she was just worried for him and what the revelation meant for his team.

Forcing himself to drag in a ragged breath and not let his fear fuel his anger and lead him to do something he would regret, he gave a sharp nod at Rose. "You didn't mean any harm."

"Really?" Rose looked at him with tentative hope, and he knew then and there that she'd cemented her place in their weird and dysfunctional family, because he knew she knew how strong their bonds were and didn't want to put Steel in a position where he had to choose sides.

They all knew which side Steel would choose and it was hers, but she didn't want that anyway.

"You're not going to try to kill her?" Steel asked skeptically.

With an irritated huff, Dragon stormed further into the room and flopped down into one of the armchairs. "You know I was never going to really try to kill her."

"Uh, I did not know that," Rose piped up, making the guys snicker in amusement, and Dragon couldn't remember the last time things had felt this light in their home. Rose wasn't just good for Steel, she was good for all of them.

"Cover up now, little ladybug," Steel growled, seemingly just remembering she was topless now that he deemed there to be no threat to her life. "I'd really love not to have to rip out all of their eyes."

"Relax, they've seen it all before, several times, and Lion was just—"

With another growl, Steel snatched Rose off her feet, crushing his mouth to hers to silence her before she could remind him that Lion had just been touching her breasts.

Laughing, the tattoo artist pressed her shirt—one of Steel's—into the other man's hands, and Steel managed to drag his lips from hers long enough to pull the shirt over her head. When she ground against the bulge in his pants, Steel appeared to remember they had an audience and set her down on her feet, guiding her arms through the sleeves with a gentleness none of them were used to witnessing.

Both were breathing hard, and unable to resist holding her in his arms, Steel sat back down, tugging Rose into his lap and wrapping his arms around her with a possessive glare at the rest of them.

As they all took their seats, Dragon fought against the direction his thoughts wanted to take. Imagining what it would be like to have Cassandra there, sitting on his lap, his arms around her, his intentions clear. She was his and everyone else should back off.

But she wasn't there.

He'd made his choice, and he had to live with the consequences.

"What did this person tell Cassandra?" Steel asked, protectiveness sharp in his dark eyes. The other guys all liked Cassandra and viewed her as a sort of younger sister.

"Apparently, she told her that Dr. Gardner doesn't just want us back because he created us, he wants to find out how we survived his experimental drugs when nobody else has. He has an antidote," he told the others, who all gasped in shock.

Rose ran a soothing hand over Steel's arms, which were banded around her. "What does that mean exactly? Can my brother undo what he did? Turn you back into who you were before? Would you even want that? Good or bad, this is who you are now."

Would he go back if he could?

Part of him would say yes, that the man he had been before was a better one than the man he was now. The other part knew even if he lost his enhanced sense of smell, it wouldn't undo the horrors they'd lived through those three years Dr. Gardner kept them captive.

"I wouldn't go back," Steel was the first to say it, and one by one the guys nodded their ascent. Rose was right, for good or bad, this was who they were now.

"Might not be an option anyway," he informed them. "According to Cassandra, this woman told her that Dr. Gardner plans on injecting us with the antidote, studying us, then reinjecting us with the same drugs as last time to try to figure out how we were able to adapt and thrive. This woman doesn't think we'd survive."

A small whimper escaped Rose's lips, and she pulled Steel's arms tighter around her, not liking the idea of losing him.

"Not going anywhere, little ladybug," Steel said, but anger danced in his gaze. "We need to find out more about this woman. We need to know who she is, how she knows about us, how she's connected to Dr. Gardner, and how she managed to figure out that Cassandra was a good way to get to us. Dragon, you need to go to Cassandra, see if you can pull more details from her."

Perfect.

That was exactly what he wanted to hear.

Maybe he wasn't strong enough to go to her on his own, but now he had the perfect excuse.

∼

January 4th
   11:34 A.M.

All morning, Cassandra had felt out of sorts.

What annoyed her the most was not knowing whether it was because she'd been accosted by a stranger or the phone call to Dragon.

To most people, one was definitely way more concerning than the other. Someone she didn't know approaching her at a deserted park after dark, where there would be no one to help her if the woman had wanted anything other than to deliver her message, was a dangerous, potentially deadly situation. Talking to Dragon on the phone was just talking to a man she'd been developing feelings for, but things burned out before they even got a chance to set alight.

"You made the right decision," she assured herself as she slipped her feet into a pair of boots.

That was true. Cassandra knew she'd done what was best for her. There was no way she could have hung around and allowed herself to get involved in whatever plans for revenge Dragon and his team had, which from what she could gather, appeared to be targeting someone close to the doctor responsible for changing their DNA. If she did, she would have been reinforcing the fears she already battled.

Of course, her family knew she'd been shaken up by the revelation that she was conceived via rape, there had been no way to mask her feelings when they were so raw and fresh. But over the last couple of months, she'd done such a good job of convincing everyone she was handling everything, dealing with everything, and moving forward with a healthy self-perception.

Only that couldn't be further from the truth.

It felt like evil ran through her veins now. She was the daughter of a rapist, a man who had killed without remorse, and who wasn't afraid to do whatever it took to protect himself. How could she not view herself differently, knowing all that?

Plus, she'd killed her own father and didn't feel any guilt over it.

There had to be something wrong with her.

Helping, or even just tacitly going along with Dragon's plans for revenge, to hurt someone who might be completely innocent, would only go further to convince her she really was her father's daughter.

A knock at her door had her straightening, a smile curving her lips up even as she rolled her eyes. It had to be one of her brothers, overprotective things that they were. Since she'd told Monique what happened last night, she'd half expected to find her half-sister and stepbrother turn up on her doorstep, even though she'd assured Monique that she was fine and safe. Or one of her other brothers, since there were no secrets in their family, and she had zero doubts that Monique had blabbed to everyone the second they ended their call.

All twelve of her brothers and one day sisters-in-law, hated the fact that she went running alone after dark at the park. Even though she'd tried to explain why she needed that time to herself to destress, all they saw were the potential things that could go wrong.

It wasn't like she could really blame them after her stepbrother Jake's now-girlfriend, Alannah, had almost been burned alive at the park a few months back.

But she needed that time, so she fought for it, assuring them nothing was ever going to happen. Now she realized how wrong she'd been, how easy it would have been for that woman to do more than just give her a warning for Dragon. Which was going to ruin her alone time, because now every day at the park she'd remember how vulnerable she'd been.

Wondering which brother hadn't been able to hold off any longer on checking up on her, Cassandra headed down the hall and flung open the door. Even though she complained about how overprotective her brothers were, she wouldn't change a single thing about any of them. They loved her, and she needed their love now more than ever, even if she kept them in the dark about how badly she was struggling.

The smile on her lips died as soon as she saw who was on the other side of her door.

It wasn't Cade, Cooper, Connor, Cole, Jake, or Jax. Wasn't Gabriella, Willow, Becca, Susanna, Alannah, or Monique either.

It was Dragon.

Here.

At her house.

Standing on her doorstep.

Staring at her with those weird violet eyes of his that seemed to see right through her charade and probe deep into her soul, finding all her secrets and leaving her feeling bare and exposed.

What was he doing here?

When she'd spoken to him last night, he hadn't mentioned flying out to see her, and she couldn't think of any reason why he would need to. If he had more questions, he could have called her on the phone like a normal person.

Seeing Dragon again hurt. She'd really liked him, and he'd been a steady presence in her life those first weeks after she learned the truth. It wasn't like he'd talked much to her, but he'd just been there. Bringing her food so she ate, sitting with her even if she was just staring into space, checking on her if she disappeared off on her own for too long.

He'd felt like an ally, a friend, and the hint of something more hung between them even if there had been only the one kiss. So the fact that he'd been able to dismiss her concerns so easily, brushing them aside like they—like *she*—meant nothing, had hurt more than she'd been willing to admit.

But now she couldn't deny it.

Now he was standing there, and she had to confront the idea that he'd hurt her deeply. All her life, she'd been brushed aside. She was the baby of the family with six overprotective big brothers. She loved them to death, and knew that protectiveness was their love language, but there had been lots of times they'd shielded her, or not taken her seriously, because to them she was always going to be the baby sister.

Of all the people she thought would never shut her down like she wasn't smart enough, or strong enough, or mature enough to handle things, it was Dragon.

Neither of them spoke.

She stared at him, he stared right back at her.

It was weird, it felt like there were things Dragon wanted to say, and yet he kept his mouth shut and stood there like an immovable mountain.

Her pain quickly morphed into frustration. Coming here was a stupid idea, and she didn't know why he'd done it. What she did know was that she wasn't standing around waiting to see what he wanted. She'd been on her way out, and she saw no reason why she should hang around now that Dragon had deemed her worthy of his time.

"I'm on my way out," she said dismissively, glad she'd already put on her shoes and that her purse hung by the front door.

Reaching back to grab it, she slung it over her shoulder, pulled the door closed, and attempted to brush past him. His hand darted out quicker than she thought a person could move, and closed around her wrist, holding her in place.

Staring at his large fingers curled around her slender wrist, Cassandra couldn't help but note that while his grip was firm, it was also gentle. He was taking care not to hurt her. This time anyway.

"Let me go." Cassandra hated that her order didn't come out strong and commanding. Instead, it sounded breathy and insubstantial. Why did this man have to affect her so deeply? Especially when she now knew he didn't feel the same way she did.

"No."

The single word was all she got, and it ignited two fires inside her. One low in her body where she couldn't help but respond to the man she was wildly attracted to, the other set her anger boiling over.

"You don't get to say no. I called you, told you what she said. I have nothing else to give you. I'm not hanging around now because you've decided that I hold some sort of value, that my words or opinions matter, when before you told me it didn't concern me and not to insert myself where I wasn't wanted or needed."

It was annoying that the pain she'd felt at being dismissed like that seeped into her tone, but she was only human, and she couldn't keep all her emotions under control all the time. It just sucked that she slipped now, letting her vulnerabilities out with the one person she knew could exploit them if he wanted.

Instead of saying anything, arguing with her, Dragon merely bent, plowed his shoulder into her stomach, and used his hold on her wrist to lift her up.

"Hey!" she squawked as she found herself hanging upside down,

Dragon's arm banded around her thighs, keeping her in place, her face right by his toned butt, which felt wildly unfair since attraction was the one thing she couldn't just shut down easily. "What do you think you're doing?"

Again, she got no answer. Dragon snatched her purse from her hands, found her keys, and let himself back into her home, carrying her in with him like he owned the place. If her anger had been boiling over before, now it was exploding out of her.

Who did he think he was?

Did he think he could push her out of his life and then stroll back in when it suited him?

Did he think she'd been sitting there pining for him these last couple of months?

Okay, she'd thought about him more than she wanted to, even attempting to get herself off while pretending he was the one touching her a couple of times, but he'd hurt her, and she knew she'd made the right choice by leaving. She didn't want him back in her life, not when she was already struggling just to hold it all together.

In her living room, Dragon tossed her purse on the couch, and then slowly lowered her back so her feet touched the ground. Before she could tell him off, he grabbed her shoulders and leaned in to crush his mouth to hers in a bruising kiss that stole her ability to think, to do anything other than feel what he was doing to her as he broke down all her walls, leaving her utterly defenseless.

CHAPTER

Four

January 4th
11:59 A.M.

This was a bad idea.

Definitely not the way to get back in Cassandra's good graces, yet as Dragon swept his tongue inside her mouth, he couldn't seem to find the strength to care.

Laying eyes on Cassandra again was everything he'd wanted and everything he'd feared.

She was angry with him, he'd known that, but worse, he'd hurt her when he hadn't listened to her concerns that going after Rose wasn't the right move. That focusing all his energy on revenge and being prepared to go to any lengths to get it would only turn him into the monster he'd spent most of his life trying so hard not to become.

Hurting her hadn't been his intention, he just hadn't been able to see past his own goals.

Even after they'd abducted Rose and started torturing her, he'd held on longer than the rest of his team, refusing to allow himself to admit that using her was wrong. Because if he had to admit that, then he had to admit he'd lost Cassandra for nothing.

When small hands shoved hard at his chest, he finally pulled back, ending the kiss before he could take things further. Which he might have been unable to stop himself from doing. This woman clouded his judgment at a time when he needed to have a clear head.

"You can't just drag me back in here and then kiss me," Cassandra snapped. Anger danced in her pretty green eyes, arousal too. Her body responded to his even though she didn't want it to.

There was no doubt that using that to his advantage would only fuel her depiction of him as a monster, but right now, standing in her presence, drowning in her sweet caramel scent, he was prepared to do anything he could to give himself the upper hand.

"We need to talk more about this woman who came up to you at the park last night," he told her, taking a step back because if he didn't, he was pretty sure he was going to have her naked and beneath him before he could blink. While he was prepared to use Cassandra's lingering attraction to him to his advantage, he wasn't going to rape her, which was what it would be because there was no way she was giving consent for anything right now.

"What is wrong with you?" Cassandra demanded, her eyes about bugging out of her head. "You hang up on me last night, then you just turn up here. You kiss me then you demand more intel."

Instead of answering, he merely took a seat in a comfortable-looking armchair and waited for Cassandra to calm down. She already knew he wasn't like normal people, he didn't have regular conversations. She'd lived at the mansion with him and his team for months, she should know by now what to expect from him.

After a tense couple of minutes of silence, Cassandra sighed and plopped down onto the couch. "Fine, if you're not going to be reasonable, let's just get this over and done with so you can leave."

Not going to happen, little rabbit.

Until I ascertain whether or not you're in danger I'm not going anywhere, so you'd better get used to seeing me around.

"I don't have any additional intel to offer you. I told you what she said. I'm sure you accessed CCTV footage from cameras in the area, so you can probably try to use facial recognition software to ID her, which will tell you more about her than I could."

They had accessed the footage already, but they hadn't been able to get a proper shot of the woman's face that could be used to identify her. They'd followed the car the woman had driven off in, but it hadn't had any plates on it, so they couldn't trace it, and they had eventually lost track of it as it disappeared between cameras. If she were smart, the mystery woman had a second vehicle stashed somewhere to make her getaway in.

"I don't know who she is, and I'm sure you know more about what she was talking about than I do. Why are you really here?"

Beneath the anger and pain, Dragon could smell a note of something else.

Hope.

Cassandra was struggling, and she wanted to believe he was there for something more than just to get more intel out of her about the woman from last night.

Wanted to believe he was there just for her.

The thing was, he *was* there because he needed to be near her. It had nothing to do with the mysterious woman, although he was concerned that someone had approached Cassandra to use her and could do so again. This had just given him the excuse to do something he was too stubborn, too cowardly, to do on his own.

"We don't know who she is, but she obviously works for a man who wants to abduct me and my team and keep experimenting on us," he said slowly, wishing he had the guts to say what he really felt.

"If she wanted to hurt me, she would have done so last night."

Fear soured his gut at the thought of her being injured when she was alone and so very vulnerable. "Maybe she didn't want to hurt you, but if she could connect the dots between us and you and go to you with a warning, then Dr. Gardner could connect those same dots."

"So ... what? You want me to move in with one of my brothers until you find this Dr. Gardner guy?" Cassandra asked, and he scented a hint of weariness in her. Almost all her life, she and her family had been burdened with the weight of what had happened to their parents, then she'd had more and more piled on top of her, it was no wonder she wanted a break. To be free to live her life.

"I think you should come back and stay with us. That way, no one will be able to get to you."

She actually laughed at that. Full on belly laugh like it was the funniest thing she'd ever heard. Grinding his teeth, Dragon waited for her to calm down, and when she wiped away a stray tear, he shot her a glare.

"Yeah, that's not going to happen," Cassandra announced. "I don't want any part of your revenge plans."

"She's fine." He huffed.

"Who is?"

"Rose. The woman we went after. Dr. Gardner's little sister. She's helping us find her brother, she's involved with Steel." Maybe if he could convince Cassandra that Rose was not in any danger, and that while they had started their plan to use her, it had all fallen apart when the feisty little redhead turned out to be nothing like they expected, then she'd stop hating him.

Knowing she viewed him as a monster, even though he himself did, left him with a hollow feeling inside he didn't know how to fill.

Brow furrowed, she looked at him quizzically. "You didn't go through with it after all?"

While he'd love to assuage her doubts about him, he couldn't. "We did. We took her, but it didn't take long to realize we went about things the wrong way. Rose has forgiven all of us for what happened."

"And this Rose woman is dating Steel?"

"He's obsessed."

"And she's helping you find her brother, who is this Dr. Gardner person that the woman last night warned you about?"

"She is."

"But you hurt her. Rose. You kidnapped her, and what? Tortured her? I can't believe I'm even asking questions like that. How is this my life? How do I know people who would abduct someone they know is innocent and plan to torture them? How can I be attra—" Cassandra cut herself off and shot him another glare.

There was no need for her to finish the sentence, though. He knew what she'd been about to say. How could she be attracted to someone who would use and abuse an innocent person just to satisfy his own craving for revenge.

Attraction alone didn't give him much to work with if he wanted to ... get Cassandra back? She'd never really been his to begin with. Was that what he wanted, though? Did he want what Steel had found with Rose? Did he want someone who didn't care that he was damaged, that he was no longer normal, that saw him anyway, the man who existed beneath the experiments that had been done to his body?

Dragon wasn't sure. All he knew was that he couldn't stand Cassandra hating him, viewing him as nothing more than a monster.

"I'm not going to go and stay with you again," Cassandra said, and from the stubborn jut of her chin, he knew that arguing with her would be pointless. She'd already made her mind up, but the thing was, he had too. At least about this.

"Then I'll stay here," he informed her.

"You are not staying in my home," she all but screeched at him.

Shrugging, Dragon pushed to his feet. "Don't need to stay inside your house to watch over you, little rabbit," he told her as he strode across the living room and out the front door.

If Cassandra didn't want to come with him, and she wouldn't let him stay with her, then he'd simply sit in his car in the street to protect her. Whatever it took, he wouldn't allow Dr. Gardner to lay a finger on the only good and pure thing he had in his life. Even if that good and pure thing currently hated his guts.

~

January 5th
2:06 A.M.

This was crazy.

Why was Dragon still sitting in his car outside her house?

He'd been out there for hours. *Hours.* He hadn't budged, other than to knock on her door twice and ask if he could use the bathroom.

Cassandra had been tempted to tell him no, just so he would have to leave for a bit, but then the thought of him not being close by temporarily paralyzed her vocal cords, and all she could do was give a single nod.

She knew him well enough to know that when his big body brushed against hers as he walked past her, it was no accident. He wanted her to be affected by his presence, and she absolutely hated that her body was.

Her body.

Not her mind.

She was clinging to control of that with every drop of strength she possessed.

While of course she was glad that the guys had stopped their plan to use this Rose woman before things got taken too far, that didn't negate the fact that they had abducted the woman and hurt her in some way. Nor did the fact that the woman had jumped sides and was now working with them, and apparently dating Steel.

Imagining the large man who could crush a human skull with his bare hands fawning all over a woman was pretty difficult. Steel was always so tightly in control, he was Delta Team's leader, and he took that responsibility seriously. She was glad he'd found someone who saw past all that. Hard to imagine or not, she was happy for the couple if they were happy.

One thing she'd always known about the men of Delta Team was that they were absolutely not the monsters they feared themselves to be. It was why she had been so adamant about leaving, and staying away, when she learned of their plans to use someone to get their revenge. Doing that made them monsters, because only monsters hurt completely innocent people.

Yet apparently, Rose had gotten over it. She wished she knew the woman's secret.

How did you get over something like that?

How did you forgive people who had tortured you?

What kind of woman was Rose Gardner?

Since she wasn't going to get answers to any of those questions, Cassandra let the curtain slip back into place as she stepped away from the window. There was absolutely zero chance that she was going back to Delta Team's Gothic mansion, so she wasn't going to meet Rose and get a chance to ask her questions.

Even though she had no intention of falling back into Dragon's orbit, she couldn't deny that she felt safe knowing he was right outside. Just because she didn't think she was in any danger from the woman who had given her the warning, it didn't hurt to be extra safe in case someone else learned of her connection to the guys and decided to exploit it. The stranger had had ample time to kill her if that was the goal, even though that would have been counterproductive since she wanted Cassandra to pass along a message, but that didn't mean this Dr. Garnder man would feel the same way.

Knowing she could potentially be in danger wasn't why she couldn't sleep, though, why she was wandering her bedroom at two in the morning.

Nope, that was all Dragon.

Why couldn't she make a clean break with her feelings the same way she could with her presence?

Distance had helped these last few months, but as soon as she saw him again, that pull that had first drawn her toward the man with the unusual eyes was tugging at her all over again.

It wasn't what she wanted, but part of the problem she'd been facing ever since she learned the truth about her conception and parentage was that she didn't know what she wanted anymore. How could you know what you wanted out of life when you were struggling to figure out who you were?

What she needed was time to herself, away from her family, to try to figure out all the tangled thoughts and emotions stuck inside her. While overbearing at times, her family loved her and she loved them back. How could she be selfish enough to disappear for a while when they'd finally shrugged out from under the burden of finding out the truth about their parents?

That had been the focus of all their lives for almost two decades. Her brothers had shouldered most of it, and they deserved this time to finally be free and focus on themselves and their partners. It would be selfish to go and make it all about her, which was why she tried so hard not to let any of them know how badly she was still struggling.

But it got lonely.

Isolating.

And the lonelier she got, the more isolated she felt, the more the darkness inside her grew.

It would be so nice to have someone who was just solely on her side. Someone she didn't have to worry about them feeling torn and having other priorities. Someone who could just be hers.

As she padded down the stairs, her gaze couldn't not stray to her front door, thinking of the man sleeping in his car in the street outside her townhouse.

Dragon had come here because of her. To try to get more intel about the woman who had accosted her at the park, but what did that mean exactly? Had he just come because he was genuinely worried that Dr. Gardner posed some sort of threat to her?

If he really thought she was in danger, she didn't doubt he would have shoved a syringe in her arm, knocked her out with a sedative, shoved her on a plane, and taken her back to his home.

As much as she hated admitting it, Cassandra didn't hate that Dragon was outside. That he'd cared enough to come. He'd also explained about Rose, was it just to prove he and his team were right about what they'd done, or did he want to find a way to smooth things over between them?

Would a man like Dragon ever really care enough about anyone, though?

Not because he was incapable of caring about another like he believed himself to be, but because he was so tightly controlled that he was afraid to let anyone get close to him.

Only he had nothing to be afraid of with her.

Why hadn't he seen that?

Why couldn't he have at least listened to her? Taken her seriously instead of just brushing her off like her opinion meant nothing?

Okay, so she wasn't part of Delta Team, but she knew those guys better than anyone else other than Eagle Oswald himself, surely that counted for something.

But it hadn't.

In the kitchen, she opened her fridge and grabbed some chicken. It was supposed to be for tonight's dinner, but she felt like popcorn chicken, and she was awake anyway so why not make it now?

After all, a midnight snack could be anything you wanted.

Engrossed as she was in chopping up the chicken into little bite sized portions, it wasn't until she moved to the pantry to grab some seasonings that she felt it.

A brush of cold air against her skin.

With a gasp, she turned to find that her back door wasn't latched closed, it hung open just enough to let cold air in.

Enough to tell her that somebody was inside her home.

There wasn't a single shred of doubt in her mind that she had closed and locked that door before going to bed. Dragon's presence had shaken her up, and she hadn't wanted to not take a potential threat seriously enough to at least confirm she was locked in tight for the night.

But someone must have picked her lock.

It was the only explanation.

It wasn't like her door could unlock and open itself.

If it was Dragon, he would have announced himself. And he wouldn't have broken in anyway. He would have just knocked on her front door and demanded she open up if she ignored him. If she persisted in ignoring him, he would have just gone ahead and broken her door down, there would have been no need for sneaking around, arrogant man that he was.

Fighting against whoever it was never even entered her mind. She wasn't going to risk it when this person—or possibly people—would be bigger and stronger than her. Sitting just outside, she already had the best defense anyone could ever ask for.

Snatching up the knife she'd just been using to cut the chicken from the kitchen counter, Cassandra darted for the front of the house. She didn't see the person hiding in the shadows until she felt the slight shift of air.

Even though she spun, lifted the knife she gripped tightly in her hand, it didn't stop the sharp sting of pain as the person who had broken into her home sliced her open with a knife of their own.

CHAPTER
Five

January 5th
   2:22 A.M.

For the first time in months, Dragon felt an element of peace slip into his soul.

Cassandra hated him, that much was clear. His decision to prioritize revenge for himself and his team over listening to her and her concerns had derailed any shot at ... anything they might have had before it even got up off the ground. She wasn't pleased to have him hanging around, nor did she think it was necessary, and yet he was there. Sitting outside her house, close enough that he could breathe in her sweet caramel scent and be content to watch over her from a distance.

Content wasn't something he could ever recall experiencing. It hadn't even been on his radar. He'd gotten so used to being unsettled, always on edge, always searching for threats, always stuck in survival mode that he'd been blinded to how badly he needed something calming in his life.

Those months when Cassandra had been in the house, he'd not just become accustomed to her presence, but the peace she brought with her. Even though she had just learned some devastating truths about how she was conceived and what her existence had led to for her family, she'd been a breath of fresh air.

She'd breathed life back into him, and it wasn't until he'd lost her that he'd even realized the full extent of what it was exactly that he had lost.

A future with someone like Cassandra should be impossible.

This wasn't like Steel with Rose. While he hated that Rose had been suffering basically since birth at the hands of her deranged family, it was all the woman had known. Darkness lived inside her the same way those years they'd lived under Ridge Gardner's thumb, kept locked in a cage, had planted darkness inside them. They might have been bred from different circumstances, but deep down, they were all the same.

It made sense that Steel and Rose clicked, even if he wasn't used to seeing one of the men he considered a brother obsessed with a woman. The two of them could barely keep their hands off each other, and Rose's presence also breathed life into their home.

But Cassandra was everything good and sweet in the world. Despite losing her parents at such a young age, being raised by her grandparents and brothers, the weight of her mom and stepdad's apparent suicides hanging heavily above them, she was pure joy. That darkness hadn't tainted her soul, and he knew that he would never be good enough for her.

She deserved the world, and all he would ever be able to offer her were the broken parts left of his soul.

Which she didn't even want.

Even if he wanted her.

And he didn't. Well, he did, but he didn't. His soul craved her light, her soothing touch, her calming scent, the peace she carried so effortlessly, but his brain knew it was never going to happen.

Never should happen.

The most he could ever have was exactly what he was doing right now, what he'd been doing ever since she packed up her stuff and went back home. Watching over her from afar, protecting her as best he could, finding a way to accept it when she found a man worthy of her and moved on with her life to find the happiness she deserved.

While he wasn't kidding himself, Cassandra wanted him gone sooner rather than later, he also knew she was affected by his presence. She kept drifting to one of the front windows of her home, looking out to see if he was still out there. Even now, in the middle of the night, he'd seen her at her bedroom window, staring out at him.

What's running through your head, little rabbit?

Do you really want me to go, or do you wish you wanted me to go?

Can you ever forgive me for pushing you away?

Will you ever see me as anything other than a monster who hurts others to get what he wants?

There were no answers to those questions, and no way he was going to voice them aloud. Because apparently, he wasn't just a monster, but a cowardly one at that.

All his life, he'd picked avoidance over confrontation. Even now, when the stakes had never felt higher.

As he sat there and watched Cassandra's house, he suddenly caught a whiff of something in the air that shouldn't be there.

Rolling down the window so he could get a clearer read on it, he smelled it again.

Blood.

There was no second-guessing himself, no taking his time to figure out what it meant, his logical mind flew out the window. Acting on pure instinct, Dragon was out of the car and running for Cassandra's house without any conscious thought whatsoever.

While Thunder's enhanced skill was speed, they all worked out every day, and they had all been given heightened endurance, able to better cope with extreme temperatures, handle no sleep, and go longer without needing food or water. He was at the door mere seconds after he'd first scented blood in the air.

Knocking wasn't even a consideration.

Again, he didn't have Steel's enhanced strength, but he was a big guy, stronger than the average man, with hours of daily weightlifting under his belt, and he simply threw himself at the door and watched as the wood splintered around him.

As soon as he was in Cassandra's living room, his gaze fell on the two shadowy figures, right by where he'd crushed his lips to his little rabbit's not even twenty-four hours earlier.

Inside, the stench of blood was stronger, and he saw one of the figures was on the ground. The other stood above them, the blade of a knife glinting in the moonlight streaming in through the hole the broken door left behind.

Likely the only thing that saved Cassandra's presence was his entrance.

The man standing above her faltered for a second when Dragon stormed into the room, and Cassandra wriggled back a little, so that when the man recovered and brought his weapon down, it missed everything vital.

Caught her skin, though, if the smell of blood growing stronger was anything to go by.

His little rabbit might be light and sunshine, but she was no wilting flower. She had six overprotective big brothers who had drilled her in self-defense training, he knew because he'd worked with her on building on those skills while she stayed with them.

Her own knife came down on the man's shoulder, and he grunted in pain.

Nothing compared to what he was going to feel when Dragon was through with him.

Not needing a weapon to take care of Cassandra's assailant, although his gun was in its holster on his hip, he launched himself at the other man.

The rage pounding inside him insisted that he make the man suffer, that he inflict as much damage as possible, that he torture him slowly to punish him for daring to touch something that didn't belong to him.

But there was a tiny whisper in the back of his mind that Cassandra was there.

She was watching.

Already she believed him to be a monster. What would she think of him once she discovered the depths of his depravity?

Somehow, Dragon managed to cling to some measure of control, and when his body collided with the intruders and he took him down to the floor, he slammed a fist into the other man's neck, crushing his windpipe in a single blow.

Unable to breathe, the man stared up at him, and Dragon could scent his fear along with his acceptance. He knew he was going to die, and there was nothing he could do about it. It would be a faster death than the man deserved, but the fact that he recognized his situation and was powerless to do anything about it soothed a little of his rage.

But the smell of blood was still strong in the room, and only one sluggishly oozing gash on the dying man's shoulder. The rest of the blood was coming from Cassandra, and he found he could hardly stomach the idea of turning on the lights and seeing how badly she was hurt.

What if she were bleeding out?

She hadn't said anything, hadn't moved from where she'd been when he threw himself at her attacker. He knew she wasn't dead, but that didn't mean that she, too, wasn't dying.

If he'd gotten in there seconds too late to save her life, all because he'd been trying to respect her wishes and stay in his car when he knew she'd be safer with him inside the house with her, trying to convince her he wasn't completely a monster even though they both knew that he was, Dragon knew he would never forgive himself.

January 5th
   2:30 A.M.

Dragon had come.

He'd known she was in trouble, and he'd come.

Killed for her.

As badly as Cassandra wanted to believe that meant something, she knew the man standing before her, his back to her, breathing heavily, would kill to save any innocent person. Especially if that person was part of the Prey family.

It didn't mean that he cared about her.

Didn't mean he respected her.

Certainly, didn't mean he was interested in any sort of … anything … with her.

Yet she couldn't seem to take her eyes off his tall frame even as the pain from her wounds began to seep back into her conscious mind. What would it be like to have someone who did kill for her because they cared so deeply about her, the thought of losing her wrecked them?

Expecting Dragon to come to her, kneel beside her, and check her wounds, when instead he headed away from her, across the room and back toward her front door, Cassandra's heart dropped.

Okay, so he didn't care about her the way she cared about him, but he wasn't seriously just going to leave her bleeding all over her living room floor while he went back to his car, was he?

"You're leaving?" she cried out at the same moment he flicked the light switch on, illuminating the room.

"What the hell, Cassandra?" he snapped as he finally turned around to face her. "Why would you ask that? You really think that little of me, that I'm that much of a monster, that I wouldn't even perform first aid and call the cops before walking away and leaving you all alone after you were almost killed?"

Remorse immediately had her cheeks heating. That wasn't how she saw Dragon. Not really. Not when she was thinking clearly. When she wasn't terrified out of her mind, she knew there wasn't a chance in hell he would leave her after what had just happened.

Because when she wasn't scared senseless or fixated on anger at being dismissed so easily, she knew the truth.

Dragon felt the same way about her as she did about him, he was just too scared to admit it.

"S-sorry," she mumbled as tremors began to wreck her body, making her teeth chatter. Suddenly, it felt like the temperature in the room had dropped about twenty degrees, and she knew it had little to do with the fact that she no longer had a front door. "I j-just p-panicked for a m-moment."

Those unusual eyes of his softened slightly, and he snatched a blanket from the back of her couch and a couple of throw pillows as he hurried back to her side. "You're bleeding," he said softly, but there was no way he couldn't have known that. Her attacker had inflicted the second wound right in front of him.

"G-got me as I c-came through th-the d-door," she told him as he slipped one of the pillows under her head, his large hand cradling her for a moment before he lowered her head down to rest on the pillow. "G-got him t-too though."

Despite the pain, the fear, the confusion, Cassandra was proud she'd fought back. Of all seven siblings, she was the only one who hadn't chosen a career in the military or some other agency like their parents had. It had been another mark against her, another way she was different than the rest of them, but it had always been the right choice for her.

She wasn't as strong and tough as the rest of them, and it showed in how she was handling the recent revelations about her conception.

"Course you did, little rabbit." There was definite pride in Dragon's voice as he knelt at her side and draped the blanket over most of her body, leaving the wound on her leg and the one on her arm exposed.

A tiny bit of warmth infused itself into her ice-cold body at hearing Dragon was proud of her. It shouldn't matter what he thought, it hadn't mattered to him what she had to say about his plans, but it did.

"This one doesn't look too deep," Dragon told her as he examined her arm, and she followed his gaze to look at the gash about five inches long in the side of her bicep.

"H-heard him a m-moment before h-he a-acted," she explained, the way her body trembled against the hard floorboards making her ache all over.

"You have good instincts. You need to learn to listen to your gut more often."

If she'd listened to her instincts, she wouldn't have stayed there tonight. She would have gone to her brother Cade's house with the intent of helping out with her five-year-old niece Esther, so she didn't feel completely useless as her oldest brother played bodyguard.

Doing that wouldn't have just put the little girl in danger, but her soon-to-be sister-in-law as well. Gabriella was four months pregnant with a high-risk pregnancy. The former nanny to little Essie had never made it this far in a pregnancy, suffering miscarriage after miscarriage, and the whole family was praying with everything they had that this time she was able to carry to term and give birth to a healthy little boy or girl.

That all could have ended if she'd been stubborn and decided not to let Dragon watch over her from his car on the street. She could have been responsible for another death, and she was pretty sure it would have sealed in Gabriella's mind that she wasn't to have biological children, and she wouldn't have tried again. That would have deprived the couple of more kids, Essie of siblings, and caused two people who had already been through so much to suffer all over again.

Maybe listening to her instincts wasn't such a good idea after all.

Maybe hers were broken.

"Is he dead?" she asked as Dragon probed the wound on her leg.

"Yes."

Swallowing the lump of emotion clogging her throat, she nodded even though he wasn't looking at her. "Th-thank you."

At her thanks, Dragon's gaze snapped up to meet hers. There was surprise in his. Did he really think that she thought he was a monster? That she would react badly to him killing the man who had broken into her home and attacked her?

She'd left because she couldn't be part of what he and his team were planning, not because she didn't understand why he wanted revenge, and certainly not because she believed him to be a monster. She thought he was a man who had been badly hurt, prepared to lash out at someone innocent if it got him closer to the guilty person. That didn't make him a monster, even though it wasn't right by any definition of the word.

"It was b-because of the w-woman, wasn't it?" she asked, her gaze now drawn to the man lying dead in her living room.

"Twenty-four hours after you were accosted by her, someone shows up at your house in the middle of the night, no way it can't be related," Dragon replied as he pushed to his feet and disappeared into her kitchen, reappearing a moment later with the first aid kit she kept under the sink.

"It had to have been this D-Dr. Gardner man, r-right? He sent that man here to k-kill me."

Dragon's gaze refused to meet hers as he knelt beside her and began to wrap a bandage around the gash on her leg. If he wouldn't look at her, it meant there was something he didn't want her to know.

But she had every right to know.

Whatever plan the guys had enacted with this Rose woman now included her. She'd been dragged into it, and she didn't want to be kept in the dark. Keeping her distance was no longer an option. She was part of this, even if she didn't have the emotional or mental capacity to deal with anything else right now.

"What?" she prompted, reaching down to grab his hands and stop him, and hissing when pain flared in her arm.

Glaring at her, Dragon's hands closed around her shoulders, and he eased her back down. "Now I get Steel's thing about no moving," he muttered, making her brows dip in confusion as she had no idea what he was talking about.

"You know something," she pushed, not willing to let him be another person in her life keeping her out of the loop to protect her. Her brothers had tried to do that for years as they dug into the past to find the truth about their parents, but it didn't make her feel protected, it made her feel like an outsider in her own family.

Cassandra knew she wasn't part of Dragon's family. He didn't really owe her answers, but she'd tried to walk away and it hadn't worked. Now she was in this whether she wanted to be or not, and she wanted to know what she was up against. What she had to be prepared to face.

"Tell me," she insisted.

"He dropped something," Dragon told her. He tucked the blanket over her legs and moved to kneel by her shoulder, gently picking up her arm and bandaging it as well.

"Dropped what?"

"A syringe."

"A syringe?" she echoed, not catching on.

Violet eyes meeting hers, for once Dragon didn't shield what he was feeling, allowing her to see it all. Fear, regret, guilt, remorse, concern, and worry. "I don't think the plan was to kill you tonight, little rabbit. I think the plan was to kidnap you and use you as bait to lure us in the same way we tried to use Rose to lure in her brother."

CHAPTER Six

January 5th
  4:39 A.M.

Exhaustion was etched into every one of Cassandra's features.

After bandaging up her wounds and leaving enough time to ensure her attacker was dead and couldn't be revived, he'd called the cops. While he would have loved to keep the guy prisoner, take him back to the mansion and interrogate him, it would be quicker for the cops to ID him and then use that to get answers.

With Cassandra's safety on the line, it wasn't the time to focus on an outlet for his rage. They needed as much intel as they could gather as quickly as they could gather it. Once they had a name to go with the man who had clearly been intending to abduct Cassandra and use her as leverage, Prey could start doing a deep dive into his background.

Somewhere in it would be a link to Dr. Gardner that they could use and exploit.

For now, though, he had to focus on the woman sitting beside him. Paramedics had stitched the deeper wound in her calf and cleaned and bandaged both wounds. She'd refused painkillers, and Dragon was pretty sure it was because she was afraid of being at a disadvantage if another attacker came after her.

It grated that she didn't have absolute faith in his ability to kill anything that presented itself as a threat, but he had to accept that he'd broken any trust between them when he'd refused to even listen to her warnings about their plan.

She'd been right.

Going after Rose was a mistake. One they might not have been able to come back from if Rose hadn't turned out to be the opposite of what they were expecting. Even though Cassandra hadn't been part of their team, she hadn't gone through what they had or grasped just how much they'd suffered at the hands of the crazed scientist, she'd earned her right to at least give her opinion because in the months she'd stayed with them, she'd become part of their family.

He'd denied her that, and he'd hurt her more deeply than he'd realized until he'd seen her again.

Was there any chance he could earn back that trust?

If he could, what did he intend to do with it?

Walk away again as soon as the threat was taken care of and he knew Cassandra was safe? Ask her out on a date? Figure out how to not be a monster so he could have some kind of future with Cassandra?

Hell, he didn't know what was going to happen after, or what he even wanted to happen after, but he knew he didn't want to spend the rest of his life walking around with this ball of anxiety in his gut. Dragon needed Cassandra's forgiveness, and at the very least, her friendship.

"Are we done?" he asked the older female cop who had been gently questioning Cassandra.

The woman shot him an annoyed frown, but nodded. "Yes, I think we have everything we need from Ms. Charleston. It was lucky you were here tonight, sir."

It was.

If he'd stayed at the mansion with the others, Cassandra wouldn't have stood a chance of getting away from the intruder, no matter how hard she fought back, and he was proud as hell of her that she had kept her wits about her enough to fight.

"Chances are this was random, Ms. Charleston," the other cop, a younger man inserted, and Dragon had to force himself not to rip out the man's eyes for the way they appreciatively roamed Cassandra's toned body.

"That's likely true," the older woman agreed, although again she looked annoyed at anyone else stepping in to speak, she seemed to like to run the show. "But without a door, and just to be safe, it might be a good idea to stay with someone else tonight. Do you have somewhere to go?"

"She'll be staying with me," he replied before Cassandra could say she'd go to one of her brothers' houses. There was no way in hell he wasn't keeping her in his line of sight until he was positive she was going to be safe.

"All right then," the woman agreed, and Dragon knew she wasn't pleased about that. The cop was annoyed that he hadn't handed over a name, but when he'd informed her he worked for Prey and that she could call and confirm he was operative Dragon, there was nothing she could do about it.

Still, it left him feeling uneasy to have more people know he existed, even if they had no way to track him down. Of course, people were aware of his existence, but they were either people from his past, people he worked with, people he was rescuing, or people he would kill, this felt different.

Cassandra's grateful eyes shifting to meet his helped to ease that discomfort, and after taking the cops' cards, they both bid them farewell. A crime scene unit would be coming out to collect evidence, but thanks to a triple murder on the other side of the city, that would be a while.

Long enough for him to get his little rabbit out of there. He didn't want any more eyes on her tonight, chances of any of these people being connected to Dr. Gardner were slim to none, but still, he couldn't be positive.

"Pack a bag," he told her once they were alone.

Wearily, she nodded, and he hated the dark circles under her eyes and the pain in her green depths. "Where are we going?"

"Motel."

"Not one of my brothers' houses?"

"Want to risk taking this to one of their homes?" It was a low blow because he knew how much she adored her big brothers, but apparently, it was a blow he was willing to make to ensure he got to keep her all to himself.

"No," she answered softly, and without another word, headed upstairs to pack.

Sighing, Dragon hated hurting her, but he was selfish enough that he kept doing it. Not a great start to his plan to win back Cassandra's trust.

Pulling out his phone, he dialed Steel's number and waited. Half expecting to catch the man in the middle of sex, because sex seemed to be pretty much all Steel and Rose were interested in, he was somewhat surprised when the call was answered on the first ring and his team leader sounded alert and focused.

"What happened?" Steel demanded.

"We have a problem," he replied.

"She wasn't happy to see you?" Blade asked, tone teasing, and it reminded Dragon how much things seemed to be changing. They never teased each other, they weren't light-hearted, they didn't laugh, they certainly didn't get obsessed with women to the point of needing a tattoo of their teeth etched onto her skin as a sort of claiming mark.

"She wasn't," he confirmed. "Wasn't convinced that she was in danger either."

"I sense a big but coming," Thunder said.

"Huge but." Gaze unable to move from the spot where Cassandra had been when he came in, Dragon pinched the bridge of his nose, willing it to release the scent of blood that had been clogging it since he first caught a whiff of it. "I told her if she didn't want to come home with me, that I'd stay and watch over her here. She didn't want me inside, so I stayed in my car. About two hours ago, I smelled blood."

"Someone came to attack her," Steel said harshly, not bothering to control his anger that Dr. Gardner would go after an innocent to get to them, even though they'd done the exact same thing with Rose.

"Is she okay?" Rose asked, and he could imagine her running her palms down Steel's pecs in an effort to soothe him.

"Two stab wounds, but she's lucky it wasn't worse," he answered. "That's not all, though."

"What else?" Voodoo asked, and he was sure the medic wanted to get his hands on Cassandra and do his thing, take her pain and heal her, or whatever it was he did that made people who should be dead survive. Not that he was sure Voodoo himself knew how he did it.

"The intruder had a syringe with him. We can get Prey to run tests, but I'm pretty sure it was a sedative." Dragon had pocketed the syringe before the cops got there, he didn't need them getting in the way of this.

"So, Cassandra is now officially a target," Lion said.

Hating that but unable to deny it, he had no choice but to agree. "She is."

"You're staying with her," Steel said, a statement, not a question. There was no doubt in anyone's mind that he'd be sticking like glue to Cassandra until he was positive that she was no longer in any danger.

What happened after that, he had no idea.

Wanting Cassandra wasn't the same as agreeing it was a good thing for him to be part of her life. He was dangerous to her in so many ways, and not all of them had to do with the experimental drugs he'd been given.

Some of his faults he'd inherited the old-fashioned way.

Through his DNA.

~

January 5th
5:05 A.M.

Three hours ago, Cassandra had been standing right in the same exact spot she was right now, staring out her window at Dragon sitting watch over her house from his car.

Back then, all she'd had to worry about were the confusing feelings it stirred up to know that Dragon was looking out for her even when she didn't think there was any need for it. Being at war with herself wasn't fun, but she would definitely prefer it to fighting for her life.

In just a few hours, she'd been stabbed twice and watched a man die right in front of her. It shouldn't make her queasy—after all, she'd killed before herself—and it didn't really, not in the sense that Dragon had killed someone. It was that he'd done it for her.

Sure, it was just one of many people he'd killed throughout his career, but this man had died because he'd broken into her house and come after her. She didn't feel responsible for his death in that she felt bad, after all, the man had come with the intent of attacking her, then injecting her with a sedative and abducting her, but she worried about Dragon's motivations.

Had he just killed because it was his instinct to kill any and all threats, or had it been more personal?

It seemed like a stupid thing to worry about, almost like splitting hairs. The man was dead, Dragon had saved her, she was safe now, and she hadn't protested when Dragon told the cops she'd be with him, even though she knew for her emotional well-being she should insist she'd go to one of her brothers' houses.

But his low blow had struck its mark.

Going to her brothers would be putting them in danger when they'd only just managed to get themselves out of the line of fire a handful of months ago. That would be extremely unfair of her, especially because the whole mess for her family had started when her rapist father's sperm had attached itself to one of her mom's eggs, resulting in her conception.

With a sigh, Cassandra let the curtain fall back into place, and much like she had three hours ago, she headed downstairs, only this time it was with an overnight bag and her treasured toy bunny from her childhood in her hands. The toy was sentimental to her because it had been given to her the day she was born by her mom and the man she desperately wished was her father, who she had believed to be her father up until a few months ago.

Throughout the months following her mom and stepdad's death, it had been a security blanket of sorts for her, and she had refused to go anywhere without it. After learning the truth about her parentage, she'd considered burning it because it felt tainted somehow, but she'd been unable to bring herself to do it.

When she went to stay with Delta Team before she'd taken it with her, for some reason unable to leave it behind, and she felt the same way today.

Dragon was waiting for her at the bottom of the stairs, and she noted how his gaze dropped to the stuffed bunny in her hand. Was that why he called her little rabbit? She'd never heard him call her that before, but the nickname had slipped out earlier, and with such ease that she assumed it was how he thought about her.

Did he think about her?

Or had he quickly moved past her brief presence in his life?

After all, he had his revenge to focus on, the one thing that seemed to consume him and be all he cared about.

Only as his gaze drifted up her body to rest on her face, she got the feeling that wasn't quite true. Because in his deep violet gaze, she could have sworn she detected concern and tenderness, maybe even affection too.

But when he spoke, his voice was brisk and detached. "You got everything you need?"

"Yeah, I think so."

"I've booked us a motel for the night, and we'll regroup after you get some proper sleep and decide what our next move is going to be."

Maybe she should ask more questions about that. Where were they going? What did he think their next move would be? Was he really going to care about her opinion anyway when he'd already proven he didn't think anything she said was of any value?

But Cassandra asked none of those questions.

Merely nodded and followed Dragon out the door and down the garden path to his rental.

Taking her bag from her hands, he left her holding the bunny and opened the passenger side door for her. Leg aching, she managed to push herself up and into the high SUV's seat, but it cost her, and her body trembled with exhaustion.

Apparently, Dragon noticed it too, because he grabbed the seatbelt before she could take it and leaned over her to snap it into place.

It took everything she had in her not to lean into his comforting scent. Dragon had strength that seemed to go on for days. He never wavered, never faltered, he was so sure of himself and every decision he made. How nice that must be.

After he'd closed her door, deposited her bag in the back of the SUV, and got into the driver's seat, she expected him to say something, but he didn't. Merely turned on the engine like she wasn't even there and took off down the street.

She really should ask where they were going, but Cassandra couldn't find it in her to care.

Truth was, she was just tapped out.

With the year she'd had, she was running on empty, and the last thing she'd needed was for Dragon's problems, which she'd already made the choice to walk away from, to come crashing into her life.

But it was what it was.

There was no going back.

This woman, who claimed to know about the drugs and Dr. Gardner's plans for Dragon and his team, knew who she was. It might not make sense that the woman would send someone after her, although they couldn't rule it out, but now Dr. Gardner seemed to know about her existence as well and her link to the guys.

That meant she would remain in danger until the guys were able to get to Dr. Gardner. She wished she knew more about who Dr. Gardner was and the details of what exactly the man had done to the Delta Team guys. She knew they'd been injected with drugs that gave them enhanced skills, but she didn't know a lot about how it had all come about.

Right now, though, she didn't have enough energy to ask questions.

Later.

When she'd recouped a little she'd be stronger.

Maybe.

She hoped.

Or maybe it would be really nice just to turn her brain off permanently, stop obsessing over who she was and what the revelation about her paternity meant. About whether killing her biological father made her more like him than she wanted to be. About why Dragon couldn't give in to the attraction that simmered between them and how easily he could dismiss her like she meant nothing.

Neither of them spoke on the drive, and she hadn't really expected

Dragon to. He had always been a quiet guy, most of the time they'd spent together had been in silence. Only this silence felt different. It felt deeper, uncomfortable, lacking the ease that had always been there before.

What if there really was no going back?

It had never been her intention to contact Dragon again after she'd left. If he found her important enough to fight for, he would have to come to her. Then again, she'd never expected to find herself in danger because of his past.

Dragon being there now felt too late. Or maybe it was because he hadn't come for her, just because she was in trouble.

When they reached a motel about forty minutes away from her house, she didn't bother to confirm they hadn't been followed. There was no way Dragon wouldn't pick up on a tail and lose it along the way.

In fact, she didn't ask anything, just allowed Dragon to unbuckle her and carry her bag for her as she trailed behind him to the room he'd rented for them. Inside, the room was small and dated, but clean, and all she needed right now.

"Taking a shower," she muttered. Without giving Dragon a chance to respond, she snagged her bag from his hand and disappeared through the door to the bathroom, closing and locking it behind her.

The lock wouldn't stop him. He'd already broken down her front door tonight, and this door was a whole lot flimsier, but she also knew he had no intention of coming after her. Slipping out of her clothes, she ignored the bandages on her arm and leg, not caring about those wounds right now, and turned on the water as hot as it would go and stepped under the spray.

Hot water burned her skin, but not enough to make her move out from under it. Instead, she tilted her face up to catch the full effect of the pounding water and let the tears she held in with a ruthlessness that often surprised her fall free.

Her life was a mess—she was a mess—and she had no idea how to get back on track.

CHAPTER
Seven

January 5th
6:27 A.M.

Clenching his fingers into fists, Dragon kept his feet planted right where they were so he didn't go storming into the bathroom.

Cassandra was crying in there.

She wasn't making a sound, but he could smell her tears, the scent hanging heavily in the air, demanding that he do something about it.

But what could he do?

Barreling in there was only going to make her angry. Already, she'd made it clear that she wasn't happy about him being back in her life for any reason and she was tolerating his presence only so she didn't bring trouble to any of her brothers' doorsteps.

At no point last night had she turned to him for comfort. She'd accepted his help with first aid, allowed him to sit beside her while she gave a statement to the cops, answered questions, and was treated by the paramedics. In the car on the drive to the motel, she hadn't spoken a single word, not even asking one of the dozens of questions he'd been expecting.

Dragon hated it, he wanted her trust even though he didn't know what to do with it.

And there lay the problem. He didn't know what he wanted beyond Cassandra no longer hating him. He wanted her to look at him the same way she used to, but he didn't know if he could ever give her what she'd once wanted from him.

So he stood there, staring at the bathroom door like it was offensive to him, when it was really himself that he loathed, and waited.

And waited.

And waited.

It was another thirty minutes before the water in the bathroom finally shut off. Another fifteen by the time the door opened, and Cassandra stepped through it. Her long chestnut brown locks were still wet, and she'd twisted them into a braid that hung down her back. She was wearing a pair of fuzzy pajamas in a pretty shade of soft pink. The skin on her face was tinted pink, and the dark circles beneath her eyes looked even darker, even as her eyes were red from tears.

Taking a step toward her wasn't a conscious thought on his part, he just had to be near her, had to offer her some sort of comfort, even as he had no idea the best way to comfort a traumatized woman.

"Don't," she whispered, taking a step back.

Hurt lanced his chest. Just because he knew she was angry with him didn't mean it didn't hurt like hell that she couldn't even stand to have him near her.

Was that fear he saw dancing in the green depths of her eyes?

What the hell?

Was she scared of him now because he'd killed someone in front of her? She had to know all he'd done was eliminate a threat. He hadn't tortured the man, even though he'd wanted to because the need to get to her, check on her, protect her was stronger.

Feigning disinterest, he nodded at her arm as he pointed to her legs. "You took a shower, pretty sure you weren't careful to keep your wounds dry. I need to dry them and rebandage them so you don't have problems with them healing."

That was all true, but it wasn't what he cared about most right now, it was just an excuse. The need to touch her was overwhelming, and he was beginning to understand how Steel had felt when they had Rose locked in the cell in the basement. How the hell had his friend managed to hold it together when they strung Rose up and whipped her to make a video to send to her brother?

With a weary sigh that said she'd rather be anywhere than near him right now, Cassandra gave a small nod, and walked over to perch on the edge of the bed.

Impotence raged inside him. Cassandra was hurting, and he couldn't just make things better for her. There was no magic answer. No way to wave a wand and eliminate the danger now swirling around her. No way to turn the clock back and return to when Cassandra first discovered they had plans to use someone to reach the man responsible for changing them, and listen to what she had to say, explain to her why they were so desperate.

If he could make it so she no longer hated him, he'd do it in a heartbeat.

Instead, he grabbed the first aid kit he'd brought with him from Cassandra's house and approached her. When he knelt before her, he noticed how her pulse picked up, but when his gaze met hers, it wasn't fear he saw swimming in those pretty eyes of hers, it was pain.

Pain that hit him so hard, his hands actually shook as he rolled up the leg of her pants so he could get to the wound. The bandage that had been placed there by the EMTs was gone, he assumed she must have taken it off in the bathroom, and the skin around the stitches was wet and soggy.

Pushing to his feet, he went into the bathroom, grabbed the towels Cassandra hadn't used, and returned with them to the bedroom. Kneeling once again beside where his little rabbit was sitting, watching his every move with a detachment he didn't like one little bit, he wrapped the towel gently around her calf.

One thing he'd quickly realized about Cassandra when she first came to stay with them was that everything she did, she did with her whole heart. She'd been hurting, doing her best to come to terms with the revelation of her paternity, but there had still been an openness to her.

Now it felt like she was shutting down, and he had no idea how he was supposed to reassure her it wasn't necessary. She was the light in the Charleston Holloway family, and they needed her even if she didn't see that.

When she tensed as he pressed gently against her wound, Dragon began to massage the back of her calf to try to relieve the tightness there. As his fingers worked her muscles, he felt Cassandra slowly relax.

Long past when he knew the wound was dry, he stayed right where he was, holding the towel pressed to the cut, massaging her tight muscles, content to soak up this small moment with the woman he couldn't stop thinking about. These small moments were all he'd have left with her. Even if she agreed to come and stay with him and his team, it wouldn't be the same as it had been before.

As badly as he wanted to go back and redo things, he couldn't, and he hated that.

He wanted things to be like they'd been before.

A soft, almost content sigh fell from Cassandra's lips, and when he glanced up at her, he saw that her expression had relaxed somewhat. She even gifted him a small smile. "Thanks, that feels good. I didn't realize how tense my muscles were."

"You're welcome." The words came out somewhat stiffly, but the tightness in his chest eased, and he felt like he'd just inched his way a little closer to Cassandra even though he still felt the emotional distance between them.

Setting the towel down, he grabbed a clean bandage and wound it around Cassandra's leg, before pulling her pant leg back down. Then he rose to sit beside her on the bed, ready to dry off her smaller wound.

"Umm, I'm not wearing anything under here," Cassandra said when he grabbed the hem of her pajama top.

"Then we'll just slip your arm through the sleeve." Circling his fingers around Cassandra's wrist, he gently eased her arm out, stretching the material so it did most of the work to minimize her pain.

Patting the gash on her arm until it was dry, Dragon could feel Cassandra's watchful gaze on him, but he refused to meet it, almost scared of what he would find there.

Judgment, he was sure. Cassandra believed he was a monster, something he'd known since he was old enough to figure out who and what his family were. Unlike the rest of his team, he had always been a monster. He hadn't been created by Dr. Gardner and the experimental drugs they were injected with.

With those probing eyes on him, it felt like he was being flayed open, all his secrets exposed, even as he knew there was no possible way Cassandra could know he was a mafia heir who had thrown away the future mapped out for him, one he'd never wanted, and instead enlisted in the military.

After enlisting, he'd never left the base, knowing it was the one place his family couldn't get to him. His entire life, he'd been a prisoner to someone. First, his family, then the military, then the crazed scientist, then hiding for his own safety. He'd never been free, didn't know how to live without anything tying him down, but Cassandra made him want to find out what it was like.

"You should get some rest," he told her briskly as he slipped her arm back into her sleeve, then stood to pull back the covers.

"Hmm, yeah, sleep," Cassandra mumbled with a yawn, and he helped her scoot back then lie down.

As he pulled the covers up to tuck her in, he couldn't help but let his fingertips trail across her shoulder. Now he could understand Steel's obsession with Rose, his need to have her close, to touch her at every opportunity. Cassandra was right in front of him, but it wasn't enough. He wanted her in his arms, wanted to bury himself inside her, wanted to tie her to him so she could never leave.

His ruthless parents hadn't broken him, special forces training hadn't broken him, Dr. Gardner hadn't broken him, but somehow it felt like a five-foot-three, green-eyed, brunette held the power to shatter him within her hands, and she didn't even know it.

~

January 5th
    3:42 P.M.

.   .   .

A few hours of sleep seemed to change everything.

Cassandra had woken up this afternoon with a clearer head and her emotions back in check.

At the back of her mind, a tiny little voice whispered that maybe it wasn't the sleep that changed things.

Maybe it was the care and attention Dragon gave her last night. His large hands had been so gentle as they dried her wounds and massaged the tight muscles in her leg. It hadn't just been the soft touches that had warmed something inside her, it was the look in his eyes while he was doing it.

While he'd aimed for nonchalance when she'd refused what she was pretty sure was going to be an uncharacteristic display of comfort, she hadn't bought it. There had been pain in his eyes when she'd taken that step back.

It wasn't her goal to hurt him, she wasn't the kind of person who wanted to lash out and hurt someone back because they'd hurt her. His dismissal of her a few months ago had hurt both because it reopened old wounds where she felt less inside her family because she didn't have as much to offer, and created new ones because she'd been sure there were feelings growing between them. But she didn't want to punish him for it, she just wanted to move forward.

Floundering wasn't a fun way to live.

Finding her footing again was imperative, and Cassandra feared she couldn't do that so long as she was around Dragon. He was dangerous to her because she cared deeply for him and wanted to shoulder some of his pain, even if he didn't believe her shoulders were strong enough to do that. But he was also dangerous to her because he showed her moments of softness that weakened her resolve.

No weakening.

She liked Dragon far too much, and her traitorous little heart was all too ready to forgive and move forward. Well, she'd probably already forgiven, because she did get that she wasn't part of Delta Team, so her voice didn't matter, but Dragon's easy dismissal had hurt too much for her to put herself back into that situation for it to happen all over again.

Maybe Dragon had feelings for her, but he was never going to open himself up to it, so even if she wanted to give them a second try, it was never going to go anywhere.

"Monique's calling," she said to Dragon when he came out of the bathroom. "Am I okay to answer? No one will be tracking us or anything?" Cassandra was so far out of her comfort zone that she had no idea what to do. Just because her parents and siblings had all served it didn't mean it was her area of expertise.

"You can talk to your sister."

With a happy little squeal, she snatched up her phone. It had stopped ringing, but she returned her sister's call and relaxed further when Monique answered.

"Are you okay?" her sister demanded without hesitation.

"Can I take it you know what happened last night?" While she hadn't called anyone, she'd been too tired, too lost in her own head, she shouldn't be surprised that Dragon had made sure her family was aware of the break-in. Just because she didn't want them to worry didn't mean she wasn't relieved, she wasn't built for keeping secrets.

"Yeah, we know, and we're all worried sick."

"Sorry." Having her family worry about her sucked. They'd done that enough these last few months, and while she got family worried about family, she wanted them to see her as strong enough to handle anything rather than the weak link.

"Don't be sorry, but tell Dragon to bring you to my and Jax's place. We'll go out to my animal sanctuary. It's remote and no one will think to look for you there."

That was actually a great plan. Cassandra didn't want to put anyone in her family in danger, but the sanctuary was beautiful, and it was where she'd first met her half-sister so it held a special place in her heart. She knew Monique loved any excuse to get out there, so it wouldn't really be like she was putting them out.

"I don't want to put you guys in danger," she admitted. If she was doing this, she needed them to know they could opt out.

"Pfft," Monique said dismissively. "Jax will watch your back, you know he'd love nothing more. And I love having a sister, so any excuse to spend time with you I'll take. Besides, I truly don't think that anyone would think to look for you there since the sanctuary isn't connected to you in any way."

"All right," she agreed, decision made. Staying with Dragon would keep her physically safe, but there was no way to protect her heart when he showed her moments of gentleness like he had this morning. Those little moments would build up quickly the longer they spent together, and she wasn't sure she could make it out the other side with her resolve intact.

"Ask Dragon if he can fly us over there on his plane before he heads back home," Monique said.

"I will, we'll get ready and head right over." Now all she had to do was break it to Dragon that she wasn't going to be staying with him. He wouldn't like it, that was for sure, but she didn't think he'd kidnap her and take her back to his house against her will.

At least she was fairly sure he wouldn't.

She hoped.

"See you soon. Love you," Monique said.

"Love you too."

As she set down her phone, she looked over to find Dragon standing on the other side of the bed, staring at her with an expression she couldn't read. He was good at that, shutting down whatever he was thinking, keeping his expression blank. While she had no intel to back it up, Cassandra couldn't shake the feeling that it was something he'd learned long before he and his team were experimented on.

"Umm, Monique said I could stay with her and Jax out at her animal sanctuary," she began a little more tentatively than she would have liked. This was her life, and she was in charge of it, but she knew she'd be hurting Dragon's feelings by rejecting his protection. "I think it should be fine. I'll be safe there, and you know Jax is trained enough to protect me. The cameras he put up when he was worried about Monique's safety are still there, and I'm sure he can link you in on them so you can watch them if it will make you feel better."

For a long moment, Dragon didn't say anything, and she tensed, half expecting him to pull out his own vial of sedatives and knock her out so he could take her back to his mansion with him.

Then he gave a single nod, walked over to grab their bags, then waited for her by the door.

Wait.

Was he going to agree to take her there without an argument?

It was what she wanted, but for some reason, it hurt a little to know that despite his insistence yesterday that he was watching over her himself, whether she liked it or not, all those hours he sat in his car outside her house, now he was prepared to just walk away and wash his hands of her.

Her hurt made no sense because it was what she wanted, for Dragon to go back to his life and leave her alone, yet her eyes stung as she searched for her shoes and shoved her feet into them.

Since Dragon had her bag, all she had to do was grab the stuffed bunny from the bed. It was stupid that, as a twenty-four-year-old woman, she still got so much comfort from the toy, but she clutched it tightly as she walked over to join Dragon by the door.

Again, she expected him to say something, but he merely opened the door, angled his body so it blocked hers, scanned the outside of the motel, and then led her to his SUV. This afternoon, he didn't pause to open her door for her or do up her seatbelt. She missed that tiny concession, a small way for him to take care of her without speaking a word, but there was no way she'd admit that out loud.

Neither of them spoke in the car, and she assumed Dragon knew where her brother lived because he didn't ask for directions, just started driving.

Despite his silence, Cassandra knew that not only did Dragon not like this, but that her rejection had indeed upset him. It would help if he just told her that, opened up just a little bit. It felt like another thing that she had to keep to herself, the knowledge that she could see more of him than he wanted her to.

The weight of all the emotions she held in was becoming too much. How much more could she hold in before the inevitable happened and she broke?

Each day, it felt like she got a little closer to breaking, and each day she pretended that she hadn't.

Lost in thought as she was, Cassandra wasn't prepared for Dragon to suddenly stiffen beside her, his nostrils flaring as he obviously caught a scent he didn't like.

Opening her mouth to ask what was going on, before she could get the words out, the car swerved wildly, veering sideways and slamming into a fence.

CHAPTER
Eight

January 5th
4:36 P.M.

The second the scent invaded his nostrils, Dragon knew they were in trouble.

It was the unmistakable smell of the brake line fluid. And the only reason he'd be able to smell it the way he could was if someone had messed with the brakes and caused them to start leaking.

With Cassandra in the car with him, he didn't have many options. She noticed when he went stiff beside her, and he felt her eyes on him. Before she could ask what was going on, the steering wheel he was gripping tight enough his knuckles had blanched white began to wobble in his grip.

Great.

They'd messed with the steering as well.

Dragon took his foot off the gas, so at least when they hit whatever they were going to hit, it would be at the lowest speed possible. Cassandra was the most precious cargo he was ever going to carry anywhere, and he only had her for a little while longer. Once he dropped her off at her sister and stepbrother's house, that was it. She'd made it clear she didn't want anything to do with him going forward, and he wasn't going to force himself on her. Neither could he stand to be around her, knowing she would never see him as anything but a monster.

So this was goodbye.

But it was going to be goodbye and not the final goodbye that signaled death.

Unable to control the vehicle in any way now, all Dragon could do was hope for the best as they slammed into a nearby fence. The impact of the crash threw his body forward, and he felt the airbag engage, but he cared only about Cassandra.

Turning sideways, he saw her slumped against her seatbelt. She wasn't moving, but he could smell her scent still strong, she wasn't dead. Still, the metallic scent of blood was also strong, and the reddening patch on her arm told him the jarring crash had reopened the wound.

"Dragon?" She moaned as she stirred.

"Right here, little rabbit. Where do you hurt?" he asked as he internally raked himself over the coals for not checking the vehicle before leaving this afternoon. It didn't matter that he hadn't thought there was any need to. There had been no tail when he drove Cassandra to the motel. He'd been as careful as he could be to ensure it because no way was he putting her at risk all over again.

The chances of them being tracked to a random motel were slim, which meant the most likely scenario was that his car had been sabotaged last night. If the man from Cassandra's house had a partner waiting in the wings for the getaway, it was possible that person had messed with his car while he was inside killing the man who dared touch Cassandra.

When he'd jumped out of his car, his only intention had been to get to his little rabbit, he hadn't even closed his door. It would have been obvious to any potential partner that someone had left the vehicle in a rush, and since he had crashed through the front door, it would be easy to assume that his vehicle belonged to someone connected to Cassandra.

"Are you okay?" Cassandra's small hand brushed against his arm, and he blinked, realizing he'd zoned out.

What the hell was wrong with him?

Zoning out after crashing the car when Cassandra could still be in danger was unacceptable. What if someone had tagged his vehicle and was following him right now.

"Where are you hurt?" he growled, making her hand fall away. Even as he wanted to mourn the loss of her touch, he couldn't rein in his anger at himself for not taking Cassandra's safety seriously enough. Instead of being there to protect her, she'd been hurt twice now on his watch. Didn't matter that her intruder had gone in through her back door, he should have been paying better attention, should have known, should have kept her safe.

"I'm not," she assured him. "Not really. Just sore. What happened? You knew we were going to crash before we did. How?"

"Smelled the brake fluid leaking," he replied as he unsnapped his seatbelt and then leaned over to undo Cassandra's as well.

"Someone sabotaged your rental. Could it have been random? Maybe something was wrong with it before you even rented it?"

Hating to dispel the note of hope in her tone, Dragon shook her head. "No way I could have driven it all the way from the airport to your place, then from your place to the motel without the line already going empty."

"So it happened while we were at the motel? If they knew we were there, why wouldn't they come in rather than just mess with your car? They could have gotten to us while we were sleeping."

"Not possible."

"How do you know? They could have just snuck in and—"

"Do you really think I would sleep while you're with me and someone is out to use you to get to me and my team?" he growled, uncertain if he should be angry that she thought so little of him, or sad that he was such a coward he hadn't let her know that he cared deeply for her.

"Oh." Cassandra's eyes were wide as she stared up at him, but he would have sworn she relaxed slightly, and he hoped it was because she was happy to know that her safety would always take priority. It was why he'd let her go without a fight. Why force her to stay when he knew he would never be someone she would be safe around?

"If the hole they made in the line was small, it would have taken a while to leak out enough to be noticeable," he explained. "And I didn't check the car to make sure it was safe this morning." Instead, he'd been throwing himself a pity party because Cassandra wanted to get away from him as quickly as she could.

"You couldn't have known, Dragon. We got all the way to the motel this morning, then the car sat there for hours. Why would you think to check it out when there was no reason to think anyone knew where we were, or that another person was involved?"

Almost more than he loved the comfort Cassandra couldn't help but offer, even though she hated him, Dragon loved that she was already putting two and two together. So often Cassandra downplayed her own strengths to build up her family, like she didn't believe she measured up. But she was an intelligent woman who was every bit as tough and strong as her siblings. She'd just chosen a different path in life.

"When it comes to your safety, I should consider every possible scenario," he told her, not willing to let himself off the hook as easily as Cassandra was apparently willing to. Before she could reply, he shoved open his door and climbed out. Other vehicles had stopped, and people were beginning to come to check on him and Cassandra.

While he didn't want anyone to get too close to her, he didn't smell anything other than worry from anyone, so he rounded the wrecked vehicle, opened Cassandra's door, and helped her out. Her legs were a little shaky, and he could see the wound on her leg had also been ripped back open, so he helped her to sit a short distance from the wreck, then stood beside her, prepared to act in an instant if a threat presented itself.

Steel's name popped up on his cell phone, and because he knew he would have to tell the guys about the crash anyway, he answered and took a step or two away so no one would overhear the call.

"We have a problem," he said as soon as he accepted the call.

"More than one, it seems," Steel said.

"There was a partner. Someone messed with the brake line and the steering of the rental. We just crashed."

"You need us to fly out there?"

"No. We're both okay. Cassandra wanted me to take her to stay with Jax and Monique. They were going to go out to her animal sanctuary."

"We're not dragging Monique into this," Lion's voice spoke, and Dragon knew he was on speaker phone. Lion and Monique had become good friends while she was staying with them, and Dragon completely agreed. There was no point bringing anyone else into this mess, he just had to convince Cassandra of that.

"I'll work on convincing her the safest place is with us," he assured his team, praying it was possible that Cassandra's love for her family outweighed her hatred for him.

"The guy who attacked her last night, he recently came into quite the sum of money," Steel informed him, and he assumed that was the reason for the call.

"So, Dr. Gardner put out a contract on her, and some mercenary decided to take him up on it," Dragon said, his blood heating as fear for Cassandra increased.

"You know what that means," Voodoo said gently.

Unfortunately, he did. It meant there was no getting Cassandra out of the line of fire without taking off the head of the snake. If there was a contract on her, it was a payday for anyone willing to try to abduct her and deliver her to the crazed scientist. It wasn't going away until the doctor was eliminated.

Convincing Cassandra to go back with him to the mansion was the only way to keep her safe, and Dragon wasn't sure he could convince her to do it.

~

January 5th
    4:40 P.M.

Unable to take her eyes off Dragon, Cassandra tried to guess how bad whatever news he'd just gotten could possibly be.

Surely it couldn't be worse than finding out there had been a second person involved in her almost abduction. That the person had tampered with their vehicle. Tampering with it didn't seem like the best idea when it had looked like her assailant wanted to abduct her, but maybe when that plan was foiled, he'd decided that just killing her was a better idea.

It was all so complicated, and her brain wasn't used to running scenarios like this.

She worked in a library. A *library*. Her life was about information, about helping people learn, about knowledge. She spent her days running toddler and preschool story time sessions, after-school programs for kids who were struggling at school, for kids who were excelling and needed to be further challenged, and for kids who didn't have someone waiting at home for them and whose parents wanted to ensure they had a safe place to go.

What she didn't spend her days doing was foiling would-be kidnappers and trying to figure out what their next move was. She was so far out of her league that her head throbbed with the beginnings of a headache.

"Are you okay, miss? Ambulance should be here soon," a well-meaning woman—who had introduced herself, but Cassandra hadn't been paying enough attention to absorb the information—assured her.

Giving a distracted nod, she watched as Dragon ended the call and slid his phone back into his pocket. Their gazes met, and for a second his violet eyes softened, and she could almost feel the gentle caress as he examined her from head to toe, likely in search of any injuries he might have missed when he helped her out of the car.

By some miracle, neither of them appeared to have been hurt, other than some bumps and bruises, but she knew that didn't mean they were safe. Dr. Gardner was a more dangerous man than she'd grasped, and it seemed she had been dragged into that mess now.

Closing the distance between them in two long strides, Dragon reached down and curled his long fingers around her elbow, gently tugging her to her feet. "We have to go," he informed her.

So the news was that bad.

There were a million questions she wanted to ask, but Cassandra got that now wasn't the time. Too many people were about, and this wasn't the kind of thing you could just talk about in front of anyone.

"Uh, I don't think you can leave the scene of an accident," a middle-aged man piped up.

Dragon shot him a glare that had the man taking a small step back, and Cassandra quickly placed a calming hand on Dragon's forearm. The last thing they needed was for him to view any of these well-meaning motorists as a threat. After all, none of them could be the mysterious partner because there had been no tail when they went to the motel, and none following them this afternoon.

"Maybe we should wait, just till the cops come," she said softly to Dragon.

"Not safe," he muttered, glancing around them like he expected someone to come jumping out at any second. Remembering his fierce declaration that when it came to her safety, he had to consider every conceivable threat, she let her fingers trail down his arm until they reached his hand, then she twined them with his.

"Safest place for me right now is here. Cops will be here soon, and medics. Besides, we don't even have a car anymore, so we'd either have to walk or call a cab or an Uber."

A low growl rumbled through his chest, causing all four of the drivers who had stopped to check on them to cast wary glances Dragon's way. If he kept behaving like this, they were going to think he was the source of danger.

"Need to get you somewhere safe."

"We can call Jax. They're expecting us anyway and—"

"No."

There was more finality in that one word than she would have expected, and the abrupt way he once again cut her off without even listening to her, especially when once again she was trying to help him, had Cassandra trying to tug her hand free from Dragon's hold.

His fingers tightened around hers, and he tugged her with him as he tried to move back from the small group of people.

"Sir, I think you should let go of her," the middle-aged man piped up again, and she wanted to yell at him to stop talking. She got that he was trying to help her, but he was only making things worse and kicking Dragon's already protective instincts into overdrive.

"It's fine," she rushed to assure him before he could do something even stupider, like actually try to physically prevent Dragon from touching her. "He's just shaken up by the accident. We aren't going to leave before the cops show up."

Ignoring Dragon's huff, she quickly led him away from the gathered group, ignoring the pain pulsing through her leg as she walked on it. The stitches had all popped in the crash, and it was going to need to be stitched again before she went to her sister and brother's house.

"Who was on the phone?" she asked once they had a few yards between them and the others.

"My team."

"And what did they want?" Sometimes getting information out of this man was like pulling teeth. But since this involved her now, she wasn't backing down without all the information. If it affected her, she deserved to know.

"The man who attacked you last night, they found out that he recently came into a large sum of money."

"Okay," she said slowly, not getting exactly what that meant. "And how does that change things from what we already knew?"

"We thought he was one of Dr. Gardner's men. In the ten years since he started experimenting on us, he hasn't stopped. The woman who came up to you the other night must be one of his employees. Maybe she's just trying to throw us off our game, maybe she really is doubting her boss' plans and decided to finally do the right thing, we don't know. But we assumed the man who broke into your place was another of Dr. Gardner's employees."

"Now you don't think that?"

"If he was one of Dr. Gardner's employees, he wouldn't have just come into a sum of money the very same day he broke into your place."

"Okay," she said once again, still struggling to follow along.

"It is highly likely that Dr. Gardner didn't send one of his own people after you."

"Then who did he send?"

"We're guessing he's put out a contract on you."

"Like to kill me?" Cassandra wasn't completely unaware of what a contract meant, past the obvious that it was one person ordering the death for money of another person. Her own biological father had put out bounties on her family. Mercenaries had started coming after them time and time again, which was how she, and then later the rest of her family, had wound up staying with Dragon and the guys to begin with.

"A contract isn't always to have someone killed. Chances are, he's put it out there on the dark web that he'll pay for your capture. Prey will keep digging, see if we can find proof of that, but from what we already know it's the most likely scenario."

Pieces of the puzzle began to click into place. "So there's more than just the partner of the man who attacked me last night after me now?"

"Which means going to Monique and Jax's house isn't just potentially bringing trouble to their door, it absolutely one hundred percent certainly is." Already Dragon had talked her out of going to stay with one of her brothers once, but then the idea of going to the sanctuary had seemed to negate that threat. Now she knew that likely wasn't the case.

"If there's money to be had from kidnapping you, then trust me, there are any number of mercenaries willing to come after you. Since we don't know the details of the contract, we don't know if you're to be delivered uninjured, or if Dr. Gardner doesn't care about your condition when he gets you so long as he gets you."

The words behind what Dragon didn't say came through just as loudly as the ones he did say.

If the scientist didn't care about her condition when he got her, it meant the men who abducted her could rape her, torture her, do whatever they wanted to her as long as she was still breathing when they handed her over.

"He had a knife last night," she whispered, feeling the blood drain from her head as shock made her feel cold and shaky. "He didn't just stick me with the syringe, he intended to hurt me first." Which meant that even without seeing exactly what Dr. Gardner had put out there, they knew he didn't care if whoever found her first hurt her.

Dragon's expression was a mixture of grim, angry, and protective. "Everything about you will be known, including the location of your family. If I take you to Jax and Monique's, then there is every chance someone could be waiting there in the hope of spotting you. It would be like handing you over on a silver platter."

"Which means I no longer have a choice." It was stay with Dragon or get him, and possibly her brothers and their partners, killed when they tried to protect her from whatever mercenaries were coming for her.

CHAPTER
Nine

January 5th
8:52 P.M.

Was he supposed to say something to her?

Offer wise words? Comfort? Reassurance?

Tell her he was sorry for not taking her opinions into consideration when she found out he and his team had something planned?

The problem was, he had no idea.

Cassandra had always seemed such an open book, it had been easy to read her emotions, but now she somehow seemed to have learned how to shield them from him. Something she shouldn't be able to do with his ability to scent emotions on people much the same way a dog could.

If it wasn't for the fact that he could still scent emotions on every other person he came into contact with, he might have thought something had happened to his heightened sense of smell. But it was just Cassandra he could no longer scent. Well, his nostrils were invaded by her soft caramel smell, it was so uniquely Cassandra to him now that he found he kept a stash of caramels in his room to eat whenever he missed her too much. They couldn't quite match her real scent, whatever sham-poo, perfume, hand cream, or whatever other girly potion she used to smell so sweet was an artificial scent, but he much preferred it over the real thing.

Now as she sat beside him in the cockpit of the small private jet Eagle had bought for him and his team to use, all he could smell was *her*. Not her emotions, just her.

It wasn't until now that he even realized how heavily he'd come to rely on the changes Dr. Gardner's experiments had done to him. As a kid, if he wanted to figure out the best way to remain safe and out of the line of fire, he had to study body language, voice inflections, and search for the tiny tells that told him he was about to be taught a brutal lesson in what it meant to be part of a mafia family.

The changes made to him gave him an edge, and now he found he struggled to read anything else. Since he couldn't scent her emotions, he had no idea how to figure out whether Cassandra was more angry or upset that he'd all but emotionally blackmailed her into coming away with him.

Not that he wasn't telling her the truth. The money transferred to her assailant indicated he'd gone after her for money and therefore wasn't an employee of Dr. Gardner's, so staying with him and his team really was the safest place for her, but still, it felt like manipulation.

Talking had never been his thing. In his family, you didn't talk about your feelings, you just squashed them down until they disappeared. There were expectations that had felt stifling, and he'd spent all his time playing along, pretending to be exactly what his family wanted him to be, while constantly counting down the days until he could escape. Then he'd jumped straight from the frying pan and into the fire. Escaping his family, only to enjoy a few years of military and special forces training, and then wind up a prisoner all over again, this time to a deranged scientist who once again wanted to mold him into the man he wanted Dragon to be.

Did he even know who he was?

There had never been time to figure it out, there'd always been bigger problems and issues to deal with. But when he was sitting beside Cassandra, her caramel scent invading his body and mind, he wanted to know what it would be like to be a normal man. One who wasn't a danger to the sweet woman that had somehow managed to find an opening he hadn't even known existed and wriggled through it to lodge her presence inside him.

"How come you didn't make me wear the blindfold?" Cassandra asked, breaking the silence that had enveloped them since they took a cab to the airport after they finished talking to the cops and she was treated for her injuries.

That was a loaded question and one he wasn't sure he was ready to answer.

All his life, he'd practiced keeping his thoughts and feelings to himself. Nobody in his family cared, he wasn't a real person to them. He was the heir to an empire he had no interest in controlling. But that didn't matter to them, playing along had become so easy that he'd lost himself in the process, and now even answering a simple question—or a not so simple one—felt like a life-or-death challenge. His family would never have killed him, he was the oldest son and heir after all, for answering a question wrong, but he would have been punished for giving the wrong answer. Severely.

Maybe his upbringing wasn't all that different from Rose's. They were more alike than he let on, and that made him feel worse about how he'd treated the feisty redhead. It wasn't Rose's fault he'd lost Cassandra, it was his own.

Now he wanted her back, but he didn't know if it was even a possibility.

What the hell is running through your mind right now, little rabbit?

It would be so much easier to adjust what he said if he knew her expectations. He could work with anger, and he could work with hurt, but he couldn't work with nothing, it left him feeling like he was floundering, and he despised that feeling.

"Not like you know where we're going anyway," he said with a nonchalant shrug. It wasn't the answer he wanted to give, but he couldn't seem to make himself be real anymore. How could he when he didn't even know what was real and what wasn't?

"I can see where we're going," she countered.

"Okay then, tell me what state we're flying over right now."

After pausing, Cassandra huffed out a breath. "Okay, fine. I don't know where we're going. Still, you never cared about that before. You guys always had a strict blindfold or sedatives policy when it comes to bringing people to your home. I don't understand what's different this time."

Although he was missing his ability to scent Cassandra's emotions, he could tell, nonetheless, that there was an undercurrent to her question. He just had no idea what the hell it was, or what she wanted from him.

Since he couldn't come up with the correct answer, he gave none at all, merely shrugging and then concentrating on flying the plane. Thing was, he hadn't discussed with his team letting Cassandra see where they lived. Of course, they knew he was bringing her home with him, but he hadn't mentioned that he didn't want blindfolds or sedatives between him and Cassandra anymore.

It made things between them feel fake, the same as everything else in his life, but what he felt for Cassandra was possibly the most real thing he'd ever felt in his life. There was no doubt he thought of the men on his team as his family, his brothers, he would die for them, he would kill for them, they had been the backbone of his existence for the last decade.

But what he felt for Cassandra exceeded what he thought he was capable of feeling.

It was terrifying because there was no chance he could ever be the soft, gentle man she needed him to be. Cassandra was sunshine, and he wasn't just a rainy day, he was the dead of night, in the middle of a violent storm.

They were never going to mix, and yet he couldn't seem to let her go.

Even if she walked after this, and of course she would, he wouldn't be able to cut her out of his life. He'd go back to watching her from afar, stalking her every move, and hope she never met someone who could give her all the things he couldn't.

It made him selfish, but it was what he was. He was absolutely the kind of man who was an if I can't have her, then no one else can type. Maybe he should just keep her at the mansion, refuse to let her leave, she could hate him for it, but at least he'd be able to have her close.

"Are you angry with me for something, Dragon?" Cassandra asked, and when he turned his head, he didn't have to rely on his temporarily malfunctioning enhanced sense of smell, or his long-lost ability to read every person and situation to know what she was thinking.

Worry wafted off her in waves, and he couldn't stop the sharp shake of his head even if he wanted to.

"No. Why would I be?" he asked. He had zero reason to be angry with Cassandra, she'd done nothing wrong. It was because of him she was now in danger, running for her life, forced out of her home and away from her family. The only one of the two of them who had a reason to be angry with the other was her.

Shrugging, she turned back to stare out the window, and his hands tightened on the controls.

A chasm was between them, and he knew for certain he wanted to cross it, but how was he supposed to find a way over to the other side to reach his little rabbit? Nothing was going to magically turn him into the kind of man Cassandra wanted, needed, or deserved.

He was the dragon, and she was the princess. Was there a way to slay himself to save her from how he'd destroy her?

～

January 6th
12:06 A.M.

They'd been driving for about an hour by the time they reached the gates of the Gothic mansion where Dragon and the guys lived. Even though she'd made this journey several times before, it seemed shorter without the blindfold on. Maybe it was because she was enjoying the gorgeous scenery as peace began to seep back into her system.

Much as it annoyed her, given the circumstances in which she'd left, coming back felt like coming home. The calm she'd been missing ever since she left returned, and she smiled as she looked down the long tree-lined driveway, already anticipating seeing the mansion that looked like it should be the set of some horror movie.

Home for her growing up had been constantly changing. While she had few memories of the first five years of her life with her mom and the man she'd thought was her father, and then her mom and stepdad, she had a few, and they were greatly treasured. After that, she'd lived with her grandparents, but with her oldest brother being ten years older than her, and the youngest six years older, they'd all been out of the house before she even hit her teenage years.

Amazing brothers that they were, they'd kept a close eye on her, helped out with her, and been active participants in raising her. But first, Cade left when she was eight, then Jake when she was nine, Cooper and Connor when she was ten, Jax when she was eleven, and finally Cole when she was twelve, taking pieces of her heart with them with each departure.

To them, she would always be the baby of the family, a little girl even though she was all grown up now. Things here had been different, though. The Delta Team guys had seen her as a burden of sorts, sure, that was why she'd been sent there, so they could look after her. But they hadn't treated her like a child who didn't know her own mind, and step in to circumvent any pain or suffering.

If her twenty-four years of life had taught her anything it was that pain and suffering abounded in this world.

"Lights are still on, I thought everyone would be asleep," she said, more to herself than Dragon as he drove them down the winding driveway, and the mansion appeared through the trees.

The only reason she caught the weird look he gave her was because she was looking over his shoulder at the house. Dragon had been weird ever since she agreed to come back there with him, and she wasn't sure if it was because he was angry with her for getting herself involved in the mess that was his life, or angry at himself for getting her involved.

"Course they're not asleep, they're waiting to see you."

"To see me?" For some reason, she'd been under the impression that the guys wouldn't be all that keen to have her there, given that she hadn't left under the best of circumstances.

"Why wouldn't they want to see you?"

Cassandra shrugged. "I don't know. I guess I just figured they were okay with me staying here again, but they weren't excited enough about it to wait up for me. I thought I'd just see them in the morning."

Apparently, she'd been dead wrong on that one. Because as Dragon pulled up out the front of the mansion, the door opened and all five of the guys piled out along with a woman with dark red hair who held Steel's hand.

That had to be Rose.

It was silly, but she was most nervous to meet the woman who had somehow captured Steel's heart. She knew these guys about as well as anyone knew them, and they were strong, quiet, keep-to-themselves kind of men. They'd been kind to her while she stayed with them, but it wasn't in their nature to be excessively friendly, and she couldn't see one of them falling in love. Well, except for Lion. She knew there was a woman from his past that he'd left behind, she just didn't know any of the details.

Although the other woman was about the same height as her, there was something intimidating about Rose, something bigger than life, a confidence in the way she held herself that told Cassandra once again she was the odd one out. What was that old Sesame Street song?

One of these things is not like the others. One of these things just doesn't belong.

Why was she always the thing that didn't belong? The different one. The lesser one.

"Welcome h—back," Steel greeted her when she pulled up her metaphorical big girl panties and managed to open her door and climb out.

Was it her imagination, or had Steel almost said welcome *home*? A slip of the tongue, it had to be. Because even though this place felt like home, it could never really become that. How could it when the guys had made it abundantly clear that she wasn't one of them and her opinion on their plans wasn't valued or wanted?

"It's always a pleasure to be here," she said politely, things feeling weird between her and the guys now. They all knew why she'd left, and it felt like that hung between them, erasing the easiness she'd felt when she stayed there last year.

"I'm so excited to meet you," Rose said, stepping up and offering her hand. "I'm Rose. I'm sorry my jerk of a brother is messing with your life, he likes to do that, thinks he's a God in the making, but I'm glad for a bit more estrogen to even things out here."

Taking Rose's offered hand, Cassandra shook it and mustered up the most genuine smile she could manage right now. Rose reminded her of the woman she'd always been before she found out the truth about her parentage. Confident, outgoing, sure in herself, all the things Cassandra now found herself lacking.

"The guys can be a lot," she agreed. There was no arguing that the six huge men standing around them practically oozed testosterone, and it hadn't escaped her notice that Steel hadn't let go of Rose's other hand, cradling it gently between his two huge ones because it was in a cast.

"Tell me about it," Rose agreed cheerfully. "But let's not stand out here talking, you must be exhausted, and it's freezing out here. Steel and I cooked you some dinner, but if you're too tired and want to go right to bed we can pack it into the fridge for leftovers."

Her stomach chose that moment to grumble loudly, and Cassandra felt her cheeks heat. "I could eat."

"Great," Rose said with a laugh. "Because I can't wait to talk and get to know you. I'll fill you in on my pretty depressing childhood, but I've never really had a friend before." Vulnerability bloomed in Rose's tone, and when Steel growled, she rolled her eyes and swatted his shoulder. "Relax, you didn't even know me then. There was nothing you could have done to stop my psycho brother."

Feeling totally lost in the conversation, because other than knowing who Rose's brother was, and that Dr. Gardner was the one responsible for giving the guys their enhanced skills, and who was now coming after her, she didn't have many details about what else the scientist had done to the guys. And she had zero idea what the man had done to his sister, although it was clearly enough for Rose to hate him and work with Delta Team to bring him down.

They all trailed inside and were halfway to the kitchen when Rose suddenly spun around to face her, tears shimmering in the woman's forest green eyes. Taking a step toward her, Rose paused, seemed to consider her options, then with a shake of her head, threw her arms around Cassandra's neck.

Caught off-guard, instinct had her returning the other woman's hug, although she wasn't quite sure what the sudden display of emotion was all about.

"Thank you," Rose whispered. "I know what you tried to do for me, that you tried to stop them. It all worked out okay, but you were the first person in my entire life to actually care about what happened to me just for me, not because you could get something out of it. I know it messed up things between you and Dragon, but I'll be forever grateful that you cared even though you didn't know me."

Her own eyes stung, not just at the sincerity in the other woman's voice, but because here she was complaining to herself that she didn't feel like she fitted in with the people in her life when she had an entire family that loved her, and Rose hadn't had anyone. And how did the woman even know about her and Dragon? It wasn't like they'd paraded around the mansion flaunting that they ... liked each other. Had made it known that feelings were developing and they were attracted to one another. Felt a connection that neither of them had done much about pursuing.

Cassandra felt like the last year had been full of grieving. Grieving for the man she thought all her life had been her father, grieving for herself and the woman she'd always thought she was, grieving for her family and the distance she felt between them that she knew was one-sided.

Grieving the loss of Dragon and what might have been.

Maybe it was time she stopped being a passive observer in her own life, stopped worrying about the differences she felt separated her from the people who loved her, stopped drowning in grief, pain, and loss, and figured out who Cassandra Charleston was going to be going forward.

If Rose could rise from the ashes and find love with a man who had abducted and tortured her and still find things to smile about and be grateful for, then she had no excuse for not putting pieces of herself back together. The new Cassandra might be different, maybe a little more jaded, not quite so sunshiny, her pieces might be bent a little, possibly even broken in spots, but in the end, she was still her.

CHAPTER

Ten

January 6th
11:23 A.M.

Something had to change.

There was being stubborn, and then there was being stupid, and Dragon knew he had firmly crossed over into the second.

If Rose could forgive Steel after what they'd all done to her and still want to be with him, there had to be a chance that Cassandra could forgive him for shutting her out. All he had to do was pray that she understood that revenge had been all he'd been thinking about from the time he was old enough to understand what it was and what his family was trying to turn him into.

Revenge against his mafia bloodline might not be in the cards, but once they got Dr. Ridge Gardner's name, making the man suffer for everything he'd put him and his team through had been all-consuming. Ignoring Cassandra when she was trying to get in the way of a revenge she could never truly understand the scope of had seemed like the only logical thing to do.

But Cassandra had been right.

Using Rose was wrong. It didn't help them get one step closer to revenge, instead it brought them one step closer to becoming the monsters Dr. Gardner had intended them to be.

Listening to Cassandra, taking that step back to examine what they were doing rather than just jumping straight in, would have saved Rose, who had already suffered so much, from being hurt all over again.

Just because things had turned out okay, that Rose had fallen for Steel, who was utterly obsessed with the redhead, didn't make what they'd done any less wrong. It was only the fact that Rose had proven to be immune to the effects of torture that had stopped his team from going any further. Despite Steel and the others wanting to back off from her, he had been the one still insistent on continuing, insistent on killing her once she lost any perceived usefulness.

Now he had to make things right before he stood even a chance at earning Cassandra's forgiveness.

Finding which room Rose was in was easy. With the number of rooms in the mansion, they'd all managed to carve out their own spaces. After spending three years locked in a reinforced glass cage together, with their every move watched and not a single second to themselves, it was no wonder that now they all craved a place to call their own. While they had some shared spaces, the main office where they planned ops, the kitchen and dining room, one of the living rooms, and the gym, the rest of the spaces were their own personal ones.

When he found Rose in the smaller office, she was sitting at the desk, a furrow in her brow as she concentrated on the piece of paper she held in her hands. None of them had known until recently that Steel had a thing for origami, something he'd learned how to do from his grandmother. He'd shared the interest with Rose, and now she was obsessed, working on perfecting her technique and learning new objects to fold and make like it was her lifeline. Not even having one of her arms in a cast stopped her.

"You going to stand there staring at me or are you interrupting me for a reason?" she finally asked without looking up from what she was doing.

Guess Steel's little ladybug was more aware of her surroundings than he'd realized. Not that he should be surprised. He and his team had chosen the lives they'd been handed, even if they hadn't had all the intel they needed to make an informed decision, but Rose had been forced to learn survival skills, or she never would have made it through being raised by her brother.

Entering the room, he moved to stand by the window, staring out at the forest surrounding the mansion. It was peaceful out there, it was one of the things he loved most about this remote retreat Eagle had found and created for them. There were no neighbors for miles, nothing out there but trees and wildlife. It was the only place he'd ever lived that felt like a home.

Maybe that wasn't due entirely to the location of the Gothic mansion, and also included the fact that the men he lived with felt like family.

They *were* his family as far as he was concerned.

And now his family had grown to include the woman watching him with dark green eyes that saw too much.

"Do I need to worry that you rethought your plan to kill me?" Rose finally asked, and he spun around to glare at her.

"You know I'm not a threat to you," he growled.

Rose just grinned. "Maybe. I also know asking that question is the best way to get you talking. What's up, Dragon? Why did you track me down when I'm not the woman you really want to be talking to?"

"Actually, you were exactly the woman I needed to talk to."

"Well, since Steel would rip your tongue out if that were true, and I think Cassandra would help, I don't think I'm where you want to be right now. Where you need to be."

"I need to apologize to you," he blurted out. The words felt weird on his tongue because he'd been raised to never apologize for his behavior. The head of a mafia family didn't waste time saying sorry to people who were below them.

"I should say you do," Rose agreed cheerfully. "Abducting me, torturing me, wanting to keep going to try to make me break, deciding killing me was better than letting me go. If anyone was ever owed the apology of all apologies, it's definitely me."

Her gentle teasing, making light of a situation he knew had caused her pain, helped him relax a little. "I'm sorry, Rose. Truly. We all should have known better than to give in to the anger inside us and go after an innocent person. I don't know how you're even able to look at any one of us, let alone do ... the stuff I smell you doing with Steel."

Rose laughed before sobering. "I'm not saying I'll ever one hundred percent get over what you all did to me," Rose said, her voice growing serious. "You gave me new scars when I already had so many, you tried to take my power over myself like my brother had been doing my entire life. But I'd be lying if I said I couldn't understand why you did it. I guess that helps me to put it in perspective, put myself in your shoes, and see things the way you did. Steel was the first person to offer me true freedom, a chance to find out who I really am when I'm not fighting against being what someone else wanted me to be."

"Yet you chose to stay here with us when given a choice of freedom."

"Sometimes being free doesn't mean being alone. If I'd left, I'd be right back where I was before, all alone in the world, trying to figure things out on my own. But here I have Steel. He's crazy, and obsessive, way too overprotective, but ..."

"You're falling in love with him," he finished for her, and she nodded.

"It's the craziest thing. I know how it looks to anyone else, but what I feel for him is real, and it's terrifying. Feelings weren't part of my childhood, and when I got away from Ridge, I thought that developing them for anyone was a weakness, something that could be used against me, but I was wrong. Feelings aren't a weakness, they're a strength. I've never felt stronger than I do knowing I have Steel at my back. The rest of you are starting to feel like brothers, and I finally feel like I belong somewhere."

So much of what Rose had just said resonated with him in a way he wasn't sure anyone else could have affected him. Their childhoods had been similar in so many ways, and he, too, felt like he didn't know who he was, and that allowing himself to feel anything for anyone else was a weakness that could get someone hurt.

"Cassandra's back, I don't know the details of what went on between you two other than she left over what you all had planned for me, but the details don't matter right now. All that matters is what you want the future to look like. I was able to forgive Steel because I made the choice to look forward instead of backward. It doesn't fix what's behind you, or make it disappear, but it makes it easier to keep moving on, and one day maybe the past will be so far behind me I can't even see it clearly anymore."

That was what he wanted. To move far enough away from the past that it could no longer keep its claws in him. Dragon wanted to find his own freedom, wanted to know who he was, who he wanted to be, and he wanted Cassandra to be part of that future.

If it wasn't already too late to make that happen.

∾

January 6th
    3:37 P.M.

The house was different than it had been last time Cassandra stayed there.

There was life in it now.

Which sounded weird because when she'd stayed last year, the thing she'd enjoyed the most was that the guys often kept to themselves and everything was so peaceful. That tranquility had been shattered when more of her family moved out there, but the craziness had all come from her family, on the whole, the guys still kept to themselves.

But not so much anymore.

Something had obviously shifted when Rose moved in. Although the rooms were all set up the same way, and she assumed the guys all retreated to their personal spaces when they needed them, there was a connection between them that had been missing before.

These men would kill for one another, she had no doubt about that, never had. They were family in every way that mattered. But they also needed their space, and unless training together or working on something in their office, they were usually on their own.

When she'd woken up a couple of hours ago, unable to get much sleep even though she was exhausted, she'd come down to the kitchen expecting to find it empty. Instead, it had been bursting at the seams. All six of the guys were there along with Rose, and there'd been chatter and laughter.

Neither had been there last time.

The guys talked, sure, they weren't mute or anything. But they used to only talk when necessary, and there was never any laughter. Today, however, they'd been talking with Rose about vegetable gardens she wanted to plant in the expanse of lawn between the mansion and the forest.

Cassandra had overheard Rose mentioning how it would be nice to do something to the space out back, and Blade had piped up about how they should put the vegetable gardens out front as a memorial to Rose's escape attempt.

Expecting mention of Rose's drive to escape the men who had abducted her to bring down the mood in the room, she'd been prepared to rush in and defend the other woman, but laughter had broken out. She could pretty much hear the eyeroll in Rose's voice when she'd sassed back that she wouldn't have needed to run if the guys had been more welcoming hosts.

Still unsure if Rose was okay or pretending for the sake of sounding strong in front of a group of tough men, when she'd stepped into the room, the woman had shot her a warm smile, and Cassandra had been shocked. She'd known that Rose was okay—well, not okay, more like accepting—of what had happened, but seeing it being talked about like it was no big deal made her feel silly.

Was she the one who had ruined what could have been with Dragon instead of him?

At the time when he'd brushed her off and told her she had no say in what he and his team did, it had felt like a big deal, only now she wasn't so sure.

It was certainly nothing in light of what Rose had gone through, and yet here the other woman was, perched on Steel's lap, wearing one of his shirts, chatting with the guys as they ate what looked like a late lunch.

Joining them all at the table felt weird. Last time she'd been the one attempting to inject chatter into the room any time they were all together. The guys always responded, but she'd known that if she wasn't there, more often than not they would have eaten in silence.

Not anymore.

Now they all seemed to communicate with each other just for fun.

Which made her feel even more like an outsider. Everyone had been happy enough to have her back, she felt that genuineness coming from all of them, but their little family unit had grown stronger with Rose's addition, and it felt like she no longer belonged.

Not that it should matter since her stay was temporary.

Only it did matter.

"You okay?"

Steel's voice startled her, and she realized she'd been standing at the window long enough for everyone else to disappear. Dragon included. It didn't seem like he was going to be interested in spending any time with her now that he had her there, and now the protectiveness she'd felt these last couple of days felt like a ruse just to get her someplace safe.

"Sure," she agreed, pasting on a smile.

These days, her smiles felt less and less genuine and more and more like an act. Last time she was there, she hadn't felt the need to keep up the act she'd been putting on with her family. She'd felt free to be more like her real self without her family's pressure. Not that her family would pressure her to be okay if she wasn't, but she put pressure on herself to not let them down by being weak when they were all so strong.

What she needed was to get out of her own head for a while.

"I think I'm going to go take a walk." Fresh air was what she needed. Cassandra might be the baby of her family and the only girl, but she had six big brothers, and she'd spent a lot of time following them all around. Since they all loved the outdoors, she grew to love it too, even if she enjoyed different things.

"There should be a coat for you in the closet by the front door," Steel informed her. "Mittens, beanie, and scarf should be hanging with it. We made sure we had it all ready for you since we know you like to go on walks."

The man turned and headed out of the kitchen, and she let out a little breath at being alone again. All her life, she'd hated to be by herself, that had been especially true after her mom and stepdad's arrests and murders. Even when she'd been there before, she'd craved company, and since she felt a pull toward Dragon, she'd gravitated to his.

But since she left there and went back home, she'd found solitude more and more appealing. When she was alone, there was no pressure to pretend that everything was okay when it felt like she was drowning in a sea of uncertainty.

Pausing at the door, Steel turned to look at her. "We're all glad you're back. It wasn't the same once you left. Dragon wasn't the same."

With that, the man disappeared, leaving her staring after him, her mouth hanging open. Dragon had really changed after she left? Why did that seem so hard to believe?

Sighing, Cassandra headed through the maze of halls to the foyer and found the coat in her size hanging in the closet by the front door, along with everyone else's. Tears stung the backs of her eyes, and for the first time in months, she didn't feel so alone. Her family made sure they contacted her regularly, came around often, and invited her over to their homes at least once a week, which meant she rarely ate dinner alone.

But she *felt* alone.

Now she felt a teeny, little bit less alone.

Shrugging into the coat, she wrapped the scarf around her neck, pulled the beanie low on her head, and shoved her hands into the mittens. Sufficiently rugged up for the cold winter afternoon, she headed outside.

Covered in snow, a magical quality was in the air that hadn't been there last time she'd stayed, and for a little while she was able to silence the doubt and uncertainty inside her and just wander through the woods she'd come to know so well.

It wasn't a conscious decision on her part, but she quickly realized she was heading toward what had become her special spot. There was a small waterfall about a thirty-minute walk from the house. She'd discovered it on a walk one day several months ago, and after that she made a point of heading out there most days. There was something soothing about the sound of the water tumbling over the rocks. Birds would sing around her, butterflies and dragonflies darted about, and sometimes she'd see deer. With it being winter now, she wouldn't see much if any wildlife, but she hoped to feel that same sense of peace once she reached it.

A large rock under a tree right by the waterfall had become her favorite spot to sit, and even though the rock would be freezing cold and was covered in a dusting of snow, Cassandra went to it and sat down, resting her back against the tree trunk.

Out here, nothing distracted her from her thoughts, but there was also no pressure. No one expected anything from her, no one expected her to bounce back to her old self despite the fact that her entire foundation of life had been shaken to the core. There was no need to pretend that she was doing better, that finding out her paternity didn't change anything, that she was going to be okay.

With that freedom came the ability to let go and stop hiding her emotions. They burst out of her with a noisy sob, but she didn't try to stop it, letting her tears stream down her cheeks like a mess of tiny ice cubes.

If she wanted to reclaim her life, the first thing she had to learn to do was stop pretending for everyone else's sake. She just wasn't sure she knew how.

CHAPTER
Eleven

January 6th
4:29 P.M.

Damn it, she was crying.

Sobbing.

Dragon froze, his confidence floundering. If Cassandra had come out here to her special place to cry, it would stand to reason that she'd want to be alone. Maybe he should leave, head back to the house, and try to talk to her another time.

He'd already turned and taken a few steps in the direction he'd just come when he realized he was running all over again. It was cowardice, pure and simple to never fight for Cassandra to stay. Now he was doing it again. Finding any excuse to delay a conversation he knew had to happen.

Do you want to lose her for good?

The question flitted through his mind with a mocking tone. It was daring him not just to admit that he didn't want to lose Cassandra from his life, but that he wanted an actual life with her. Wanted to find a way to become someone who wouldn't hurt her, who could maybe even cherish her. He had no idea how to be that person, but the more time he spent in Cassandra's presence, the more he couldn't lie to himself about it anymore. He wanted to figure out how to be what she deserved.

Which meant he couldn't give in to the urge to run and hide. Not this time.

Resolutely, Dragon turned once again and stepped out of the trees, alerting Cassandra to his presence. He knew the exact second she saw him because she choked on a sob, and he thought she was going to quickly stuff her feelings down, wipe away her tears, maybe offer him a small chuckle, or at least some words to convince him that she was okay.

But she wasn't okay.

Not even close.

Only this time, Cassandra didn't try to stop her tears or offer him a smile, their gazes met, and she held his, allowing tears to continue to flood down her cheeks.

Those tears did something to him, tore something wide open inside his chest. A rush of emotions he could identify but wasn't sure he'd ever experienced before came flooding out. Tenderness, affection, softness, a desire to go over there and wrap her in his arms, kiss away those tears, then hold her on his lap so she would know she wasn't facing the uncertainties of the world all alone.

Still holding her gaze, Dragon closed the small distance between them. Instead of pulling Cassandra into his lap, he sat on the rock beside her, close enough that their bodies touched, and he soaked up the feel of her against him.

"I never told you this before, but this was where I always used to come when I needed to be alone, but also needed the grounding of nature around me," he admitted. Growing up in a mafia family, there was no time to play or enjoy the beauty of the grounds surrounding the family home. Besides schoolwork, he was expected to learn the family businesses, shadow his father, and work out in the gym. There had been no time for his caged soul to fly free, not until he moved out there and had the freedom to do whatever he wanted whenever he wanted to do it.

"This is your special spot, too?" Cassandra asked, lifting a mittened hand to brush away her tears.

Snapping out a hand, his fingers circled her wrist before she could get the moisture on her gloves. In the cold temperatures, that small amount of moisture would freeze into icy little crystals, making her hands too cold.

Her surprised eyes stared at the fingers gently holding her wrist, then his other hand as it reached out to capture her tears. Like it was mesmerized, her gaze didn't break away as he brought his fingers, covered in her tears, to his lips. If he could take her pain that easily he would in a heartbeat.

What was more pain and suffering when it was all he'd ever known?

Cassandra was pure, she was innocent, she was light. Anything that dared to touch her made him want to tear the entire world down to punish it.

"My special spot," he agreed as he kept his hold on her, only letting his fingers slide down to hold hers rather than her wrist.

"I never knew that, you never told me."

"Never told anyone." The guys all had their spots around the house and grounds that they escaped to when the raging fire inside them got too big to handle and they needed to disconnect and get themselves back under control.

It was in the first weeks of living there that he'd found this small waterfall. In those earlier days, he'd struggled to tame his anger in a way the guys hadn't. They might not have all lived perfect lives before they joined the military, but none of them had been raised to be the head of a mafia family. None of them had their childhoods stolen from them, and the resulting seed of anger long since planted.

Finding Cassandra at the spot where he sat when he needed to calm himself filled him with a sort of pride he hadn't been expecting. It was almost like she'd sought it out because it was his, even though he knew she couldn't smell his scent there the same way he could smell the lingering scent that marked this place as his.

"We signed up for Dr. Gardner's program willingly," he told her. She knew bits and pieces about what had happened to his team, but he no longer wanted to keep the rest of it from her. If they were going to have a chance at being ... something ... then he didn't want anything between them.

"You don't have to tell me what happened. I know I'm not part of this, part of you. You were right when you said what I thought didn't matter, that it wasn't relevant."

"Actually," he said the word slowly, but he hadn't been so certain of anything for a long time. "You matter more than I was ready to admit. I want to tell you, Cassandra, if you want to hear." For once, Dragon didn't fight against the moment of uncertainty that nudged inside him, urging him to retreat.

"I want to hear." Her fingers squeezed around his and held on, giving him the strength he needed.

"Back then, we were young, arrogant, and enticed by the idea of being the best of the best. We didn't know Dr. Gardner's name, he was just Doctor. I was excited when we got those first shots. I wanted to have enhanced skills, it was a heady rush to know we'd be unbeatable."

"When did things change?"

"It wasn't long until we all started experiencing uncontrollable rage, followed by suicidal thoughts."

Cassandra gasped, her fingers tightening almost convulsively around his. Wanting to soothe her, Dragon began to rub small circles across her knuckles. This desire to calm someone else was new to him, but he didn't fight against it.

He was done fighting against what he wanted.

"None of us gave in to it, little rabbit," he reminded her, even though she knew that they were all alive and well. "We discussed it amongst ourselves, the possibility that we should back out, but Dr. Gardner convinced us it would pass. We believed him, continued with the treatments, but it only got worse. When Dr. Gardner told us he'd figured out what had gone wrong and how to undo it, we all offered ourselves up like lambs to the slaughter."

"What did he do?" Cassandra whispered.

"He sedated us. When we woke up, we were all naked and locked inside a bulletproof glass cage. There were beds, and a table and chairs, but nothing else. He had put shock collars on us to control us, although he only let us out a handful of times. We were like his own personal kill squad, completely at his mercy."

"How long?"

"Three years."

"Dragon," she murmured, pain in her tone, and she pressed closer against him. "I'm so sorry. How did you get away?"

"New guy messed up, he didn't lock the door. We got out, killed everyone there, waited for Dr. Gardner to return, but he never came back. After a few weeks, we left the facility, stayed on the run for the next year before we chanced making contact with Eagle. He brought us in, set us up here, and gave us jobs. We owe him everything. He even found us the name of the doctor who had played God with our lives."

"Rose's brother."

"Rose's brother. We couldn't get a lead on him. Wherever he's hidden himself away, he's off the grid. Nothing in his name, nothing to trace."

"That's why you decided to use Rose."

"It felt like the only thing to do if we wanted to stand a chance at getting to her brother."

"I didn't—"

"Don't," he cut off whatever excuse or apology she was going to give. "You were right, Cassandra. We shouldn't have gone after Rose. It was wrong. She was an innocent, and going after her proved we were the monsters we'd fought for so many years not to become."

Pausing, he drew in a breath. He'd come this far, there was no point in backing out now.

"It's not just what was done to me that turned me into a monster," he admitted.

"You're not a monster, Dragon."

Holding a finger to her lips, he gently shushed her. "I know what I am, little rabbit. And what I am is a monster. I was one long before I joined the military and wound up in Dr. Gardner's experimental program. My family is a well-known mafia one, and I was raised from birth to become the next head of the family. Any gentleness, softness, goodness that might have been inside me when I was born, despite my DNA, has long since been beaten out of me. I didn't need Dr. Gardner's drugs to make me lose my ability to feel emotions, to erase my conscience. I'd shut down any emotion by the time I started school because it was the only way to survive."

The finger he held to Cassandra's lips brushed absently back and

forth. Since he wasn't wearing gloves, didn't need the additional protection from the weather, he enjoyed the feel of her soft skin beneath the
calloused pad of his finger.

"You are everything that is good about this world, and I'm everything that isn't. You're good and sweet and pure, I can't ever be the man
you deserve. Everything you want, I can never give you."

At his revelation, he'd expected her to either offer assurances that he
could be what she wanted or confirm that he couldn't.

What he didn't expect was for another sob to break free as she
tugged herself out of his grip and ran off into the forest.

~

January 6th
6:14 P.M.

Running hadn't been her smartest decision.

Especially since Dragon had opened up to her and told her about
what happened to him and his team. Instead of offering him the
comfort he needed, she'd panicked because he'd dug at a wound he
didn't even know existed.

Nobody knew.

Because to the rest of the world, she was always sweet Cassandra
Charleston. Tragically, she'd lost both her parents by the time she was
five, had six overprotective big brothers who all her girlfriends had
crushes on, and all her boyfriends were scared of. She was a librarian,
who spent her days surrounded by books and working with kids. She
was bright, bubbly, and sunshiny.

All of that was true, but beneath lurked a secret.

One she hadn't shared with anyone she knew.

One that had haunted her since she learned the truth about what
happened to her mom and how she was conceived.

Would Dragon still want her if he knew the truth? Knew what she
craved deep down in the secret places of her soul?

The answer had to be no.

The only reason he was interested in her was because he thought she represented everything he'd never had but always wanted. Her allure was the sweet, innocent girl everyone thought she was. If he knew that she had much darker fantasies lurking beneath that bubbly exterior of hers, he'd regret ever wasting a second on her.

Still running had been childish.

Even if he'd just confirmed that whatever she hadn't allowed herself to hope for between her and Dragon would never happen because he wanted someone who didn't really exist.

Despite that, she should have thanked him for opening up to her. She knew how hard that must have been for him to let in someone who was an outsider. She doubted anyone at Prey outside of Eagle Oswald himself knew the whole truth about the Delta Team guys, she was sure her brothers didn't.

Now, after hours of wandering aimlessly through the grounds, Cassandra had come back to the house. She couldn't stay outside forever, it was already dark and getting colder by the second.

It was time to face Dragon and the mistake she'd made in running.

Walking into the house was like stepping into an oven. She was immediately surrounded by a wall of heat that made her cheeks sting as she began removing her outer clothing. Slipping off her boots, she padded lightly through the house, heading for the kitchen. She'd had a late lunch, but Cassandra was hungry again.

As a peace offering, she should ask Dragon if he'd like her to cook him—and the others—something for dinner. She enjoyed cooking. Since her grandparents had been older by the time they took in her and her brothers, she'd often stepped up to help with chores to give them a break. Especially after her brothers all graduated from high school and went off to enlist in the military or college.

"It didn't rise," Dragon said from the kitchen as she approached, disappointment heavy in his voice.

"She won't care," Rose said back.

"True, D, she won't," Steel added.

"I wanted everything to be perfect," Dragon huffed, and she could hear pots and pans being clanged about, although she had no idea what he was making.

"She doesn't care about perfect," Rose said soothingly. "She'll appreciate the effort. I swear it won't matter to her that the bread didn't rise."

Bread? Dragon was making her homemade bread?

That had been one of her favorite winter hobbies ever since she hit her teens. She'd bake a fresh batch of bread in the afternoon, and then for dinner she'd eat it warm, straight from the oven, or sometimes toast it and spread her grandmother's fresh homemade strawberry jam on it. The smell of baking bread always gave her that warm and fuzzy feeling she associated with home.

When she'd stayed there before, she'd baked bread no more than a handful of times. How had Dragon figured out it held such emotional significance to her?

"The jam turned out perfect," Steel piped up, and Cassandra's heart swelled as tears clouded her eyes.

Even after she'd thrown his revelation back in his face by running, he still wanted to do something so unbelievably sweet for her. And the man thought he didn't feel emotions and had no conscience.

Hurrying the rest of the way into the kitchen, she found Dragon trying to scoop out the dough that hadn't risen from the mixing bowl. All three heads snapped around to look at her as her socked feet skidded to a stop.

"You made me homemade bread and jam?" she asked Dragon, uncaring of the fact that they had an audience.

The big man shrugged, and a slight blush darkened his tanned skin. He looked somewhat sheepish about it, but it was one of the nicest things anyone had done for her in a long time. Part of playing the role of someone who had it all together was that people believed you. Her brothers would forever be her protectors, but they were building new lives, and while she knew they would never ever forget about her, she was going to play a less prominent role in their futures as the women they'd fallen in love with took center stage.

As it should be. There wasn't a hint of jealousy inside her, her brothers deserved their happy endings, she just felt lonely and left out.

Or she had.

Until now, anyway.

Without hesitation, Cassandra hurried over to Dragon and threw her arms around his waist, uncaring of the fact that he was covered in flour, which now smeared all over her clothes and face, even getting in her hair.

"Thank you," she whispered, pressing her face into his chest and breathing in deeply Dragon's slight woodsy scent, now softened with the sweetness of strawberries, and the doughiness of rising bread.

Slowly, his arms came up to wrap around her. "The bread didn't rise. I messed it up somehow. I followed the recipe I found exactly so I don't know why."

Smiling, she pulled back a little while remaining in the circle of his embrace. "I could teach you my recipe if you want?"

Those unusual eyes of his searched hers as though he didn't quite believe her. "You want to?"

"I'd love to. This is one of the sweetest things anyone has ever done for me."

"You have six brothers who spoil you rotten," he reminded her.

"Do you have any idea what it's like to grow up with six crazily overprotective brothers? No boy asked me out until I was in college because one of my brothers would always be hanging around to scare them off. I don't know how they managed it since they were all in the military, but one of them always seemed to be home. I had to throw the biggest tantrum to convince them to let the boy I liked ask me to go to prom."

"They love you." Dragon's hand brushed some flour off her cheek, and she couldn't not think of the gentle way he'd wiped away her tears when he found her sobbing in her—no *their*—special place in the forest.

Or the way his finger had felt against her lips.

"They do," she agreed. "They drive me crazy, but I'm so lucky to have them in my life. They're the best big brothers any girl could ever wish for. Dragon." Her fingers curled into his T-shirt, grabbing fistfuls of it and praying he believed her. "Me running, it wasn't because of you."

"Sure," he said, clearly not believing her.

When he went to move away, she tightened her grip. "I swear. I'm so grateful you opened up to me, shared the horrors you endured. It helped me to understand why you were so adamant about your decision and why you didn't want me interfering."

That violet gaze of his searched her eyes again, assessing the truthfulness of her words, and she could see his nostrils flaring as he obviously used his enhanced scent to try to do the same.

"You're not a monster. Not now and not ever. You might be scared to let your emotions out because of how you were brought up and then what happened, but you still feel them in here." Keeping one fistful of T-shirt in her fingers, she placed her other palm above his heart. "What you're doing right now, making me bread and jam, even after I ran off, proves that you are a good man who cares about the people in his life. Who cares about me."

"You don't have to explain—"

Pressing her fingertips to his lips, the same way he'd silenced her earlier when she was going to tell him she was sorry she'd interfered, even if she could never endorse hurting an innocent woman, she shushed him. "I want to explain. When I ran it had nothing to do with you or what you'd just told me."

Taking in a deep breath, Cassandra wondered how much to say. There was no way she was comfortable telling Dragon all about her darkest fantasies, because once she told him, she shattered his illusion of her and lost him forever. For now, she needed the grounding his feelings gave her, even though that was incredibly selfish of her.

"I'm not the innocent girl everyone thinks I am," she admitted, dropping her gaze because she knew there would be doubt in Dragon's.

He wouldn't believe her if she told him the truth, nobody would. And Cassandra didn't know how to express the side of herself she kept hidden. If people knew the truth, especially those who knew what had happened to her mom, they would realize just how broken inside she really was.

CHAPTER
Twelve

January 6th
8:51 P.M.

Today felt like the first day of something new.

A new life, maybe?

That felt too cheesy, and Dragon wasn't comfortable being quite that sappy. Still, he couldn't deny that spending the last couple of hours in the kitchen with Cassandra had left him feeling lighter, freer than he ever had before.

His world had never been full of choices. His family's expectations, the military's, Dr. Gardner's, then having to live in hiding so the crazed doctor couldn't come after him until they had enough intel to bring him down. He'd never had an opportunity to figure out who he wanted to be and how he wanted to live his life.

He still didn't have all those answers, but as he looked at the warm flush on Cassandra's cheeks, and the twinkle in her eyes, he knew he wanted more of this.

More light moments like those they'd shared in the kitchen as she taught him how to make bread. More joy as he listened to her giggle, to her ramble on about old memories of all the times she'd made this meal with her grandparents, and the crazy things her brothers had done when they were all younger.

It didn't make him miss his own brothers. He could quite happily live the rest of his life without ever seeing his two younger brothers again, although he did feel sorry for his sister, who would be sold off to another family to strengthen a bond. He hadn't shared the same kind of familial bond with his own siblings, so he didn't miss their absence in his life. Besides, the next brother in line for the throne was exactly what his father wanted him to become, a ruthless, cold-hearted, selfish man to carry on the family empire.

"You still have a little flour here," Cassandra told him as she stepped up close enough that her body brushed against his. Her fingers were gentle as they found the spot on his forehead and brushed it free.

Every cell in his body wanted to wrap his arms around her, drag her up against him, grind his growing erection into her hot center, crush his lips to hers, and kiss her until neither of them could breathe. Only he couldn't do that. Not only did Cassandra deserve a sweetness and softness he wasn't sure he had in him, but she'd run earlier.

Even though she said she hadn't run from him, because of what he'd told her, he was having a hard time believing it. Her scent said she was being honest as had the clearness in her eyes, and the tone of her voice, and yet for once, he wasn't able to put blind faith in his ability to smell other people's emotions.

Like she was feeling the same tension simmering between them, Cassandra let her fingertips drop slowly. Trailing down his cheek and brushing across his lips before dropping down to hang by her side.

He ached at the loss of her touch, but he resisted the desire to grab her hand and bring her fingers back to his lips. Suck each one into his mouth and fantasize about what she would taste like if he could strip her naked and bury his face between her legs.

For his little rabbit, he was prepared to tame his darker instincts, find a way to learn to be gentle and soft, and give her what she needed. If it meant keeping her, he'd do whatever he had to do, including keeping himself on a leash.

After all, wasn't that what he'd spent his entire life doing?

While he yearned to be free, to not have to hide any parts of himself, for the gorgeous woman smiling shyly at him, he'd do anything. Literally anything. What was taming himself when it meant he got to keep this ray of sunshine by his side?

"Hey, lovebirds, we're hungry," Thunder called out from the dining room.

Usually, they ate at the smaller table in the kitchen, but tonight Cassandra had set the dining room table, added candles and a vase of origami flowers that Rose had made and handed over, beaming with pride. It felt nice to spend some time together. Before Dragon had always craved solitude, because he knew the darkness inside him was different from what lived inside his teammates, his brothers.

But tonight, differences didn't matter.

Tonight, he was focusing more on what bound them together than what had the ability to tear them all apart. He had no idea how his team would react to finding out he was supposed to be the head of a mafia family. As much as he'd like to believe that they would accept that he'd had no choice in what family he was born into, that sliver of doubt had him keeping quiet.

"Guess we'd better feed the hungry hoards," Cassandra said with a giggle as she took a step back.

Before he could rein in his instincts, he growled at the distance she'd put between them and grabbed her hips, dragging her back toward him. Since he knew Cassandra wasn't ready for the ravishing kiss he'd plant on her lips, he leaned down and touched his lips to her forehead instead, allowing them to linger as he grounded himself with her caramel scent.

"Yeah, guess we'd better feed them," he muttered, releasing her even though it was the last thing he wanted. But if he didn't, he was going to have her spread naked before him, eating her out until she was screaming his name, without a care in the world that his team would hear everything.

With a last heated glance, Cassandra picked up the loaves of bread they'd baked together. There was the homemade jam he'd made when he came back to the house after Cassandra had run off. Wanting a way to draw her back in, see him not as a monster but as someone who could worship her if she let him, he'd remembered her stories about the homemade bread and jam she'd make with her grandparents and decided to make some. Luckily, the jam had turned out great, even if his first go at bread hadn't risen.

Since his team was joining them for dinner, they'd also thrown some meat in the oven, and prepared everything else they'd need to make burgers with the bread instead of buns. Although he knew both he and Cassandra would be eating the bread with jam.

"Okay, okay, hungry animals," Cassandra teased as she carried in the bread while he brought the meat. Everything else was already on the table, including drinks and his jam. "Here's your food."

"About time," Voodoo said with a grin, making Cassandra's smile widen.

The desolation he'd felt coming off her in waves ever since she'd first come to stay with them had receded a little. There was a lightness back to her, and she was smiling more, smiles that reached her eyes and didn't feel fake.

"It smells amazing," Rose gushed from where she was perched on Steel's lap. The man could hardly stand not to be touching her, and Dragon was starting to understand what that felt like. Cassandra had taken the seat beside him, and yet it felt like an entire ocean was between them.

"Thank you," Cassandra said, blushing even as she beamed in delight at the compliment.

"I've made bread a thousand times before, but it was always just a chore, and I swear it never smelled as good as this," Rose continued, and he could see a firm friendship developing between the two women.

Hopefully, another point in his favor to Cassandra giving him a chance.

Everyone agreed and began helping themselves to slices of bread. Then, to his surprise, they started passing the jar of strawberry jam he'd made around the table. The meat sat there, as they all slathered jam on slices of the still-warm bread, and then took huge bites, offering him congratulations on what was apparently delicious jam.

As Cassandra took a bite of her own bread, her happy gaze locked onto his, he felt rather than scented her joy. He'd learned to rely on his sense of smell for everything, but for once it was nice to take a step back and feel something instead.

And the longer he stared at Cassandra, the more he felt.

It was like his chest was swelling as emotion built up there. It was the strangest feeling, he had no idea emotion could be experienced in this way. But those feelings lodged there, and they weren't unpleasant. There was warmth to them, echoed by the laughing, chattering voices of his team as they enjoyed the meal.

Only he and Cassandra remained quiet. But it was a nice quiet, a connected quiet, one they shared amidst the hustle and bustle of what was happening around them. Their gazes remained locked, and he felt no desire to let it go.

His darkness needed her light, and now that he'd taken that plunge, he was determined to do whatever it took to ease the doubts Cassandra had about him and make her his.

~

January 7th
7:00 A.M.

As she padded barefoot down through the corridors of the mansion, Cassandra felt more like her old self than she had in months.

Learning how she'd been conceived had rocked her foundation so badly that she'd started to feel like she could never go back to the bright and bubbly young woman she'd been before.

But last night something had shifted.

Baking bread in the kitchen with Dragon had been exactly what she needed. It reminded her that even though her life felt rocky right now, there were still things she could cling to. Happy memories from her past, old hobbies she had neglected for far too long. A man who had laid himself bare before her.

Dragon was trying, he was making an effort to open himself up to her. Sharing not just details on what had happened to him and his team, but about his family and what his life had been like as a child, was a big step for him, and she knew it, respected it, and felt a little more for him because he'd done it.

It was also bittersweet.

Because beneath the words he'd given her were the ones he hadn't. She saw it in the way he looked at her, though. He looked at her like he was trapped in the dark, and she was a ray of light that would lead him out.

What happened when he learned that she had her own darkness?

That she wanted to join him sometimes in the darkness.

Just because she had chosen not to follow in her parents' footsteps and head into some kind of military service didn't mean that she was darkness-free. She just liked her darkness contained in one particular area of her life, one that she could control, that could satiate her needs and leave her free to spend the rest of her time in the lighter parts of the world.

When Dragon looked at her, he saw spun glass. Something he had to be careful with, treat like it was breakable. But she wasn't breakable, and if they ever took their budding relationship to the next level, she didn't want to be treated like some porcelain doll that could shatter if he wasn't careful.

She was pretty sure Dragon would freak out more than all her brothers combined if they ever found out that while she was in college, she had frequented an on-campus group that participated in rough sex. The kind where you tied each other up and inflicted a little pain along with a whole bunch of orgasms.

It was the wildest thing she'd ever done, and back then she hadn't quite grasped the consequences of what she was doing. It wasn't until she dated a guy she met through someone she'd known in the club after she'd graduated that she realized the potential dangers of the kind of rough, dark, dirty sex she craved with someone she couldn't one hundred percent trust.

That particular lesson had left behind a few scars when the guy had neglected proper aftercare, and she'd realized that she either had to lock away her dark fantasies or find someone she could trust her body with.

Dragon was that man.

Part of her had known that from the second she first laid eyes on him. The darkness inside him called out to the darkness inside her, and she'd wanted so badly for him to see past everything else, the perceptions everybody else had of her, and just see ... her.

But he hadn't.

Maybe more of the blame for that fell on her shoulders, though, because she'd been so busy just trying to survive. To figure out how her paternity changed her so she could discover who she was going forward and what she wanted.

When she reached the conservatory at the back of the house, where she'd done yoga every morning she'd spent there other than the day before, and that was only because she'd slept until after noon, she came to an abrupt stop.

The room wasn't empty as she'd been expecting.

Dragon was standing in the thin, first rays of dawn shining through the glass walls. He was wearing nothing but a pair of gray sweatpants that hung low on his hips and nothing else, giving her a perfect view of all that delicious, tanned skin and perfectly defined muscles.

Darn, he was droolworthy.

Too bad they weren't at a place yet where they could openly drool over one another. Might never get to that place.

So for now, it was look but don't touch.

"What are you doing here?" she asked as she walked over to him like she wasn't growing wetter between her legs by the second.

"What are you doing here?" he shot back.

Narrowing her eyes at him, she held out the rolled-up mat she carried with her. "You know what I'm doing. Same thing I always do to start my day. Yoga."

Nodding at the mat already on the floor, he shot her a smirk. "Same."

"You don't start your day with yoga."

"I do today."

When he moved over a little to give her space to lay out her own mat, his muscles seemed to ripple, and it took all her self-restraint not to reach out and trace them with her fingertips. Or the tip of her tongue. "Do you know, or is it an accident?"

"Huh?"

"Never mind."

His hand grabbed her wrist as she bent down to set her mat on the ground. "Tell me."

There was a slight command in his tone, but that wasn't what had her giving an answer. It was the sliver of doubt in his eyes. Her running yesterday had made him doubt himself, and she wasn't sure how to rectify that without sharing her secrets with him, and she wasn't ready to do that yet.

"The sweatpants," she explained.

"What about them?" His brow furrowed as he looked down at them and then back up at her. "I thought they would be good for yoga, but I can change if it's not appropriate."

She snorted at his words. Gray sweatpants weren't appropriate for yoga, or for anything when you wore them with nothing else. Obviously, he had no idea that gray sweatpants were like the sexiest thing a guy could wear and turned girls on faster than any foreplay ever could.

"They're fine to wear," she muttered.

"I don't get what the problem is then."

"I know you don't, and that only makes you cuter."

"Cuter?" Dragon made a face at that, and since he still held her wrist in his hand, he brushed the calloused pad of a thumb over where her pulse was fluttering wildly. His nostrils flared, and then a smile broke out on his face. "Ah," he nodded in understanding. "Now I get it. For some reason, my sweatpants turn you on."

Knowing he could smell her arousal didn't help, and even though she definitely felt embarrassed, she also got a whole lot wetter. This man turned her on more than any other ever had, and she'd even dial back her dark fantasies if it meant giving him the soft, sweet sex he wanted from her.

She could learn to like it vanilla if it meant having Dragon, couldn't she?

"Do we have to talk about this?" She groaned, sure her cheeks were flaming red, and it was only half from mortification, the rest was pure desire.

Using his hold on her wrist, he tugged her off-balance so she stumbled forward and planted her free hand against his chest to keep from falling. His free hand curled around her backside, and since his hands were huge, the position left his fingers brushing achingly close to where she longed to feel them.

He'd set her on fire, it seemed only fair he should put it out.

Smoky arousal flared in his violet eyes, and she was positive he was going to crush his mouth to hers. So sure in fact that the tip of her tongue swept along her bottom lip, already anticipating what it was going to feel like to kiss Dragon. Properly kiss him, not the chaste little kiss they'd shared last Thanksgiving.

But he didn't kiss her.

At least not where she wanted.

Instead, he brought her hand to his mouth and pressed his lips to her palm. Then his fingers brushed across her center before he released her and took a step back.

Darn him and his restraint.

How did she get him to realize she didn't want restraint? She wanted him to let go, unleash the monster he believed lived inside of him, and take anything and everything he wanted from her. She wanted to be possessed, claimed, owned. She wanted him to tear her apart and then put her back together again afterward.

Cassandra didn't necessarily want to want all of that. It felt so wrong now that she knew her mom had been held down and gang raped by four men who thought they could do whatever they wanted without consequence.

But wrong or not, she couldn't deny that her darkest fantasy was to be chased, then caught. Tied up and held down. Clothes ripped from her body as she was spread open to be taken roughly until her body was littered with bruises, and pleasure built so high inside her it could no longer be contained.

If Dragon knew the thoughts running through her mind, he'd be disgusted with her.

Everybody would.

There was something wrong with a woman conceived via rape wanting to, for all intents and purposes, be raped herself.

Something was wrong with her.

CHAPTER

Thirteen

January 7th
    12:18 P.M.

How was he supposed to focus on anything that wasn't Cassandra?

Joining her for yoga had been a bad idea.

But how was he to know that wearing sweatpants was apparently some girl secret language turn-on code?

Looking around at the guys sitting at the large conference desk they had in their office, he wondered if they'd ever heard that girls liked sweatpants. They didn't discuss their sex lives with one another.

Ever since they'd had their DNA altered by Dr. Gardner, Dragon had never looked for a woman to have sex with, he'd always thought it was too dangerous. Mafia family rules meant he'd had his first sexual encounter at thirteen with his father watching on. The woman was a prostitute, at least he hoped she'd been, because as he grew older, he'd suspected that she was in fact a human trafficking victim, although he had no way to verify that. Once he escaped and joined the military, he'd kept himself on base so there hadn't been options for sex.

Prostitutes had been his only option as a teenager, and he'd never felt entirely comfortable with it because the older he got, the more he understood what his family was and the more he believed those women were not there by choice. So while he'd had enough sex to satisfy his father that he saw women as something to be used for his own pleasure, he actually hadn't had much sex at all, where he was free to explore what it meant to share that intimate act with another person.

He didn't need to be the most experienced guy to know that Cassandra had been burning hot for him this morning. Didn't need to have enhanced scent to smell her arousal, which had flooded the room the second she saw him waiting for her.

There wasn't a doubt in his mind that every single one of his teammates was more experienced sexually than he was. No one brought girls back here, but that didn't mean they didn't travel into the nearest town to find a sexual partner. Maybe they did, maybe they didn't, although he doubted Lion did, the man was still hung up on the woman he'd left behind. And Steel had Rose now, so he wouldn't be looking at anyone else.

"Did you know about sweatpants?" he blurted out, causing all five sets of eyes to turn to stare at him quizzically.

"Sweatpants?" Blade asked.

"What about them?" Thunder asked.

"Why are we talking about clothing in the middle of what is supposed to be an important intel gathering session?" Steel demanded.

Shrugging, Dragon felt bad about derailing their work, not that they'd been making much progress anyway, but he didn't back down from his question. If he was going to do his best to fight against his instincts and his fears and embrace this whole pursuing Cassandra thing, then he figured part of that was embracing the brother bonds he had with these men.

"I know what he's asking, and yeah, D, I know," Lion told him. There were shadows in the man's eyes, the pain of leaving behind someone he loved not having dimmed over the last decade, but there were the remnants of fond moments from what he was sure felt like another life to Lion.

"Well, I still don't know what in the hell we're talking about," Voodoo said, looking utterly lost.

Lion rolled his eyes at all of them. "You all really that stupid? You never noticed that girls go crazy about gray sweatpants? Does something to mess with their libido."

"It does?" Steel looked intrigued by the idea, and he had no doubt the man would be buying gray sweatpants as soon as they finished up here.

"As if Rose needs another reason to have sex with you," Blade said with a mock shudder. "I swear all I hear these days are the sounds of you two going at it."

Steel just grinned. "What can I say? My girl is insatiable, and I can't look at her without wanting to be buried inside her. Too bad I can't stay that way." Steel's voice conveyed true regret as he said that, and it went without saying that the rest of them were grateful that it wasn't a viable possibility. Being happy for Steel and Rose was one thing, wanting to see the man they considered a brother, and the woman they were beginning to see as a baby sister having sex was quite another.

"I wore sweatpants to do yoga with Cassandra this morning, and she suddenly got all weird and started on about sweatpants. Took a while for me to get out of her what she was talking about," he explained, feeling extremely odd to be having this conversation. In his house growing up, conversations revolved around making more money, dealing with staying off the cops' radar, and dealing with those who betrayed the family. They did not involve discussing a girl he was obsessed with.

"So, you guys ended up doing some active yoga?" Thunder teased.

"Actually, we didn't. She wanted to, and damn did I want to. But Cassandra is so innocent, so perfect, I don't want to do anything until I'm sure I can control myself. The last thing I want to do is hurt her."

"Then maybe we should all be focusing on what we're supposed to be doing. Once Dr. Gardner is dead, I think we'll all feel better about controlling the anger inside us," Steel said, but it was clear from the look in his eyes that as soon as they were done here, he'd be tracking down Rose, stripping her naked, and having his way with her.

That was actually true, though, so Dragon picked up the sketch Cassandra had given them of the woman who had accosted her. Since the man who had attacked her in her home was a mercenary without any attachment to Ridge Gardner other than wanting the money for delivering Cassandra to him, they were focusing on the woman to try to get a lead on Dr. Gardner. They had a few possibilities on who Cassandra's assailant's partner might be, but again, that wasn't going to lead them to the crazed scientist.

"What do we think of her?" he asked. The woman looking back at him was yet to be identified, but she had soft blonde waves that hung just past her shoulders and wide blue eyes. She also looked young. Too young to be working with the doctor, and yet she knew about what had been done to them, the doctor's experiments, and what would happen if they were caught again. There was no denying she was involved despite her seeming too young.

"She has to be an employee," Voodoo said. "One of them."

"No one else is bothered by the age thing?" Thunder asked. "Because I am. She knew about us, but from her looks she's barely twenty. How could she know about things that would have happened when she was a kid? She doesn't even look old enough to have graduated from college, and I can't see someone like Dr. Gardner hiring anyone who wasn't the best of the best."

"Looks can be deceiving," Blade reminded them. "Just because she looks young doesn't mean she is."

"Still, she'd have to be at least in her thirties to have been a recent graduate working for Dr. Gardner back then," Lion piped up. "And I don't remember there being anyone younger than us."

"Cassandra only saw her in the dark," Dragon said. "I'm not doubting her description of the woman, but in the dark, with the woman all in black, and her being totally unprepared to be approached, she could have gotten the aging wrong in her sketch."

"And it's not like we don't know for certain she's involved," Voodoo said. "She knew everything, and she was there with a warning, so she's in on it all."

"Or maybe a relative?" Thunder suggested.

"Just because we didn't find any evidence of it doesn't mean that Dr. Gardner doesn't have a kid out there," Lion said. "Maybe this girl is his daughter, and she knows what her dad is up to but isn't involved in it all."

The problem was, there were too many options, and they had no way to narrow anything down because they couldn't get a hit on this woman on any database they searched or any CCTV camera they hacked. It was like she had randomly materialized out of nowhere and then disappeared once again after delivering her warning to Cassandra.

"She did go to Cass to warn her, to try to save us," Blade said. "Maybe she was on the doctor's side, but now she's flipped."

"I wish we'd been able to follow her longer, figure out where she went after talking to Cassandra," Steel said, and they all nodded their agreement.

This woman was like a ghost. No one out there seemed to match her description, and yet she existed. He'd seen her with his own two eyes, although at the time he'd thought she might have been a drug dealer.

"Until we can ID her, we need to focus only on facts," Steel said. "Anything else is merely conjecture and not going to be conducive to finding out who she is, how she connects to Dr. Gardner, and finding out where she is now. All we know for certain is that this woman knows who we are, knows we work for Prey, and figured out that Cassandra is also connected to us. We know she knows that we were injected with the experimental drugs, knows that we're the only ones who survived, and knows the doctor's plans for us if he were able to capture us again."

"Which he won't," Voodoo injected confidently.

"Whoever and wherever she is, I don't think we're the only ones looking for her," Dragon said slowly. "Cassandra was attacked only after the woman spoke to her, so likely unintentionally, she led Dr. Gardner right to Cassandra. If she wanted to hurt her, there was nothing stopping her from doing it when she tracked her to the park, and it would be counterproductive anyway if she wanted to ensure the message got to us. I think Blade is right. I think this mystery woman used to work for Dr. Gardner, but now she's flipped sides. Which means if we can get our hands on her before the doctor finds her, we can get enough intel out of her to find Dr. Gardner's hideout and end this once and for all."

"Any way we have to get it," Blade agreed, and they all nodded.

This woman might have changed sides, but it was too little too late if she thought it was going to save her from their wrath.

～

January 7th
    10:49 P.M.

Was there a way to delay the inevitable ending for the evening?

Cassandra wasn't sure. If she had to guess, however, the answer would be no.

It wasn't like they were doing anything particularly special. She was just sitting in a huge cinema room, which they hadn't used once in the months she'd stayed there before watching some movie that Rose had chosen. It had been the other woman's idea to have a movie night, and while she'd been expecting Steel to immediately agree, he seemed to be prepared to do anything to make Rose happy, she had been surprised when the others all readily agreed as well.

So, movie night it was. Complete with popcorn, soda, and an assortment of candy. With her stomach pleasantly full after dinner and then way too much junk, Cassandra had been more content to watch the man sitting beside her than the movie.

The first time she'd stayed there, she'd been attracted to Dragon, but when she'd left, she was sure that the whole attraction thing she'd felt between them was completely one-sided. These last couple of months, she had been absolutely positive she never wanted to see Dragon again, that the whole thing had been a mistake, and she just wanted to put it behind her.

That Dragon had come when he thought she might be in danger helped a little, but it was everything he'd done since then that told her she'd been wrong in thinking things were one-sided. Gentle touches, sweet gestures, opening up about his past. How was she supposed to resist any of that?

The truth was, she didn't even want to.

Why would she?

Dragon was a strong, loyal man who seemed to actually care about her. Sure, they both had some issues that needed to be addressed, but they could do that while exploring whatever this thing between them was.

"Thanks for hanging with me tonight," Rose said when the credits began to roll.

"Everyone always enjoys your company, but now you're mine for the rest of the night," Steel said, scooping Rose into his arms as he stood and making her squeal and then giggle.

The couple was utterly adorable, and Cassandra watched them as Steel ran out of the room holding Rose with a wistfulness that she hadn't quite been expecting. Falling in love and having her own family had always been something she wanted. From the time she was the littlest girl, she'd played weddings and moms and dads. Maybe it was her small mind trying to recreate what she'd lost.

As she got older, her darker desires started to make themselves known, and she quickly realized she was a little different than the other girls her age. Still, it had always seemed inevitable that one day she would find a prince charming who liked things rough in the bedroom but sweet the rest of the time.

Until last year when her paternity came to light.

Now she hated the part of herself she had always accepted so easily, even more so now that she knew that Dragon wanted her because he thought she was the soft, sweet, innocent girl she was in other aspects of her life.

"I'll walk you to your room," Dragon told her as he stood and held out his hand.

Slipping hers into his was the easiest thing in the world, and he tugged her gently to her feet. In high school, no boys ever offered to walk her to class or home at the end of the day because they were all scared of her brothers. She'd always felt like she missed out on some of the high school experiences, even though she'd enjoyed those four years.

"Night," she called over her shoulder to the others, but her gaze was only for the man beside her. As much as she loved the tender way he held her hand, she wanted to yell at him that he didn't have to be so gentle with her all the time. She wasn't going to break.

If she could survive learning her father was a rapist, and then shooting him, she could survive anything.

Sure, the revelation had rocked her entire world, leaving her feeling lost and adrift, but the more time she spent with Dragon, the more she found the pieces of herself that she'd thought had disappeared. Her smiles were becoming more genuine. The lack of strength she feared separated her from her family felt more like her imagination. And Dragon's presence made her feel a whole lot less alone.

"You knew about the woman at the park before I called to tell you," she said as they headed up the stairs.

His violet gaze met hers, and then he gave a single nod. "I knew someone came up to you at the park, but not what she said to you or what she wanted."

"You were watching me."

"I was."

"The whole time I was gone." It made sense. She'd always had that feeling of being watched, but she'd assumed it was just a result of her own insecurity and that nobody was ever really there. Well, nobody had really been there, but the feeling was because Dragon had been watching over her the entire time.

"You weren't okay when you left here."

"Everybody else thought I was. My family believed me when I said I was coping with everything we'd learned."

"Your family might have fallen for your sweet, little lies, but I'm not them. I saw right through your act."

"How?" If even the people who knew her best in the world, who had helped to raise her, had been fooled when she pasted on a smile and assured them she was dealing with everything, then how had Dragon seen the truth?

His free hand reached over the tapped the tip of her nose. "I could smell the truth a mile away, little rabbit."

"You can smell all my emotions?" It was so weird, like she got that dogs had the ability to scent things in humans related to their emotions, but Dragon had to be the first ever person who could do it. His enhanced sense of smell was an amazing thing, even if it did leave her feeling vulnerable before him. He had an edge in figuring her out that she didn't have when it came to him.

"Most of the time. With everyone else I always can, but with you ... sometimes it's like I'm the old me and I have to figure you out by watching you, listening to you, and trusting my gut the old-fashioned way."

"So, I'm special?" she asked, only half teasing.

"Special," he agreed, sending a flush of warmth through her system.

They'd reached her room, and Cassandra wanted so badly to ask Dragon to come in with her. It was only the fear of rejection that held her back. Would he still want her if he found out she wasn't the angel he seemed to think she was?

Before she could make up her mind if the risk was worth the potential rejection, Dragon leaned in and brushed his lips to hers. The kiss was sweet enough to cause cavities, and although it had arousal thrumming between her legs, she wanted so much more. Wanted to tangle her fingers in his hair, wanted their tongues to duel, wanted his hands on her body, roughly massaging her breasts, then his fingers plunging inside her. She wanted him to take what he needed from her instead of being so worried about what he should give her. Because his pleasure would be her own.

But the kiss didn't progress anywhere, and her hope dimmed as he straightened and reached around her to open her door for her. He was never going to be comfortable giving her the kind of intimacy she craved.

"Sleep well, little rabbit."

Since she didn't want to embarrass herself, she nodded and hurried into her room, closing the door behind her. She had to figure out a way to enjoy what Dragon wanted from her, or she was going to lose him forever, and she didn't want that.

Stripping out of her clothes, Cassandra headed into the bathroom, turning on the shower and stepping under the spray, making an attempt to keep her stitches dry. As warm water rained down upon her, she slipped her hand between her legs. Her bundle of nerves was already throbbing with need, and if she could just make herself come with nothing more than touching it, then maybe she stood a chance at giving Dragon what he wanted.

Circling her bud, she tried to find her rhythm. Pleasure built in her system, she grew wet and thrust a finger inside herself. Finding that magical spot she knew was in there, she brushed her fingertips against it

with each thrust, and her thumb worked her bud, as she chased the pleasure that seemed to remain just out of reach.

Tears of frustration built as she tried so hard to climb to the peak,
but the more she tried, the further away it seemed to get, until she gave
up with a frustrated groan. This was useless. She couldn't come from
just a little touching, and she'd never come if the sex didn't involve
bruising grips, a sting of pain, a dominating, demanding lover who
commanded her pleasure like it was their right to do so.

"Dragon," she whispered helplessly to the empty room. "How can
you not want me the way I need to be wanted?"

CHAPTER

Fourteen

January 7th
   11:15 P.M.

He was still standing outside Cassandra's door.

Unable to move away.

She was in there, and she wanted him, and it had taken all his self-control not to deepen the kiss, ravish her mouth until she couldn't think straight. Desire didn't just pulse through his system, it pounded through it, consuming him.

But if he allowed it to consume him, he'd have her naked beneath him, pounding into her until he lost control and took what he needed without keeping a clear enough head to ensure that she got what she needed as well.

That was a line he couldn't allow himself to cross.

There was no way he would ever do anything that would jeopardize her safety and her well-being. She'd been through a lot these last few months, and he knew she'd been holding on by a single thread even if no one else in her family had realized it.

He had been the only one not to fall for her act, and it seemed to be working, having her there with him. With his team. She had a family who loved her unquestionably, who would move heaven and earth for her, he had no doubt about that, and he knew Cassandra didn't either.

But he and his team offered her something else.

They offered her freedom from being seen as the baby of the family. The somewhat spoiled, but ever sweet and bubbly little sister who needed to be protected and coddled. Her family saw her decision not to join any form of law enforcement or military as her being weaker than the rest of them. Not in a bad way, he doubted they even saw that they did it, but their protective instincts had been kicked into high gear, losing their parents the way they had, and because she hadn't had formal training like they had, they continued to protect her as though she were still a five-year-old girl.

Only the woman who had just walked away from him was the strongest he'd ever met. Strength came in all different shapes and sizes, and that his little rabbit could learn she was the biological child of a rapist who tried to kill her family, and then was the one who took him out in the end, proved that you could be small and sweet but still strong.

"Remember that, little rabbit," he murmured as he pressed his palm to the door separating him from what he wanted, what he craved. "Don't ever forget that you are strong enough to do anything. Don't let anyone ever make you feel weak. You can conquer the world, and you can do it with a smile on your face, and nobody will even see it coming."

Arousal began to filter through to him.

The scent was heavy with caramel, and he knew his little rabbit had been left hanging tonight.

"Sorry, Cassandra, but I won't take you until I know I can do it the way you deserve."

Because his strength only went so far, Dragon turned his back on the door to his little rabbit's room and headed downstairs. If he stayed, he'd throw caution to the wind and find Cassandra in the shower and show her that only he controlled her pleasure. That she came when he told her to, and how hard he told her to. He would show her an entire world of pleasure she didn't even know existed.

But not yet.

Not until he got himself under control.

Since arousal consumed his system, and he needed a way to let it out without taking the stairs three at a time and breaking down Cassandra's door, Dragon headed for the gym. He'd go a few rounds with the bag and hope that was enough to work out the excess energy buzzing through his veins. He could always go to his room, hop in the shower, and get himself off to thoughts of his little rabbit doing the same thing a floor beneath him, but for some reason, finding pleasure without Cassandra felt like a betrayal.

So, the gym it was.

It was quiet in there. Everyone else had either retired to their rooms for the night or were lurking somewhere else in the Gothic mansion. Time alone was exactly what he needed, he had to find a way to cling to the self-control he'd found tonight if he was going to pursue a relationship with Cassandra.

Just because he could never be what she deserved, both nature and nurture were working against him on that one, and that was without even adding in the experimental drugs he'd been given that had forever changed him, it didn't mean he could let her go again.

When she returned, she'd walked right into a snare, and now he was never going to let her go. Couldn't. She was his light in the darkness, she was sweetness in the bitterness of his soul. He was in awe of her strength, her beauty, and her ability to smile and search for the best in people and situations. She was a glorious angel who had done the one thing no one else ever had; she'd made him feel things that weren't just anger and vengeance.

Letting her go was impossible, and while it seemed too good to be true, she seemed to see something in him that she liked.

Too good a thing not to take advantage of.

Hands taped and gloves on, Dragon attacked the bag like it was the sole reason he wasn't upstairs with his girl right now. Like the punching bag was responsible for raising him to be a monster, then messing with his DNA to ensure that it stuck.

If only he was like the other guys on his team, if only he'd had a somewhat normal childhood, known love and affection, done normal things. If he could erase the hits he'd witnessed before he reached double digits, erase the agonized screams of men being tortured, he'd do it in a heartbeat. If he could find a way to inject even a tiny bit of love into the small childish heart that had once longed for someone to wrap him up in a warm embrace and just hold him, then he would.

Not for him. He had long since accepted that his family were demons walking the earth in human skin, but he wished for an ounce of softness inside him so he could offer it up to Cassandra and assure her he'd learn to be what she needed no matter what it took.

Time lost all meaning as he pummeled the bag.

Thoughts ran through his mind, the past, the present, the future.

What he wanted, what he wished he could change, how he wanted to be going forward. It was a terrifying thing to open himself up to someone when he'd been taught since birth to hold everything inside.

By the time he took a step back, he was breathing hard, his heart hammering in his chest, pulse pounding in his ears. Maybe that was why he didn't realize he had an audience until he turned around.

"What did that bag ever do to you?" Lion asked, watching him with an amused smile. But beneath that smile, he could see the pain, the loss, the regret. They all knew there was a woman Lion had never gotten over, and he wished there was a way for the man to go after that woman and see if she still had feelings for him and could forgive him for leaving in an attempt to protect her.

He'd never really understood that level of love for another person. How could he? There was no love in his family. Everything was transactional and born from expectations. But Cassandra made him want to be a better man, to find where his heart was buried under layers of pain and anger, dig it out, and figure out how to use it.

"Better than the alternative," he said as he yanked off his gloves and began to unwind the tape.

"Cassandra?"

"It's crazy, right? I don't deserve her, I know that. I'll never be good enough for her. She's been through so much, and I don't want to hurt her. I can't help but feel like I will somehow, someway. How could I not?"

Being vulnerable with another person was hard for anyone, but for someone like him, it felt as though he was tearing himself open, literally peeling off his layers of skin to expose what was underneath. But if he said he wanted to change, find his heart, and work toward being what Cassandra deserved, then he had to fight through his instincts that were screaming at him to backtrack.

"How could you not take that risk?" Lion countered. "How could you throw away a chance with a woman we all know likes you, cares deeply for you, could maybe even fall in love with you? Do you want to end up like me, alone and full of regrets?"

With that, his friend turned and disappeared, leaving Dragon staring after him. It was the first time the other man had been so open about the fact that he had a lost love out there somewhere.

The question posed to him was an easy one to answer.

There were no guarantees he and Cassandra would work out, and no guarantees he could ever become what she needed or wanted. But he absolutely didn't want to walk away again without fighting for his little rabbit with everything he had in him.

~

January 8th
5:27 P.M.

Despite last night's frustrations at being unable to make herself come with just her fingers, today had been a good day.

Cassandra had expected to be told no when the guys had announced after breakfast and their early morning workout that they were going to run intel for a few hours and she asked to sit in with them, but Dragon had immediately agreed. In fact, he'd even smirked when she'd planted her hands on her hips right after asking and prepared herself to argue her point.

No need to get your feathers ruffled, little rabbit.

That's what he'd told her. Before she could stop herself, she'd sassed right back at him that rabbits had fur not feathers, and he'd gone and laughed.

Laughed.

It was the first time she'd ever heard such a sound come from Dragon, and she'd just stood there, open-mouthed, staring at him, soaking in the carefree laugh she knew he never found much cause to make. Couldn't imagine there had been much to laugh about when he was growing up either. Being part of a mafia family sounded terrifying, especially for someone like her who had grown up with the love of parents, siblings, and grandparents.

Not only had she been pleased to be included in the guy's intel gathering session, not that she had much to contribute, unlike Rose, she didn't even know all the key players well enough to be helpful, but Dragon and the others had been completely open with her. They'd shared with her more details about what had happened to them after they were injected with the experimental drugs, and she knew that was no small feat.

While she didn't want to get her hopes up, mainly because she wasn't sure whether she'd stay there with Dragon after she was no longer in danger, or if he even wanted her to, she knew it meant they were accepting her. Welcoming her into their little family and making sure there was nothing left between them.

Clearing the way for her and Dragon.

If she was brave enough to take those steps toward what she wanted. And it *was* what she wanted, she was just scared. Because there was no way to try having a relationship with Dragon and not be honest about her sexual preferences.

Even if she pretended that she could have sex the normal way, Dragon would notice that she never came. Of course she could fake it, but somehow, she was pretty sure that he would either figure it out because he'd be the kind of guy to feel that her body didn't orgasm, or maybe he'd be able to smell it.

Either way, she didn't see faking it as a long-term solution. Which only left telling him the truth and facing his judgment and rejection.

"You're quiet tonight," Dragon said from beside her as they worked on dinner together in the kitchen.

"Just thinking," she said honestly. The silence between them had been comfortable, she'd been relaxed enough to let her mind wander and not succumb to her usual need to fill any quiet with chatter. Since growing up with her brothers, all moving out one after the other, eventually leaving her alone with their elderly grandparents, she'd missed the noise and commotion as each brother left. So she'd overcompensated and started filling any and all silences.

Except tonight.

Except with Dragon.

When she'd stayed there before, she'd quickly found that whenever she was alone with Dragon, she never felt the need to chatter. Being with Dragon filled her with contentment that didn't need anything else.

Her phone rang, and when she saw it was Cade's name on the screen, she smiled as she wiped her hands on a dish towel and snatched it up. She knew her phone was safe to use, the location services had been turned off, and the guys had gone through it to ensure it was clean, so no one could track her location. Not even her brothers.

"It's Cade," she told Dragon as she accepted the call. "Hey, big brother. How's my absolute favorite brother today?"

"Hi, boo," he said, using the nickname she hated. Her phase of hiding and jumping out to scare her brothers, yelling out 'boo' at the top of her little lungs had stuck even though she hadn't done it since she was eight, resulting in the silly nickname. "And I'm only your favorite because I'm the one talking to you, you're a fickle little thing, baby sister."

Cassandra laughed because that was true. She'd always called whatever brother she was talking to her favorite, except if they were all together, then it was whichever one did something nice for her. Everyone knew she didn't really have a favorite. She loved every one of her brothers, biological or step, equally.

"How's my favorite niece? Is Essie still excited to be the flower girl at the wedding?" The five-year-old had been obsessed with weddings and being a flower girl ever since her daddy proposed to her nanny.

"You know she is, more so since we got her the dress, she's driving Gabriella crazy asking to wear it all the time."

Although she smiled because she could absolutely picture her niece harassing the woman she already called Mom, something in her brother's voice had the hairs on the back of her neck standing up.

Something told her this wasn't a social call or a check-in to see how she was doing.

Apparently, she was giving off those vibes—or scent—because Dragon stopped what he was doing and moved closer.

"What's wrong, Cade?"

Her oldest brother sighed, long and low. "I hate to be the one who has to tell you this, boo, but something happened last night?"

"Gabriella and the baby are okay?" Her first fear was for her soon-to-be sister-in-law's pregnancy, because she'd had so many miscarriages in the past and never been able to carry to term. Gabriella's pregnancy might be running smoothly so far but that fear was still there, and they were all counting down the days until she could give birth to a healthy baby.

"Both fine. This is about you, baby sister." Another sigh from Cade, and she found herself holding her breath and bracing for bad news. "It's your house, Cassandra. Someone torched it in the early hours of this morning."

Her house?

Torched?

It wasn't until Dragon's big body pressed up against hers that Cassandra realized she'd started shaking. Leaning into his warmth and solid strength felt like the easiest thing in the world.

"How bad?" she whispered, although her voice trembled a little.

"Pretty bad. I don't think much will be salvageable. I'm so sorry, boo. I hate this for you. You've already been through so much. Learning about mom, about that man, what you did to end it for all of us." Cade sounded more frustrated with each word, and she could picture him raking his fingers through his hair.

She, on the other hand, felt empty.

Another burden.

Another thing she would pretend didn't break her heart wide open.

Another weight of grief as she lost photos and mementos of her parents and her childhood.

At least she'd brought her bunny with her when she packed that bag and left with Dragon.

"It's not your fault, Cade," she reminded him, injecting as much calm into her tone as she could manage. "I'll be okay. It's just stuff after all. What's that saying? No use crying about spilled milk. What's done is done. Hopefully, at least the cops can get something from it that will help Dragon and the guys link these people to the woman who came up to me and her boss."

"It's okay to be upset, Cass, it might be just stuff, but it's *your* stuff."

"I'll be okay," she repeated firmly, even though that was feeling less and less likely. Just as she started regaining her footing, feeling more like her old self, something else happened to knock her off again. "Call please if you find anything else."

Before her brother could protest or offer more platitudes that weren't going to help, she hung up and set her phone back down. Dragon's hands closed around her shoulders, and he turned her to face him.

"What happened?"

"My house burned down. Someone set it on fire." Was it punishment for her sexual preferences? Because she liked rough sex and her mom had been raped? That was wrong, she knew it, maybe the universe knew it too.

"Little rabbit," Dragon murmured, and his expression grew tender, but it was the opposite of what she needed right now.

All of this was her fault.

Her punishment.

She'd been judgmental with Dragon and his team about their plans, without knowing all the details—not that she would ever have approved of using Rose that way—but she'd been self-righteous when she was the biggest hypocrite of all.

"I'm sorry we dragged you into this, Cassandra. We'll get them, I swear we will. And they will pay for everything they did to Rose, to us, to you."

Breaking free from Dragon's hold, she shook her head and started for the door. No platitudes, no reassurances, no pity.

She didn't deserve any of it.

Running out of the room, she headed straight for the front door, needing to be outside, alone. Tears streamed down her cheeks, blurring her vision, but she knew her way through the house, and once she burst out the door it didn't matter where she ran, all that mattered was that she needed to get away, needed to be alone.

She didn't deserve comfort when she was such a sick and twisted young woman.

CHAPTER
Fifteen

January 8th
   5:59 P.M.

That look was worse than the emptiness on Cassandra's face when she agreed to come out here.

She'd looked guilty.

What in the hell would Cassandra have to be guilty about? She hadn't burned down her own house, she'd been states away here with him. She hadn't asked the people hunting him and his team to go to her and drag her into this. She didn't know who the partner of her assailant was or a way to contact him, and even if she did, why would she ask him to destroy pretty much everything she owned?

There was literally no reason for her to feel guilty, and yet Dragon would have sworn that was the predominant emotion he could see and scent on her before she'd gone running out of there like she was the one set on fire.

Of course, he'd followed after her, yelling at her to wait, to talk to him.

Not that she'd stopped. Hadn't even slowed down. Throwing open the front door and running out into the dark, snowy woods, without shoes on her feet, a coat, or anything else to protect her from the cold.

Growling, he snatched up her things from the coat closet by the door and debated whether he wanted to waste time running up to her room to find a pair of shoes. In the end, he decided it didn't matter, as soon as he found her, he'd pick her up and carry her back inside.

If she was angry, that was fine, she could yell and scream, rant about how unfair it was. If she was devastated, she could weep and sob, grieve for the loss of her belongings. If she felt guilty, she could explain to him why the hell that was so he could understand and assure her that she had done nothing wrong, certainly nothing deserving of being attacked and losing her home.

Whatever she needed to express, she needed to get it out, she couldn't let those emotions fester. Life had been unfair to her lately. She'd been through too much, had learned things about how she was conceived that would upset anyone, and taking a life—no matter how justified—left its own scars behind. Everything life had thrown at her she'd dealt with, but she kept refusing to let anyone in and seemed to be of the belief that she had to handle it all on her own or people would think less of her, doubt her strength.

"Like hell, little rabbit," he muttered as he stomped out of the house and slammed the door shut behind him.

It wasn't hard to follow her trail even though she'd disappeared into the forest. All he had to do was sniff the air and let the sweet scent of caramel lead him right to the woman he was prepared to tear down his own walls for to keep her in his life. Walls he'd spent literally all his life erecting, since he was old enough to recognize his thoughts. Walls that were the only protection he had against his family, against what had been done to him.

Now they had to come down if he wanted Cassandra, and he wanted her.

More than he'd ever wanted anything else.

Which meant learning how to be vulnerable, to be open, to share the darker parts of his soul, he tried his best to keep hidden.

"You can't run from me, little rabbit," he yelled as he stepped within the cover of the trees, his boots stomping across the scattered snow as he zeroed in on his prey. "Don't you know the wolf always catches the rabbit?"

She was still running, he could tell from her scent, she was crying, too, and her tears did crazy things to his insides. It was like they had the ability to sear through his flesh and make him feel her pain. There had never been another person to make him feel the way Cassandra did. Hell, he'd still been willing to torture Rose even knowing Steel had grown attached to her because revenge had been the only thing keeping him somewhat sane.

"Stop running, little rabbit," he growled as he got close enough to her to hear her winded breathing and soft weeping. "You know you're going to get caught."

Dragon would have sworn he heard her gasp at his words, and he hoped he hadn't scared her. He wanted her to know that he was there for her, that she could talk to him. Maybe he wouldn't say the right things, maybe he'd be a little clumsy in his attempts to offer comfort, but he would flatten the world to fix things for her.

Sensing her unease, he picked up the pace, and a moment later, he spotted her moving through the trees a mere ten yards or so away from him. She'd slowed right down, and even from where he was, he could see that she was shaking.

Why had she run when she had a whole house full of people who would have offered her their support? They had been stripped of their consciences, their ability to feel emotions normally, at least that's what they'd spent the last decade believing, but more and more Dragon was starting to see that wasn't true. Even he, who had been raised from birth to feel nothing for anyone, had the ability to feel everything when it came to the brunette still trying to get away from him.

Tired of this game, angry at seeing her socked feet pounding the cold, unforgiving ground, and driven by a need he didn't even under-stand to wrap his body around his little rabbit's and protect her from anything and everything, including herself, Dragon picked up his pace.

He was on her a moment later.

Snatching her up off the ground, she fought against him like a wild animal caught in a trap, and since he was fairly certain she would have done the same thing even if he'd been one of her brothers, he tried not to take it personally.

"Stop fighting me," he ordered as he did his best to contain her small but strong body as she did her best to find a way out of his hold. There wasn't one, and the quicker she accepted it, the quicker he could get the coat, gloves, scarf, and beanie on her, and get her back inside where it was warm. "You have injuries, and you're going to split them open again if you keep doing that."

"Let me go," she wailed, still trying to get free.

"No," he said simply. "I don't want to hurt you, little rabbit, so please stop fighting me."

Apparently, that was the wrong thing to say, although he had no idea why, because she began to sob and beat her small fists against his chest. "I'm not going to break," she screamed into the otherwise quiet evening.

"Of course you're not," he agreed. Why would he think she would? Cassandra Charleston might not look it on the outside, but inside she had a spine of steel.

"Then stop treating me like I'm made of glass," she snarled, and even in the dark, he could see fire burning in her green eyes. "You're just like everybody else, like my brothers, their partners, you think I'm soft, weak. You treat me like I'm still a child, one who needs to be protected and coddled."

"I sure as hell do not see you as a child," he snarled right back at her. Nothing about the fantasies he had of the woman still struggling to get away from him implied she was a child. If he thought he could be a gentle enough lover, he would have joined her in the shower last night, showing her exactly how he thought of her.

"Prove it," she challenged, arching a brow and finally stilling.

"Prove it?" How the hell was he supposed to prove to her that he didn't see her as a child, or as someone who was made of glass?

Cassandra nodded. "Prove to me that you don't think I'm weak and pathetic."

Hearing her say those words about herself made a growl rumble through his chest. Nobody, not even Cassandra herself, got to say that about the only woman he'd ever been obsessed with.

"You left without putting on your coat," he said, wondering if he could maintain his hold on her without hurting her while also wrangling her into the coat.

"Weak."

"And you didn't put on any shoes. It's too cold out here to be running through the forest in nothing but a pair of fuzzy socks."

"Weak," she said again, louder this time, angrier.

"Your hair is still damp from your bath, and the temperatures have to be in the twenties."

"Weak," she screamed into the night, a wildness in her gaze that reminded him of the wildness that lived beneath his own surface, one he fought daily to keep under control.

"Stop saying that about yourself," he screamed back at her.

"Make me," she ordered as her fists once again beat at his chest. "I told you to prove to me that you don't think I'm weak and pathetic, but all you've done is prove that's exactly how you see me, the only way you'll ever see me, the only way anyone will ever see me. You only want me if I'm this meek and mild, sweet and innocent, perfect little angel that you think I am."

None of that made any sense to him, although it was clear by how agitated she was that it meant something important to Cassandra. Not knowing any other way to make her stop talking about herself that way, Dragon backed up so he had her pinned between a tree trunk and his body, kept one arm wrapped around her while his other hand circled both her wrists and held them tight. Then he nipped at her bottom lip to get her to part those lush lips of hers she'd pressed into a thin line, and when she did, he stuck his tongue in her mouth and kissed her like he'd been dreaming of since the first time he laid eyes on her.

～

January 8th
   6:11 P.M.

The kiss short-circuited her brain.

Finally, Dragon was giving her what she craved.

Even though Cassandra knew it wouldn't last, for now she let her heart and soul plunge into the kiss. Let it consume her, pouring everything she felt and was too afraid to put into words, even to herself, into it.

Against her back, the feel of the rough bark called out to the primal side of her, and the tight way Dragon kept her hands pinned together and held tight against his chest, while her body was trapped between his and the tree, had her arousal spiking.

This was what she craved.

Domination, rough kisses, the sting of pain in her lip from where his teeth had nipped at it. It might be everything she desired, but how long could it last?

Shivering at the way Dragon's kiss plundered her lips, her mouth, her heart, her soul, she mindlessly rocked her hips, seeking relief for the fire pulsing between her legs.

When Dragon abruptly pulled back, she let out a moan of disappointment. Was it over already? That was only enough to turn her on, not nearly enough for her to get off, or even to finish things on her own back at the mansion. It was like for a few beautiful seconds he'd teased her with everything she wanted, only to snatch it back again.

"Sorry," he muttered, and she both saw and heard true deep regret.

"Why are you sorry?" she asked, forcing herself not to give in to the hurt, the shame, the disappointment that urged her to tuck tail and run. To hold onto her secrets because nobody was ever going to understand them.

But if she did that, she was all but signing herself up for a life of loneliness.

Dragon was what she wanted, who she wanted. Losing him was almost a foregone conclusion, but what if she was wrong? What if he could accept her as she was?

If he could accept her without judgment, then maybe one day she could even learn to stop judging herself and find a way to accept herself again like she used to before she learned the truth about her mom.

"You're shaking, cold, hurt, upset, just got devastating news, and instead of taking care of you, supporting you, I'm pawing at you like an animal."

"You *are* taking care of me," she said softly. Cassandra wanted so badly to be honest and open about what she needed, but every time she tried to say the words, it was like they got stuck in a knot of guilt.

"I'm kissing you, I'm hurting you." His gaze dropped to where his large hands circled both her wrists, pinning them in place. For a split second that hold tightened, before he slowly uncurled his fingers one by one. His brow furrowed when he looked back up and saw her ravished lips. The nip had left her with a tiny cut, the metallic taste of blood told her that, but the devastated look on Dragon's face confirmed it.

This was one of those now-or-never moments.

Either she kept following the same path she'd placed herself on. Accepted that her family was always going to see her as nothing more than a sweet little girl they had to protect, and that Dragon saw her the same way.

Or she could pull up her big girl panties and for once in her life be honest.

It wasn't her job to play the role her brothers wanted to keep her in. She was twenty-four years old, all grown up, and until she learned her mom had been raped, had been confident in her sexual desires.

What if the universe wasn't trying to punish her? What if it was trying to make her see that in stifling who she was, she was punishing herself for something she'd had no control over?

"I liked it," she blurted out before she could talk herself out of it or second-guess her decision.

"Liked what?"

"The pain," she admitted softly, timidly, nothing like the girl who had once boldly joined a club none of her family knew about and took what she needed without shame. "I wasn't shaking because I was cold. I was shaking because I was turned on."

Those violet eyes studied her, trying to figure out if she was telling him the truth or trying to spare his feelings.

The thing was, though, for once in her life she was putting her own feelings first.

No one could deny she was spoiled, with six big brothers it

happened, but she'd always been a people pleaser, always looking for ways to ease others' burdens, to make them smile and laugh, and bring a little brightness to their day. Sometimes, in doing that, she lost herself a little along the way. Learned to keep quiet when she should have spoken up, to portray the character she believed others wanted her to play.

It was time she stopped acting and became comfortable being herself.

"Smell me," she ordered.

"Smell you?"

"So you can see I'm telling you the truth. I like it rough, Dragon. I'm sorry I can't be the sweet and innocent girl you want. I can't get off that way. I've tried, it doesn't work. I need more. I need to be held down, need my partner to take what they want. I want to feel pain, I want to feel dominated, I want to have my body used in the most deliciously dark ways. I want to see bruises the next morning, I want to see my blood paint my skin red. I want someone to take control and use me."

Her rambled words hung between them like a barrier. Cassandra braced herself for the coming disbelief, then disgust as she described the horrors her mother had lived through and admitted that she liked it. Not what had happened to her mom, that was wrong, and she fully understood the difference between rape and consent. Her mom hadn't given consent, and no one had stopped when she said no. That wasn't what turned her on, Cassandra never wanted to go through what her mom had suffered. But she wanted to hand over her consent and her trust for someone to do whatever they wanted with her body, then experience the intimacy on the other side through aftercare and cuddling.

It was too much to ask.

She was being greedy.

Hoping for the impossible.

Then all of a sudden, the arm bracing her backside moved and Dragon's hand circled her neck, while keeping her wrists pinned to his chest. The only thing keeping her from slipping to the ground was Dragon's big body pressed against hers, trapping her against the tree trunk. The bark pressed harder into her skin, and she sighed as that fire between her legs raged.

Leaning in, he touched his nose to her neck, behind her ear, and she felt him drag in her scent. Trailing down the column of her throat, he shifted the hand around her neck enough that the tip of his nose could brush across her pulse point.

When he pulled back, the hand on her neck tightened. "You enjoy pain," he said like he almost couldn't dare to hope that it was true. But that couldn't be right, could it? Dragon liked her *because* he thought she was soft and sweet.

Nodding as best she could with his hand pinning her in place. "I-it's wrong," she stammered.

"Wrong?" Dragon cocked his head, his expression clearly demanding an explanation.

"My mom was ... and I like it ..."

Cutting her off with a snarl. "It's not the same, and you know it. Consent means everything, little rabbit."

"Before I learned about my mom, I used to agree. I knew it was different, even if people might not get it. But then I found out how I was conceived, and now it's ... wrong. I'm wrong. There's something wrong with—"

"If you finish that sentence, it's going to come with a punishment," Dragon warned as the hand on her neck tightened until she could barely draw in any air.

Instead of panicking, her body heated all over again until she could hardly stand it. Cassandra whimpered as her hips sought any sort of friction that would help.

"You need some pain, little rabbit?" Dragon asked as the hand pinning her wrists let go and grabbed one of her breasts, kneading it harshly before pinching her nipple and making her yelp.

The sting seemed to send little electrical currents straight between her legs, and she whimpered again, needing a whole lot more than he was giving her.

"You really like that." There was wonder in his tone as though he had never considered this as a possibility, and yet was so glad it was.

"Mmhmm." She nodded, feeling both heavy with desire as well as light with lust.

Reaching into his back pocket, he pulled out a pair of plastic zip ties, making her laugh.

"Why do you have those on you?"

"Habit. Always be prepared. Never know when you might need them," he told her as he lowered her down to her feet and spun her around so her chest now pressed into the rough bark of the tree. "Like right now." Grasping first one arm and then the other, he brought them behind her back and tightened the plastic around her wrists.

If she'd thought he was going to hold back, she would have been mistaken.

The zip tie was tight enough that it would cut off circulation to her hands, dig into her skin and make her bleed, and her shoulders were pulled awkwardly in a way that felt like if she moved wrong, they would pop right out of the sockets.

Again, though, there was no fear, only excitement, only arousal.

Yanking down her leggings, exposing her skin to the elements, she felt Dragon press up against her back, the heat of him chasing away any cold she might have felt.

"If we're doing this, I'm taking what I need from you, little rabbit. Taking, not giving. That means you might not come."

"Oh, I'll come," she assured him. In fact, Cassandra was pretty sure she was going to combust the second he slid inside her.

"I don't like knowing that you're so certain of that," he whispered, his breath hot against her ear. "It means someone else has touched what's mine. That won't happen again will it, little rabbit?" he asked as his hand slipped inside her panties and his thumb pressed against her bud, making her squirm. When she didn't answer, he flicked her bundle of nerves, hard, making her yelp. "Asked you a question. Is anyone else going to touch what's mine?"

"No," she murmured, arching her back, so she could look over her shoulder. The tenderness in Dragon's expression loosened something in her chest. There was no judgment, he wasn't watching her with condemnation as though something was wrong with her.

The sound of a zipper was the only warning she got before Dragon literally ripped her panties from her body and buried himself inside her with a single thrust.

Cassandra cried out at the sudden intrusion, she wasn't prepared for anyone, let alone someone of his size. Although she'd been wet for him, that could only carry her so far, and she felt a sharp sting, like she was being ripped open. But it hurt in the most delicious way, and her cries quickly turned to moans as he set a punishing pace.

"Scream for me, little rabbit," Dragon ordered as his fingers roamed her body, pinching at her nipples and then her bud as his teeth scraped along her neck. "Scream so the entire world knows who you belong to."

"You," she quickly agreed. The more his fingers caused pain, the tighter her body wound as it prepared to fling her into an ecstasy-fueled universe.

Grabbing a fistful of her hair, he yanked her head back until she was forced to stare up at the sky. Teeth nipping at her, he thrust into her with an almost manic pace. "Mine," he growled in her ear.

All she could do was whimper her agreement as his fingers flicked at her bundle of nerves and his thumb breached her back hole. Caught off-guard, and totally unprepared for that particular intrusion, pain stabbed through her, but it was the catalyst for everything she needed, and Cassandra didn't hold back, screaming her pleasure into the empty forest.

Dragon hit his own release at the same time, and his teeth sank into her skin on the curve of her neck where it met her shoulder, emptying himself inside her, and never in her life had Cassandra ever felt so perfectly full.

CHAPTER

Sixteen

January 8th
    6:22 P.M.

It wasn't until the haze of pleasure began to ebb and fade that Dragon realized the full extent of what he'd done.

Something wet dripped onto his stomach just above where he was buried so deeply inside Cassandra that it felt like he had to have imprinted on her very soul. Since he was still inside her, it wasn't evidence of what he could only describe as a reckless mistake.

Which meant it could only be ...

Damn.

Blood.

From where he'd bound her wrists so tightly, he was sure she'd lost all feeling in them long before now.

His fingers were still tangled in her long chestnut locks, her head pulled back so she was staring up at the sky. He still had his thumb inside her back hole, which he had breached without a single ounce of preparation, which had no doubt made Cassandra feel like she was being ripped open, and his fingers still rested against her bud.

While shame and anger at himself thudded through his system with a steady beat, if he wasn't still buried inside her, he wouldn't feel the fluttering of her internal muscles around his softening length.

She'd come.

The little rabbit had come from his rough taking of her, just like she said she would.

Uncertain how to proceed, whether he should apologize, beat himself up for being so rough with something so precious, or praise this stunning creature who had bared her soul to him, Dragon pulled out of her slowly. Regretfully. Now fully aware of why Steel felt like he wanted to spend his time permanently inside the woman he was obsessed with.

Untangling his fingers from Cassandra's hair, she moaned slightly as she straightened, and he felt her tense as she obviously floated down from her own high. Was realization coming back for her as well? Was she regretting what they'd done? Was she hurting? Did she wish she'd asked him to be gentler instead of giving the monster inside of him permission to come roaring out?

"If you apologize to me, I won't let you do that again." Cassandra's voice was soft, and yet there was a firmness to it. No hint of regret that he could detect, and when he sniffed the air, he couldn't scent anything other than the mingled scents of their joint arousal.

"That was really what you wanted?" he said, somewhat in awe as he reached for the knife he always carried with him. A single slice cut through the zip ties, and he let them fall to the ground at their feet as he scooped Cassandra into his arms, balancing her in one, while he began to gently massage her hands to restore blood flow.

"Did you think I'd lied? That I didn't know my own body and what it likes?"

Since she sounded insulted by the notion, Dragon rushed to reassure her. "No, not at all. I just ... I've spent the last several months achingly hard every time I think about you, how beautiful you are, how strong and brave. How you managed to keep the essence of who you are intact, even though you kept receiving blow after blow. I kept reminding myself that I could never be good enough for you, that I wouldn't be able to give you the soft and sweet you deserved. Last night, when I walked away from your room and smelled what you were doing in the shower, I wanted so badly to go to you. But I thought I would take you like this, and it would be the opposite of what you wanted, needed."

"Then maybe you should have asked."

Those simple words, spoken so matter-of-factly, surprised a chuckle out of him. "Maybe I should have. You really liked this?"

"Did I come?"

"You did."

"Then I liked it."

"I made you bleed," he said, nodding at her wrists where he was still massaging her hands.

"Yep," she agreed.

"And I will have left bruises on your perfect skin."

"I know." Now she sounded pleased as punch.

"You're a wild one beneath all the sunshine, aren't you, little rabbit?"

Doubt crept into her expression, and he felt her deflate a little, curl in on herself. "Is that okay?"

That she had any doubt at all that he was obsessed with every single part of her, even the parts she was uncertain about frustrated him. Growling, he abandoned his work on her hands and instead spun them slightly so her back was back up against the tree. Then he crushed his mouth to hers and poured every single drop of what he felt for her into it.

At least he hoped he did.

Because Cassandra wasn't the only one with doubts.

"I told you what would happen if I ever heard you talk badly about yourself again," he reminded her. "You said it yourself, little rabbit. There is a difference between your mom being gang raped, and you choosing to like rough sex. They aren't the same. You aren't doing anything wrong by taking what you need."

In the dark, he could still see her searching his expression, searching for the truth. She must have found it because she gave a small nod and relaxed against him.

Good.

He'd earned another piece of her trust. Now it was time for him to show her that trust was well deserved. That he wouldn't do anything to jeopardize it.

"We didn't use protection," he reminded her as he set her down on her feet.

"I'm on birth control, and I'm clean," she assured him.

Surprised by his disappointment that he likely hadn't impregnated her, he knew it wasn't the right time, yet the thought of Cassandra's belly swollen with their child had him realizing it was absolutely something he wanted. "I'm clean too," he promised as he scooped up her ruined panties and the zip ties and stuck both in his pocket, because it turned out that when he let himself, he was a bit of a sentimentalist. Then he grabbed her leggings and carefully guided her legs through them, pulling them up for her. The coat he'd brought with him went on next, and then he added the scarf, mittens, and beanie.

"What?" he asked when he found her watching him with a soft expression as he tugged the beanie down to cover as much of her ears as possible.

"You never let anyone see this gentler side of you. Dragon the caretaker, I like it."

Unsure how to respond, he said nothing, just scooped her up again, and began to walk with her back to the house. There was no way the others wouldn't know what they'd been up to out there. They both smelled of sex, although he had to remind himself nobody else could scent things the same way he did.

Once inside, he was halfway to the stairs when Steel and Rose approached.

"Everything okay?" Steel asked.

"You really have to ask?" Rose said as she smiled over at them. "See how she looks at him? They're okay. Better than okay."

Better than okay.

Those words repeated themselves in his mind as he carried Cassandra up the stairs. There was no way he was taking her to the room she'd been using. If they were doing this, then she was staying with him in his bed from here on out.

In his room, he headed straight for the attached bathroom, setting Cassandra down on the counter while he ran her a bath. He didn't have any girly products to use, but he'd move all of her things up tomorrow.

Tonight, though, he was taking care of his little rabbit.

While the bath filled, he pulled out his first aid kit from under the sink, already running through everything he needed to do. Clean her wounds, bathe her, put her in his clothes, and then in his bed. Feed her, make sure she drank enough water, then tuck her under the covers and hold her while she slept.

The expression on his little rabbit's face was soft and warm as he took one of her hands in his and began to clean away the blood from the ragged wounds on her wrists. They would heal, likely not even leave scars, although he had a feeling that if they did, Cassandra would wear those scars like badges of honor.

"Thank you," she whispered as he set the supplies aside, ready to add antibiotic ointment and bandages after the bath.

"For what? Taking care of you?"

"Not everybody does that," she told him, making him growl.

"Later, you'll tell me who didn't perform adequate aftercare, and I'll make sure I teach them a lesson about how we treat people."

Cassandra laughed. "You can't kill someone just because they didn't take care of me afterward."

"I can, and I will," he corrected as he stripped off her clothes and set her in the bath. Moving to the shower, he grabbed his shampoo and then knelt by the bath, pouring a generous amount into the palm of his hand, and then massaged it into her long locks.

Giving a contented sigh, Cassandra slipped further under the water as he worked the shampoo through her hair. Taking care of her like this eased old hurts. There had never been anyone who had taken care of him when he was a child, he'd been taught to be independent from the youngest age, and he'd worried he had never learned these skills.

Before, it had never mattered. Who had been around for him to take care of?

Other than his team, and the way he cared for them was keeping his anger on a leash and watching their backs, there hadn't been anyone else.

Now there was.

And whether he possessed the right skills to care for his little rabbit or not, he was going to do his best to show her that he could give her everything she needed, and pray it was enough.

~

January 9th
    9:27 A.M.

As she sat watching the guys tap away on keyboards, stare at screens, and scroll through intel, Cassandra kept fiddling with the bandages taped around her wrists.

Every time she looked at them, she got butterflies in her stomach.

Not only had Dragon given her perfect, rough, leave-behind bruises and make her skin bleed sex, but he'd also provided her with the sweetest aftercare. The bath, the tender way he cleaned her wounds, how he shampooed her hair and smoothed out every tangle. Even though she'd told him she didn't need to, he insisted she take some painkillers, and he'd dressed her in his clothes and tucked her into his bed like she was the most precious thing in the world.

It was different than treating her like she was breakable, and she'd felt cared for and protected as he brought up more food than the two of them could ever hope to eat, even with Dragon's appetite. They'd gone to bed early, and she'd easily fallen asleep in his arms.

Perfect.

There was no other way to describe it. It was everything she ever could have hoped for. There wasn't a single box that she could have had on her list that he hadn't ticked off. Even down to his lack of judgment and assurances that her need for rough sex didn't mean she should be punished in light of the revelation about her mom.

The only thing she wasn't sure of was what happened next.

This morning, Dragon had still been attentive. Checking in with her on how she was feeling, where she was hurting, insisting on more painkillers even though it really wasn't necessary, and cleaning and rebandaging her wounds even though the cuts from the zip ties were nothing serious and would heal on their own without any attention.

Despite how gentle he was with her, he hadn't argued when she said she wanted to come and sit in on their intel gathering session this morning. In fact, he'd gone one better and given her something to look through. A database that he hoped might help them identify the woman who had come up to her at the park to ask her to warn Dragon and the others.

While all six of the Delta Team guys were adamant that the woman was a problem that needed to be eliminated, Cassandra couldn't help but feel that was wrong. The woman had information she could only have if she was closely involved in Dr. Gardner's experimental trials, there was no denying that, but she'd sensed a weariness in the other woman.

And all of that aside, Cassandra had something personally to be grateful to the woman for. Without that woman seeking her out, she never would have contacted Dragon again. Her pride and hurt would have led to her keeping her distance, and she wouldn't be where she was at this moment.

Which felt like right on the cusp of something amazing.

Don't get scared and back out on me, Dragon.

I know you think you were born a monster first and then it was made so much worse by what that man did to you, but no monster could have cared for me so sweetly last night.

When the phone rang, she looked up from the screen she was absently staring at, and her fingers stopped fiddling with her bandages.

Last time she'd gotten a phone call it hadn't been good news.

Although, to be fair, the evening had turned out a whole lot better than it should have after learning that her house with pretty much everything she owned inside had been burned down.

It didn't surprise her in the least, that Dragon immediately stopped what he was doing and reached over to ghost a hand over her hair. For someone who viewed himself as a monster, he had taken to the role of protective caretaker like a duck to water.

Steel picked up his ringing phone and answered it. The rest of them watched him like a hawk, and he rolled his eyes at them, but reached for Rose and tugged her up and onto his lap. The other woman went easily, and it gave Cassandra hope that if both she and Dragon kept making an effort to fight through their personal fears, soon they could be as easy with one another as Steel and Rose had become.

"Hey, Connor," Steel said, and Cassandra knew the verbal greeting was for her benefit, so she would know this was likely about her and she could prepare herself.

If her brother was calling Steel with this intel and not her, it had to be about her house, and she realized maybe she hadn't done as good a job as she'd hoped of convincing Cade she was fine when he called last night.

Maybe that was a good thing.

Maybe it was time she stopped pretending that she was okay when she wasn't. Just because her brothers had new lives they were building, it didn't mean they wouldn't still be there for her. It was definitely well past time she let them in and allowed the people in her life to support her as she struggled to make sense of her new identity.

Whatever Connor was telling Steel, he was nodding along, his expression inscrutable, as he listened to her brother. The mostly one-sided conversation went on for a solid five minutes, with Steel asking minimal questions, certainly not enough for her to figure out if it was good news or bad.

When Steel's eyes finally met hers, he held her gaze. "Just so you know, I'm going to be telling your sister all of this," he said calmly. After a pause, he nodded. "Damn right she can handle anything. Thanks, Connor."

"What did he want?" she asked as soon as Steel set down his phone.

"Cops got the man who set fire to your house. Fire investigators were doing their job at the scene, when they noticed a man hanging around watching. He looked nervous, odd, out of place, so they called the cops, who took him in for an interview. He confessed to being the partner of the man who broke into your place. Said he was desperate, and his brother-in-law promised him this would be an easy job. He backed out last minute on going inside that night, said he'd be the getaway driver instead."

"Coward," Dragon muttered.

"When he realized his brother-in-law was dead, he admitted to tampering with Dragon's car. Said it was just supposed to kill you, for punishment, revenge. When he didn't hear any reports of a car crash killing two people, he assumed you were still alive and decided to try to draw you out. Decided he may as well go for the money since he wouldn't have to split it two ways anymore."

"He folded quickly. He wasn't the mastermind," Blade noted.

"He get paid an advance as well?" Thunder asked, his fingers already poised above his keyboard, ready to input whatever information Steel gave.

"He did." Steel rattled off some banking information, and Thunder went to work.

Cassandra waited for the relief to come, knowing that the person who had set fire to her house was in prison, but it didn't come. Instead, she rifled through the intel she'd been looking at on the screen for the last hour. Any database the guys could get their hands on they'd been searching to ID the woman from the park.

They'd had no luck, and neither had she.

Only ...

"What are you thinking, Cassandra?" Voodoo asked, studying her.

Suddenly, all eyes were on her, and she squirmed. "Nothing much."

"We don't do that here," Dragon told her. "If one of us has an idea, we share it and talk it through."

"It's probably nothing," she cautioned. After all, she was the one who didn't know what she was doing. If the guys hadn't picked up on it, she doubted it was anything significant.

"Or maybe it's the missing piece," Lion reminded her.

Nodding slowly, she flicked through the images on the database she'd been searching and stopped at one in particular. "This woman. She reminded me of the one we're looking for. I discounted her because she was too old, but maybe ... I don't know," she finished somewhat lamely.

Picking up her laptop, Steel studied it for a moment and then began to read whatever he'd found. "She'd be old enough to be the woman's mother," he told the others. "She used to work for a pharmaceutical company but retired about a decade ago."

"She would have been young to retire," Blade noted.

"She would," Steel agreed. "And the company went under not long after."

"Went under or changed hands?" Lion asked, and she shot him a quizzical glance. "If this woman is somehow related to the one who gave you the warning, and she worked for a pharmaceutical company, then that's two possible connections to Dr. Gardner."

"What's the name of the company?" Thunder interrupted.

As soon as Steel gave the name, Thunder's fingers flew over his keyboard all over again. Had she found something useful? Had she been helpful in pointing out the woman who had caught her attention?

"Just because the woman who kind of reminds me of that girl works for a drug company doesn't mean anything," she cautioned, worried she was getting her own hopes up.

"Doesn't matter if it does or it doesn't, we work it through, and if it goes nowhere, no harm, no foul," Dragon told her.

"You shouldn't doubt yourself, Cassandra," Thunder said with a grin as he turned his laptop around so everyone could see it, only she wasn't sure what she was supposed to be looking at. "For a company that's been out of business for almost a decade, they just made two bank transfers."

"To them?" she asked, stunned that she'd actually contributed something this big.

"To them," Thunder confirmed. "Two transfers to the man Dragon killed in your house and the one who set it on fire. There is no way in hell that's a coincidence. From Nature, is the company's name, and Dr. Gardner was always on about how his experimental drugs were derived from all-natural ingredients. That he was merely utilizing nature as it had always been intended."

"So this woman really is connected?" she asked.

"Maybe she really is the woman's mother," Lion said.

"There's an address," Blade said. "Only one way to get our answers."

"I'm coming too," Cassandra blurted out before anyone had a chance to say otherwise.

"Oh, I am in total agreement with that," Rose quickly piped up.

"There is no way in hell you are coming with us to check out an address that may be connected to the man who wants us back under his control and who put out a contract on you," Dragon said, so calmly that it spiked her anger.

"Yeah? And how do you plan on stopping me?" she snapped back. All her life, she'd let other people take the lead. She'd never stepped up and helped her brothers try to unravel the truth of what had happened to their parents. This time, she wasn't sitting quietly in a corner and letting everyone else handle things. "I care about you, and I want you to get answers. Besides, this was *my* lead, and I'm following through on it whether you like it or not."

CHAPTER
Seventeen

January 9th
    7:40 P.M.

"Are you going to stop sulking any time soon?"

It would be completely inappropriate and unprofessional to stick his tongue out, and yet Dragon had to fight against the urge. Although he was barely able to rein it in, he was able to keep his expression neutral, impassive, a mask for the terror raging beneath his skin.

Bringing Cassandra with them was a mistake.

A mistake of epic proportions.

Even Rose shouldn't be there, this wasn't like last time when they'd needed her help to reel in her brother. At least Rose had been raised to know how to defend herself. She was capable with a weapon, gun or knife, she had good hand-to-hand combat skills, and she knew how to use her much smaller size to her advantage to still be able to take down an attacker much larger than she was.

But Cassandra ...

"I know how to protect myself," Cassandra said, her voice softer this time, more reassuring. "You're forgetting who raised me. Six big brothers. Six. Do you think any one of them would have allowed me anywhere near a boy if I didn't know self-defense? And weapons training was on the itinerary. I never really enjoyed it, but I know how to handle a gun, and I can hit what I shoot at. Besides, I think once again six is my lucky number because I have six highly trained men with me who aren't going to let anything happen."

The words should reassure him, but they didn't.

Sure, he and his team were highly trained former special forces operators. Sure, they worked out virtually every day, kept their bodies highly toned, and ran training drills. Add in their combined enhanced skills and they were definitely a force to be reckoned with.

But that didn't eliminate every scenario that could go wrong.

A sniper bullet could take out any one of them, and there would be nothing they could do to stop it. An explosion or a fire could wipe them out. Or a small army could still outnumber them.

Nothing was set in stone, and he had never been so aware of that fact as he was right now with Cassandra sitting beside him in the back of an SUV.

If something went wrong today, he would lose the most important thing in his life.

Perhaps the only important thing he'd ever had in his life.

The men with him were the first family he'd ever really had, the first people to ever truly care about him in any meaningful way. But Cassandra was the first person he'd really let into his heart, and the thought of losing her ...

"Nothing bad is going to happen," Cassandra soothed as her hands smoothed up and down his arm.

"You can't know that," he reminded her.

"No, I can't. But that means you can't know that something bad will happen either. We don't even know if this building is occupied. Chances are, it's either empty or has long since been turned into something else."

"Probably not turned into something else since they're still using the address," Blade inserted, causing Cassandra to shoot him an irritated frown.

"Are you helping me right now with that talk?" she demanded. "Can't you see how worried he is?"

"I can see that both Dragon and Steel are about to snap," Blade replied.

"Watch it, Blade, one day soon you might be the one so obsessed with a woman that the thought of anything happening to her makes your chest so tight you can't breathe," Steel said, expressing exactly how Dragon felt.

"Aww, that's very romantic, Steel," Rose teased, although her tone implied that she was pleased with Steel's declaration.

"Not going to happen," Blade said with a confidence that said his mind was made up.

If Dragon had been forced to accept one thing over the last several days, it was that nothing was ever as simple as you tried to make it.

For years, he had been adamant that nothing in him could ever love another person. He'd been born a monster, raised a monster, and made a monster. Letting anyone get close to him was asking for disaster.

But nothing could have stopped his feelings for Cassandra. Not his beliefs about who and what he was, not his determination to protect her from himself, not his mistakes in pushing her away rather than valuing her opinion.

Nothing.

From the moment he laid eyes on her, this had become a foregone conclusion.

Which was why it was so terrifying to have Cassandra there with him. It wasn't a sexist thing, women could be and were warriors, it was about hating the idea of something so precious to him now being in danger. It didn't matter that there was likely no sniper or army waiting for them, he was taking his little rabbit into a situation he couldn't control, and that meant a lifetime of learning to control his fear was quickly unraveling.

"Too late to take it back now anyway," Thunder announced as he pulled the large SUV to a stop outside what looked like an innocuous warehouse. "We're here."

"It's not too late," he contradicted, reaching over and unsnapping Cassandra's seatbelt so he could haul her over and into his lap. "Say the word, and we'll drive you and Rose somewhere safe and then come back here."

"There's nowhere safer in the world than with you," Cassandra said.

The words were so simple, and he could scent that she meant them with the utmost sincerity, but she had no idea what they meant to him. No one had ever trusted him the way she was right now. His family had molded him, the military had trained him, Dr. Gardner had tried to manipulate him, his team relied on him, but Cassandra had offered him her body in trust last night, and now she offered him her life.

As badly as he wanted to ignore her wishes and send her back home, as badly as he wished he'd gone with his instincts and sedated her back at the mansion and dealt with her anger later, he also wanted to prove to her that her trust in him wasn't misplaced.

"You're sure?" he asked as his hands framed her face, holding it still so he could search her eyes for the truth.

"Positive." She offered him an encouraging smile and then leaned in to rest her forehead against his. "I trust you, I believe in you, I want so badly for you to trust me, too."

"Oh, little rabbit, I do." This wasn't about not trusting her, it was about not trusting himself. All his life he'd believed he would break anything precious, so he'd avoided caring about anyone or anything.

But caring for Cassandra was as natural as breathing.

Stopping himself was impossible.

"Then smell me, see I'm not lying. I'm part of this now, and I'm not sitting back and hiding and letting everyone else do the hard things. I may not be part of your team, but I care about you, and I want to help, even if it's just by supporting you."

Pressing his nose to her neck, he dragged in her scent, detecting nothing but a desire to feel part of a family, a team, to no longer sit on the outside but jump all in. Trailing his nose down her neck, he paused above the bite mark hidden beneath the high collar of the jacket she was wearing.

Her trust in him floored him, humbled him, and if he let it, it could also empower him.

Dr. Gardner was going down. The man had signed his own death warrant when his experiments worked, and he tried to keep them as caged animals. For everything he'd done to them, to Rose, and to Cassandra meant Dragon would stop at nothing to destroy him.

Capturing her chin between his thumb and forefinger, he held it tight enough to cause pain and then crushed his lips to hers. When he kissed her, it felt like all the doubts about himself disappeared. Just melted away into nothingness. If a woman like Cassandra could fall for him, then maybe he wasn't the monster he'd always feared.

"H-hmm."

If Lion hadn't cleared his throat, Dragon probably would have remained lost in the kiss. When he pulled away, he saw that he and Cassandra weren't the only ones kissing. Steel had Rose in his arms, and they were also pulling away from each other, both breathing hard.

"We breaking up into teams?" Voodoo asked as they all climbed out of the vehicle.

"No," Steel said quickly, his gaze on Rose.

"Too dangerous," Dragon added, his fingers finding Cassandra's. Normally, they would pair off to breach three different doors at the same time. But that weakened them today, it meant there would only be him and one of his teammates to protect Cassandra if things went bad.

With an ache in his chest and a sense of unease that he prayed didn't mean things were about to go bad, Dragon kept Cassandra close as they approached the innocuous-looking building.

∼

January 9th
8:03 P.M.

She should be a whole lot more scared than she was.

Cassandra stuck close to Dragon as the eight of them crossed the dark parking lot toward the building sitting before them. The warehouse was somewhat remote, the property was large, and there were more buildings out the back that she was sure they would thoroughly examine before leaving.

In her hand, her weapon felt heavy, unfamiliar. She hadn't been lying when she said she knew how to shoot, she did, and she hit what she aimed at even if she couldn't make a kill shot every single time, but that didn't mean she was as comfortable with a gun as the men and woman standing around her were.

Still, she wasn't going to be any more of a weak link than she already was. She had no idea what exactly it was they were looking for, beyond the exceedingly obvious like someone who worked there or a computer full of details, but that didn't matter. At least she wasn't sitting back at home, safe and sound, while the people in her life put themselves in danger to gather intel that would save all of them.

There was no going back to be more involved in the search for answers about what happened to her parents, but this time she was determined to be involved every step of the way. Just because she had never personally met this Dr. Gardner man, he'd brought her into it when he sent people to her home to try to abduct her.

If she was involved, she was helping.

So she carried her weapon, stuck close to Dragon, and sucked in a small breath as Thunder opened a window around the back of the building and climbed inside.

"I don't need help," she muttered to Dragon when he scooped her up before she could jump up and swing a leg over the windowsill. It wasn't high, and there didn't appear to be much of a drop on the other side, given how the others had climbed in.

Ignoring her, Dragon merely passed her through the open window to Blade, who had followed Thunder in. The man snorted a small laugh as he took her and set her on her feet.

"Indulge him," Blade told her.

"He's lucky he has other qualities I like because the overprotective-ness is going to get real old real quick," she grumbled back. But she'd spent her entire life dealing with overprotective men, and since she knew it came from a place of genuine care and fear for all the bad things that could happen to her, she would deal with it again with Dragon.

The guys didn't communicate again out loud. Once they were all in, Voodoo simply eased the window closed again, and then they all started moving. While she knew what her brothers did for a living, knew they'd all been in danger in their various military careers before joining Prey, and then put their lives on the line in every op they went on, she'd never thought much about what that actually looked like.

How many times had her brothers worked in perfect coordination just like this?

It was something to behold, that was for sure. None of them needed to say anything, they just knew what to do and did it. Was every team this in sync or did the Delta Team's special abilities take them to a whole other level?

There had been no lights on in the building when they approached, and now that they were inside, she couldn't hear any sounds at all. It was like nobody was there, but from the thick smell of bleach in the air, it was obvious that someone had been there quite recently. Even without any training at all, she knew enough to know that.

Following along with the others, it didn't escape Cassandra's notice that the guys kept her and Rose in the center of their little circle. From the slightly annoyed expression on her face, it was clear that irritated Rose, but she wasn't going to complain about it. She was there although she knew nobody had been pleased about it, she wasn't stupid enough to think that she was any sort of asset, so she wasn't going to push her luck.

Besides, it did make her feel safer. Just because it didn't seem like anyone was there didn't mean someone wasn't hiding, waiting, ready to make their move.

They passed several rooms that looked like labs and offices. Each one was cleared carefully by the guys, but there was nothing in any of them beyond furniture. Desks, tables, chairs, but nothing more than that. The labs didn't seem to have any scientific equipment set out, nor did the offices have computers or paperwork anywhere.

It gave the whole place an eerie feel, like it had been deliberately cleaned down and cleared out because somebody knew they were coming.

Only no one had known they were coming.

Had they?

The smell of bleach and the lack of any signs of life meant that someone had indeed deliberately tried to erase any evidence of their presence or the work that had been done in the building. But had it been done because someone thought they might link the building to the company that paid money to the mercenaries who had come after her, or was it all just one great big coincidence?

As they moved down silent hallway after silent hallway, the guys clearing empty room after empty room, Cassandra began to lose track of time. Her heart hammered in her chest, and her palms were sweaty. It was a good thing she was wearing a pair of black gloves, otherwise she might have lost her grip on the weapon she clutched tightly enough that her fingers ached.

The sound of her weapon hitting the ground would be much too loud in this way-too-quiet building. The guys moved without making a sound, and Rose seemed to be able to do the same thing. The only sounds were her feet touching the floor with each step she took, and she'd already decided that once they got home, she would ask Dragon to teach her how to walk without creating any sound at all.

Home.

It seemed like it was automatic to think of Dragon's house as her home. It had started last year when she spent months living there, and when she'd gone back to her house, she hadn't been able to make it feel like her home again.

Would Dragon be okay with her living there permanently?

There had been no time for them to discuss the future, and it seemed like it was way too soon for them to be living together as anything more than friends. But she didn't want to go back to her house and sort out insurance and getting it fixed or sold and buy a new one, although she had no idea what she would do for a job if she moved in with Dragon and his team, how she would contribute.

When Dragon suddenly stopped in front of her, Cassandra had no choice but to throw out her free hand to brace on his back, so she didn't slam into him and wind up on the ground looking more foolish than she already felt being there with these highly trained experts.

Grateful at least for the night vision goggles the guys had loaned her so she wasn't stumbling about in the dark, she looked up at Dragon as he turned to face her. His expression screamed frustration, but she knew it wasn't aimed at her or at any of them. They'd all hoped to find something there, and instead, to find nothing more than an empty building meant they couldn't take this lead any further.

Not that any of them would give up.

There had to be a way to find the identity of the woman who had come up to her, even if the lead with the woman who looked like an older version of her hadn't led them anywhere so far. Well, it had led them there, to this suspiciously clean building, but would it lead them to the scientist who wanted to do more experiments on Dragon and his team?

"The bleach is messing with my ability to scent anything," Dragon said, breaking the silence.

"I'm struggling to hear anything," Blade added. "I'm guessing there's some sort of white noise generator somewhere in the building. Every time I think I pick up on something, I can't get a good enough read on it to confirm it's not just us."

"What does that mean?" she whispered, although her voice sounded much louder than theirs had.

"It means that someone doesn't want us here," Voodoo said softly.

"Even I know the bleach means someone cleaned this place down," she said. "That means they knew we were coming, right?"

"If my brother knew you were going to be here, I think he would have had an entire army waiting," Rose piped up. "He knows better than anyone else how dangerous you all are, and you already took out his team when we tried to trap him. He wouldn't have just cleared this place up, doused it in bleach, and left."

"What does that mean?" Cassandra asked, feeling like she was missing something important that the others all seemed to get.

"It means that if this lab was used by Dr. Gardner, he wasn't expecting us to find it, but someone else was. Someone who didn't want us finding what they'd been working on and getting access to it," Dragon replied.

"Who?" she asked.

"Only other person I can think of is the woman who tried to warn you," he answered.

CHAPTER
Eighteen

January 9th
    8:49 P.M.

That was the only thing that made sense to Dragon.

The woman who accosted Cassandra at the park had to be the one responsible for cleaning out the lab. Dr. Gardner might move locations, but if he thought there was even an inkling that they could link the payments to the mercenaries to this building, he would be there waiting for them with an army.

Which, by process of elimination, left only the mystery woman.

But why would she clear everything out and then wash everything down with bleach?

So much bleach had been used that it was messing with his ability to smell anything else. Even the scents of the seven people standing right beside him didn't properly register. It was more than obvious that nobody wanted them to find a single shred of intel there, and it was working.

There were still more buildings out the back to search, and he wouldn't say he had completely given up hope that they'd find anything, but it was getting less and less likely. You didn't do this thorough a job of cleaning up only to then get sloppy and leave something behind.

"So what do we do next?" Cassandra asked. "We still don't know who this woman is, and while the woman I thought reminded me of her led us here, to this warehouse lab that's been cleaned, that woman doesn't have any kids, so they can't be related. The woman doesn't have any sisters, cousins, or nieces either. So they really can't be related."

Sensing her frustration, Dragon took a step closer, brushing a hand down her back. She was holding up so much better than he could have hoped. No part of him wanted her there, he wouldn't feel better until he got her safely tucked away back at the mansion, and he could tell from the way Steel's gaze kept darting to Rose that their team leader felt the same way.

But she was there, and she was doing everything he had told her to, keeping up, staying behind them, keeping quiet, and her weapon in her hand was held with an unwavering grip. It was time he stopped underestimating her ability to handle everything life threw at her. Cassandra had been underestimated her entire life, the fact that she was so sweet and sunshiny made her seem like she might be weak, but she wasn't.

And if he kept treating her like she was, he would lose her.

Guaranteed.

"Next, we finish searching this place, and then we move on to the other buildings here. Even if we don't find anything, we know that this place was connected to Dr. Gardner, the coincidence is too big to come to any other conclusions. That means we go back home and dig into everything we can find out about this building. Even though it doesn't feel like it right now, answers are out there somewhere, and we will find them," he vowed.

Nothing else could be allowed.

Not when the stakes were this high.

"And I can keep looking for the woman," Cassandra said, straightening her spine and meeting his gaze squarely, showing him she was still all in on this and ready to handle whatever needed handling.

"We'll find her. She exists, you spoke to her, I saw it happen, and she knows things that she could only know if she was involved in this," Dragon said.

"Unless ..." Voodoo said slowly. When all eyes turned to land on him, he shrugged. "I was just thinking that the only way she got to Cassandra was by breaking ranks. She went against her boss, and we all know how Dr. Gardner feels when he's not in control."

"Do we ever," Rose muttered. Of all of them, she had suffered the most at her brother's hand. Her entire childhood had been one of abuse, and she bore the scars, physical and psychological.

"There's no doubt he found out she's flipped and gone rogue, because he sent people after Cassandra," Voodoo continued. "We don't know how he found out, but maybe it was through the mystery woman. He could have her, be holding her prisoner, torturing her, possibly even killed her already. She might turn out quite literally to be a dead end."

That might sound cold, but Dragon didn't disagree with what his friend had just said, even if the wording was harsh. This woman had been involved in what happened to them, she was no innocent. She was an enemy and worse, she'd dragged Cassandra into this mess.

None of them cared about what happened to the woman, but they would all like to get their hands on her, drag out of her whatever intel they could before they ended her life if Dr. Gardner had left her alive.

Blade suddenly cocked his head, and they all turned their attention to the man. If he said he was unable to pick up any other sounds, then his assertion that there might be a white noise generator somewhere in the building made sense.

But if somebody had gone to the trouble of setting one up, it had to mean they were still there.

Shifting closer to Cassandra, Dragon scanned the hall they were in. They'd just cleared what had been a lab at some point, and he focused on it now.

"Someone is here," he said, and Blade nodded. "No other reason for trying to distort Blade's abilities."

"Has to be the woman," Blade said. "She ordered this cleaned down, and if she's still here, it makes sense she doesn't want us to know. She was involved so she knows what she's up against. Has to know what we're going to do to her if we get our hands on her."

"If it's not her, it's someone who works for her," Thunder added. "Either way, we need to find them, disarm them, and take them home with us."

"Rose and Cassandra, you two are going to wait for us in there," Steel said, nodding to the same lab that had caught his attention.

"But—"

"No, little ladybug, no buts," Steel said, cutting her off. "We agreed before we left, that if need be, you two would hide and let us do what we need to do without having to worry about protecting you as well."

"Technically, I didn't agree," Rose muttered, but it was clear from her tone that she knew she was fighting a losing battle.

"You're going to, though," Steel said confidently.

"Only if you promise to be careful." The slight wobble in Rose's voice betrayed her fear for the man who had managed to capture her heart despite their crazy beginning.

"Nothing in the world will stop me from being as careful as possible, knowing that my little ladybug needs me."

"Don't need anyone," Rose said, but she said it with affection and stepped closer to Steel, pushing up onto tiptoes to kiss Steel's cheek.

"You're not—"

"Arguing," Cassandra finished for him. "I know I can't hold my own with you guys."

The others kept watch while he and Steel re-cleared the lab they'd only just cleared. Leaving Cassandra behind felt wrong, but he also knew it was the only thing to do. The room was empty, the girls would lock the door behind them, and they were both armed.

Still ...

"Dragon?" Cassandra caught his hand as he went to leave. "I know it's .... The timing is .... But we don't know what will happen, and .... Why do you call me little rabbit? Is it because of my old stuffed animal?"

The question caught him off-guard, but it was an easy one to answer. "You're intelligent and curious, friendly and affectionate, playful and outgoing. You're innocent and sometimes vulnerable, you're loyal, and yet you defend yourself with the skills you have. You're my perfect little rabbit."

"Yours?"

"If you'll have me." Maybe he should be embarrassed or apprehensive to be this vulnerable in front of not just Cassandra, but Steel and Rose as well. But he wasn't. Cassandra was worth risking everything for.

Stepping up against him, she reached up and grabbed his shoulders, guiding him down so she could kiss him. "I'll have you," she whispered against his lips.

Her declaration and the kiss made it that much harder to turn his back on her, and he was glad Steel reminded them to lock the door, because he was having a hard time focusing on anything other than his churning gut.

Was it telling him something was wrong, or was it just having his little rabbit out in the field?

Moving in perfect sync, he and his team didn't need to talk to know what they had to do. They kept moving forward. There wasn't much of the building left to clear, but Blade had heard something, and the idea of a white noise generator confirmed they weren't alone.

They were about seven corridors away when he smelled it.

The faint scent of dynamite in the air.

It meant only one thing.

"Place is going to blow," he yelled the warning, already starting to run back toward the room where Cassandra and Rose were hiding.

But he couldn't get there fast enough.

The world around them exploded.

~

January 9th
9:06 P.M.

"Come on, wake up."

The words seemed to pierce right through her skull.

Something gentle touched her face, and she moaned and tried to pull away from it.

Everything hurt.

Pain like she'd never experienced before.

Cassandra had always led a fairly safe kind of life. Unwilling to put herself out there, unsure of what always held her back, but something did. Something kept her sticking to things that weren't going to hurt her.

Which made her sexual needs so incongruent with the rest of her.

But ever since she'd shared those secrets with Dragon, she didn't feel afraid anymore. Now she felt like she could conquer the world. She was stronger than she'd ever given herself credit for, and maybe now that she had acknowledged her own strength, she would stop projecting weakness to her family so they saw her as strong too.

No more hiding, no more pretending, no more underestimating herself.

"Wake up, Cassandra. Now," an insistent voice persisted.

"No," she muttered, waking up would make the pain worse. Somehow, she knew that even though she had no recollection of what had happened or why she was hurting so badly.

"Yes," the voice countered. "Please."

There was a note in that last word that stirred her further into consciousness. The note was fear, and whether she'd gained a newfound sense of confidence or not, she hated for anyone to be hurting and wanted to do whatever she could to soothe them.

Blinking open her eyes, she found nothing but darkness all around her except for the shadowy face of someone leaning over her.

Suddenly, everything came back.

They were searching a warehouse they believed had or still did belong to Dr. Gardner and his team of scientists. The place had been bleached, and someone had been using a white noise generator to make it harder for the guys to use their enhanced skills. But still, Blade had heard something, and the guys had told her and Rose to hide while they went hunting.

The two of them had been talking in hushed whispers when suddenly the world around them exploded.

"Are you okay?" she asked, her voice shaky and insubstantial as she tried to take stock of her body and figure out what injuries she'd sustained. In the fall, she must have lost her night vision goggles, because she could no longer see with that eerie green light. Still, she could make out Rose's face, and she knew why the other woman had sounded scared. She'd heard all about how Rose had tried to escape the basement when the guys were holding her hostage and had wound up bringing the ceiling down with her.

"Yeah, hurting all over but ... just brings back memories," Rose answered, her voice soft and more uncertain than Cassandra had ever heard it before. "I've never been claustrophobic, couldn't have because my brother would have quickly figured out any weaknesses and exploited them. But now ..."

"You were buried alive," Cassandra reminded her as she slowly pushed herself up, fighting off a wave of dizziness and nausea that made her want to curl up in a ball and forget all about what was going on around her.

But she couldn't.

The guys were still out there somewhere, and she had no idea if they had been closer or further away from wherever the explosives had been set.

If they'd been closer ...

No.

She wasn't going to allow herself to go there right now. Rose was freaked out after the explosion, they were both hurt, and they had to find a way out so they could go looking for the guys.

"Thought I was going to die," Rose murmured. "But then Steel looked for me. Saved me." The woman paused, dragging in a deep breath. "We have to find a way to get out of here so we can find them. What if they're trapped and need us?"

"We're stuck in here?" she asked. Rose had obviously regained consciousness before she had, or never passed out at all, but she had no idea how long she'd been out and if Rose had managed to gather intel while she was passed out.

"Half the ceiling and walls came down," Rose replied. "Total flashback vibes. Although at least this time I'm not pinned down and helpless."

"Totally not helpless," she said, infusing as much confidence into her tone as she could manage. Just because she'd decided to stop pretending to her family that she was handling her paternity revelation just fine, didn't mean she didn't recognize this was a time when she had to fake it till she made it. Her life, Rose's life, and the lives of Dragon and the other Delta Team guys might depend on it.

"We got this," Rose said, sounding more like the woman she was getting to know.

"Of course we do. If we don't, then Dragon and Steel are never going to let us do anything fun."

Rose laughed at her joke, but it ended on a groan, and she knew the other woman was hurt. Asking how badly seemed kind of pointless. It didn't matter what injuries they had, they still had to find a way out.

Pushing herself up to her knees, the world spun sickeningly around her, but Cassandra did her best to shake it off. There was something sticky on the side of her head, and she assumed she'd struck it when she'd been thrown down.

"Do you have your night vision goggles?" she asked Rose as she blinked and tried to get her eyes to adjust to the darkness.

"No, lost them. My weapon too."

"Oh yeah." Cassandra realized she'd lost that as well. That was a major disadvantage if the person they suspected was still there had survived the explosion. Still, they had to be the person who set it, so the chances that they'd stick around to get caught up in it seemed slim.

"Where was the door?" she asked, looking around the room but unable to see anything other than shadowy piles of what she assumed was rubble. Since she'd been thrown down, she'd lost all sense of direction and had no idea where the way out was supposed to be.

"It was over here," Rose answered confidently, and Cassandra followed her to where a pile of concrete blocked what she could now make out had once been the door.

Without discussion, they both reached down and began to move the debris. It was slow going and they had to work together. The pieces were too heavy for them to move alone, even if they weren't injured.

What felt like hours later, but couldn't have been more than ten minutes at the most, Cassandra heard something that had her freezing and spinning around.

"Did you—?"

"I did," she answered Rose's question before the other woman could even get it out.

"Was there another entrance to the lab?" Rose asked, heading closer to where they had both heard a sound.

"I didn't see one, the guys didn't mention one either," she replied.

"A secret entrance then? If this was a lab run by my brother, I wouldn't put it past him to have secret entrances and exits just in case the place was ever raided. Ridge was a paranoid guy," Rose muttered.

Abandoning where they'd been working, Cassandra followed Rose. "Maybe the guys found it."

"I hope so."

In Rose's voice were the same emotions she was feeling. Fear, worry, restlessness. Rose wanted to get to Steel as badly as she wanted to get to Dragon. Of course, she didn't want any of the guys to be hurt—or worse—but the need to get to Dragon was unlike anything she'd experienced before. It pulsed beneath her skin, like an itch she couldn't scratch, and she prayed like she'd never prayed before that Dragon was about to come through the wall, strong and unharmed.

Another sound, one that definitely sounded like a person moving rubble out of the way, came from a corner of the room, and they zeroed in on it.

"There," Cassandra said, pointing to a small hole in the wall. "There was a hidden door right there."

"I see it."

"It has to be them, right?" Just because she didn't see why someone would set explosives, then hang around in the blast zone, didn't mean there wasn't someone else in the building.

"Wish I had my weapon," Rose muttered, and the anxiety in the room seemed to amp up.

If it was whoever had set the explosives, she and Rose were sitting ducks. They were trapped in there, they wouldn't be able to get through the debris to safety before whoever was coming got in.

"It's them," she said confidently, trying to convince both Rose and herself.

Before either of them could say another word, someone grunted, and the rubble in front of the hidden door tumbled down as the beam of a flashlight danced over them, temporarily blinding them.

"Huh, wasn't expecting two of you. The sister and the girl, two for one. My lucky day," a strange voice spoke, and Cassandra's blood ran cold.

CHAPTER
Nineteen

January 9th
9:10 P.M.

Consciousness returned far too slowly.

With it, a pulsing pain that was difficult to ignore.

Nothing compared to the raging fear that immediately flooded his system.

Cassandra.

That one word screamed through his mind, and Dragon jerked upright, his gaze immediately scanning the area for his team.

Thankfully, the night vision goggles were still on his head, and his weapon was strapped to his body, so he was armed and able to see around him.

It looked like the set of a bad action movie. Piles of rubble were littered about, the previously wide corridor was now mostly blocked, and he could see the bodies of his teammates strewn among the debris.

He ached to get to Cassandra, having no idea if she was injured or possibly even dead. The explosives could have been closer to them or to the room where the two girls were hiding, there was no way to know until they got there, but he couldn't go until he checked on his team.

They were family. The first one he'd ever had, and for all he knew, Cassandra was fine, that part of the building could be mostly undamaged. Even if she was injured, he would need his team to help dig through the rubble to get to her.

Still, he was torn as he shoved to his feet. The way his body weaved wasn't a good sign, but he wasn't going to waste time worrying about it. It didn't matter if he was injured, he had to check on his team, had to get to Cassandra.

What if the person responsible for cleaning down the lab really was still there?

It didn't make sense because it would mean they'd kept themselves in the blast zone, but then again, maybe they hadn't expected his team to find this place so quickly. After all, if the smell of bleach had been that strong that it messed with his ability to scent anything else, it meant the place had been cleaned down a mere couple of hours before they got there.

Stumbling through the debris, Dragon found Blade first and dropped to his knees beside the far too still man. There was blood on his friend's face, and Blade was lying awkwardly on his side, but the second he reached out and pressed his fingers to Blade's neck to check for a pulse, the other man growled and snapped out a hand, closing it around his wrist.

"Good, you're alive," he said, unfazed by the man's weak attempt at an attack, and merely pulled his hand free, shoving back to his feet and searching for the next closest teammate.

No, not just teammates.

These men *were* his family, they were his brothers, they had been the only thing that kept him sane, as well as giving him his first sense of what it meant to have people who actually cared about him. He couldn't imagine his life without every single one of them in it. His future was with Cassandra, he was done pretending he could stay away from her, but that didn't mean he would ever leave his team. Maybe they weren't the monsters they feared they had been turned into, but they still battled rage, still had enhanced skills, still would never be normal.

"What the hell happened?" Blade asked from behind him. If his friend couldn't remember what had happened, that didn't bode well for his mental state, he likely had a concussion, but at least he was still alive.

"Explosion. Smelled it too late," Dragon muttered as he shoved some debris out of the way so he could get to Thunder. Seeing the man with enhanced speed so still was definitely unsettling. Even if they all survived this, and so far that was up for debate, there was no way he would forgive himself for this failure.

It didn't matter if the bleach had impeded his abilities, he should have found a way to work around it. Hell, he should have known that if the smell of bleach was too strong, then there was a reason for it, and they needed to pull back and evaluate.

Still, there was no going back.

What was done was done, he just had to hope he hadn't lost any of the people he cared about.

Loved.

Although he wouldn't say that word aloud, wasn't in that place yet, it didn't change the facts.

"Not your fault. Couldn't hear anything either," Blade muttered, and he could hear his friend stumbling behind him.

Thunder was lying sprawled on his back, with what looked like a heavy piece of rubble pinning his legs in place.

Without exchanging a word, both he and Blade went to work removing the chunks of concrete. Thunder didn't stir, but this time around, Dragon didn't need to check if the man was alive, he could smell that he was. Blade, too, seemed to be able to hear the beating of Thunder's heart because he didn't check for a pulse either.

They were about halfway through when he suddenly smelled something behind them.

Some*one.*

Already reaching for his weapon, he was spinning around right as a howl echoed through the hall.

Blade spun around, too, and they both moved so they were using their bodies as a shield for Thunder, who groaned behind them, obviously roused by the growl of fury.

A pile of rubble suddenly went flying, and Steel emerged from it. Their team leader was breathing hard, his eyes wild. Covered in a thick layer of dust, he looked like some sort of furious avenging ghost warrior.

"It's us, Dragon and Blade," he called out, and Steel's gaze snapped toward them.

"Rose," Steel howled, voice ragged.

"We'll get to her, to them," Dragon assured his friend, uncomfortable with the role reversal. Given his past and the anger already planted in him from birth, he'd always been the most volatile. Usually, it was Steel working to calm him down before he did something rash, but for once he was the voice of reason.

It was clear Steel was doing everything he could to rein in his terror for the woman he loved, same way he was. After a few tense seconds where Dragon wondered if he could knock down his team leader before the much stronger man could use his enhanced strength to crush him like a bug, Steel dropped his head and dragged in a breath they could all hear.

When Steel looked back up, Dragon could see he'd gotten himself back under control.

"The others?" Steel asked as he staggered toward them.

"Thunder is pinned," he replied.

"Thunder is fine," the man in question said on a groan, and they all turned back to find him pushing up and reaching down to shove off the last of the concrete on his legs.

"Voodoo and Lion?" Steel asked.

A loud cough echoed through the space, and movement a little further down the hall from where they were revealed Lion pushing to his feet. "Voodoo is down," he called out.

Blade helped Thunder up, and all four of them climbed over the debris to get to where Lion was now up and on his knees, leaning over Voodoo. Even with the eerie green of the night vision goggles, Dragon could tell that the color of Voodoo's skin was off.

"Alive?" he asked as he dropped to his knees beside Lion and Voodoo.

"Barely," Lion replied.

"Look." Thunder pointed to a piece of piping that had embedded itself in Voodoo's side.

On anyone else, it would be enough to kill them, but Voodoo was different. They all had enhanced healing, but Voodoo was something else. He'd seen some crazy things when it came to this man. Both in healing himself and dragging others back from the brink.

"Pull it out," Steel ordered.

"It might kill him," Blade protested.

"It won't." Steel said it so confidently that Lion seemed to automatically move a hand to grasp the pipe.

After a brief hesitation, the man yanked, and Voodoo's entire body jerked as though in pain, although the man's eyes didn't open, his lashes didn't so much as flutter on his cheeks.

"You guys go, find the girls, I'll stay with him," Lion said as he lifted Voodoo's clothes to get access to the wound.

As badly as he wanted to get to Cassandra, ease the fiery itch under his skin, Dragon's gaze locked on the wound. "What the hell? It's healing already, look."

Before their very eyes, the gash in Voodoo's stomach, a huge hole at least two inches in diameter, began to close. It was like watching magic happen.

Seconds later, Voodoo groaned and lifted a hand toward the wound. "Damn, that hurt."

"You should be dead, man," Thunder said softly.

"Yet I'm not," Voodoo replied.

"Think you should stay still for a bit," Lion said when Voodoo tried to sit.

"Can't. The girls, we have to get to them. I feel … something is wrong."

Nobody attempted to argue with the man. Voodoo knew things sometimes before the rest of them. At the same time Dragon pulled in a deep breath through his nose, Blade cocked his head to the side.

Beneath the lingering scent of bleach, beneath the heavy smell of the dust and debris, he could smell something else. Another person. More than that, he could smell fear. Cassandra's fear.

"Someone else is with them," Blade announced, coming to the same conclusion he had.

Whoever had set those explosives was still in the building, and he'd found Cassandra and Rose. Depending on their motivations and who they were working for, that person could either kill both the women outright, or abduct them and take them to Dr. Gardner or the mystery woman.

~

January 9th
   9:25 P.M.

There was nowhere to go.

They were trapped.

Cassandra scanned the ground in the thin light of the flashlight, praying that both hers and Rose's lost weapons would suddenly become visible, and she could make a dive for them.

Without those guns, they were sitting ducks.

There was absolutely nothing stopping this man from doing exactly what he came to do. Which was kill them or take them.

She was leaning toward taking them. That had been the plan for the man who had broken into her home. That night felt like a lifetime ago, and yet in reality, it wasn't even quite a week yet.

Six days that had changed her life, though.

Made her realize things about herself that she hadn't known, admitted truths she'd been too scared to share, made decisions about what she wanted from life that a mere week ago she would have denied until her dying breath.

There was no way in heck she was losing that by going with that man.

Beside her, she felt Rose stiffen, felt determination flow back into her as her fear of being buried alive receded with this new threat. While Ridge Gardner might have decided to set his sights on her because the mystery woman had identified her as a way to get to Delta Team, he had a personal grudge against his sister after Rose had betrayed him.

This man would do whatever it took to leave here with both of them, she was sure of it.

Still, it was two against one, which gave them at least some advantage, right?

"Didn't think hanging around here would pay off," the man said, tone conversational as though they were discussing something mundane instead of him all but admitting he was there to abduct them.

It was hard to see anything past the glare of the flashlight, but Cassandra could make out the shadowy figure of the man. He was huge, not quite as big as Dragon and the others, but big enough that it would be hard for them to take him down, even two against one. Self-defense moves were helpful to know, but they didn't overcome a massive size difference.

Plus, the man would be armed, no way he'd come here without a weapon.

There was no sign of their lost guns, and Cassandra didn't know what she should do. She was woefully unprepared for a situation like this, and she now realized with horrifying clarity why Dragon had been so adamant that she not come.

Why had it seemed so important to prove that she wasn't going to sit back and let everyone else handle the threat against what was starting to feel like a new family? This threat wasn't even really about her, it was about the guys. She was only part of it because the mystery woman had somehow figured out her connection to Delta Team.

"Don't think I was meant to figure out the connection to this place," the man continued as he advanced on them. "Someone had cleaned it out when I got here. I watched the team dressed all in white leaving in vans as I pulled up. Almost left then and there, assumed this idea was a washout. But I waited, and lo and behold, I watched another vehicle pull up not long later."

That meant that this guy was just a mercenary, out to collect on the money Rose's brother had put up to have her delivered to him. He wasn't the one responsible for cleaning out the building with bleach, or the white noise generator, so he likely wasn't the one responsible for setting the explosions either.

If he wasn't then someone else was.

Someone who could also still be out there.

Be safe, Dragon.

"Have to be the luckiest guy around, right?" the man said, chuckling a little as he kept advancing on them. He was in the room now, backing them both up against the far wall as they retreated with each step he took.

There wasn't much further for them to go.

Still, Cassandra was clinging to the idea that the man couldn't grab both of them at once. If he wanted the money, he had to bring her to Dr. Gardner alive. If he knew who Rose was, it made sense that there was a contract out on her, too.

"Two for one, means double the pay," the man said, greed edging into his tone, and she knew there would be no point in trying to talk him out of doing what he'd come here to do. "Might even be room for a little negotiating. I'm sure I can have a little fun playing with you both while I make a new deal with the doctor."

A shiver rocketed through her body.

There was no need to guess what he meant.

Instead of immediately delivering them to Dr. Gardner, he was going to take them somewhere else and rape them while he worked to get himself the most amount of money he could wring out of the crazed scientist.

When her back bumped against the piles of rubble they'd been clearing when they first heard the man's approach, Cassandra realized it was over.

There was nowhere else to go.

The end of the line.

Rose's hand suddenly landed on her thigh, fingers spread wide. At first, Cassandra thought the other woman was just drawing comfort from her presence, from the fact that they were in this together.

But then she felt one of Rose's fingers move.

A moment later, another disappeared.

And it clicked.

Countdown.

The other woman had something planned, and whatever it was, she was going to enact it when she counted down from five.

The man continued to talk, but Cassandra was no longer listening. Every muscle in her aching body tensed, and she prepared herself to follow Rose's lead. They had to assume that the mercenary had a weapon, and while he might not want to kill them, he wanted his payday too badly to risk it, that didn't mean he couldn't shoot to incapacitate.

Still, she would follow whatever Rose had planned.

Two fingers still touched her leg.

The man continued to advance, confident he had them where he wanted them.

One finger.

She rocked on the balls of her feet, wishing she'd been able to spot one of the guns. If she could get to it, she wouldn't hesitate to shoot the same way she hadn't hesitated to shoot her own father when it was clear he was going to kill her and her sister.

The second that final finger moved, Rose darted forward. With practiced ease, she went in low, below the light's beam, and caught their would-be kidnapper around the legs, taking them both down.

As he fell, the man lost his grip on the flashlight, and it clattered to the ground, rolling off somewhere.

"Get the light, find the guns," Rose shouted, and Cassandra didn't hesitate to follow her order.

While the other two tussled, she battled against her fear for Rose and quickly scrambled for the flashlight. Once her fingers curled around it, she quickly moved the beam around the area where she'd fallen when the explosion went off.

There.

Something glinted in the light.

Behind her, Rose cried out, and for a second, Cassandra faltered. Maybe she should go to Rose and help her. There were still two of them against the man, and since he hadn't fired any shots yet, maybe he didn't have a weapon on him.

Deciding her best move was to go for the gun like Rose had told her to, she ran for it, dropping down and snatching it up into her hand. It felt heavy, but in a good way, it provided not just protection but could be the difference between life and death.

Another grunt from behind her, and then she heard Rose cry out again.

"Cassandra, syringe, he drug ..." Rose's voice wavered and faded as whatever she'd just been injected with obviously began to work quickly.

It didn't matter, though, she had the gun and the flashlight.

Aiming the light right in the man's face as he pushed to his feet, leaving Rose's limp body lying beside him, she didn't hesitate to raise her weapon. She wasn't going for anything less than a kill shot. There was no time to play around. She didn't know if the guys were okay, or if there really was someone else there, she had to be smart and protect herself and Rose.

Pulling the trigger as the man moved toward her, there was no crack as the bullet fired, just a click and then nothing.

What the heck?

Again and again she pulled the trigger, but nothing happened. The weapon must have been damaged somehow in the explosion.

The man chuckled as his body collided with her, sending her slamming into the ground, pain flaring through her already aching body.

"Too bad, little one, you lose." The man chuckled, his much larger body pressing her into the ground, rubble digging into her back.

Not yet she didn't.

The weapon hadn't fired, but it was still in her hand. Raising it, she slammed it into the side of the man's head with every drop of strength she had poured into the hit.

Grunting, the man stumbled sideways enough that she could scramble out from under his body. Swinging the weapon again, she connected with his temple a second time, and then she was up on her feet and running.

Debating whether she should try to drag Rose's unconscious body along with her, Cassandra knew she couldn't. Not realistically. The man was down, but he wasn't out, and she had no time to waste looking for the other weapon to try to finish the job.

She'd have to pray the man didn't hurt Rose while she tried to find the others.

Heading for the area where the secret door had been, she was halfway through it when, with a growl, the man threw himself at her. It wasn't the fresh wave of pain rolling through her that she focused on, though, it was the sharp scratch as she felt something pierce her skin.

A syringe.

She'd just been drugged as well, and the edges of her vision were already swimming.

CHAPTER

Twenty

January 9th
    9:37 P.M.

Finally.

The door to the room where Rose and Cassandra had been hiding came into view as they rounded a corridor.

It was still closed, and Dragon prayed the girls were still in there.

They wouldn't have wandered off to look for him and his team, would they? Honestly, he didn't think they would, they had no idea where to find them, and they had to know the safest place for them was locked inside that room.

Scanning the hall, he didn't see anyone else, but there was another scent in the air, one he didn't recognize, and he could still smell Cassandra's fear. In front of the door was a pile of rubble that didn't appear to be disturbed. Was whoever he could smell inside there with his little rabbit and Rose, or had the person terrorized the girls from the hall and they'd refused to let him in?

"Something feels off," Steel said as he scanned the corridor.

"I smell him, but I don't see him," Dragon said, completely frustrated. Someone was there, that wasn't in dispute. He could quite clearly distinguish nine distinct scents, yet he didn't see how anyone could have gotten into the room with the girls with the door closed and the debris from the explosion still in front of it. "I smell blood as well."

"We're all covered in blood," Thunder reminded him. "Chances are, both Cassandra and Rose are too. The explosives were a little closer to our position, but this part of the building is damaged as well, they didn't avoid getting caught up in it."

Although nothing his friend had just said was untrue, Dragon felt a growl rumble through his chest. He didn't want to think about Cassandra being injured, blood staining her beautiful skin.

"They're not in there," Blade suddenly announced.

"They have to be," he growled, closing the distance to the door and ignoring the rubble to reach for the handle. It didn't turn, the door was still locked.

"They're not," Blade insisted.

"Then where else could they be, and how is the door still locked?" Dragon demanded. He would have accepted the possibility that the girls had somehow managed to get out the door without disturbing the rubble, it didn't seem likely, especially since they would both be injured, but it wasn't impossible. But how was the door still locked from the inside if no one was in there?

"Don't know," Blade replied like it was an actual question instead of a rhetorical one. "But I don't hear them in there. My ears are still ringing so I can't get a read on how far away they are."

Damn explosion was messing up everything.

If it wasn't for that, he and the others would have either found or not found whoever had been in the building then returned. Now they were separated, lacking vital intel, and both Cassandra and Rose were in more danger than they'd been in before.

With a roar, Steel suddenly leaned down and began to fling large chunks of concrete out of the way like they were mere pebbles, and less than a minute later, the man was slamming his foot through the wooden door, splintering it.

As Steel stepped through the ruined door, Dragon hurried to follow, desperate to prove Blade wrong, find whoever was in there with his little rabbit, and tear the man to pieces.

But just like Blade had said, the room was empty.

Panic threatened to overwhelm him. The need to scream out his rage into the universe and punish anything and everyone for tearing Cassandra from him was almost all he could think about.

Only one thing kept him from tumbling over the edge.

The fact that he was to blame for what happened.

Ignoring his instincts and bringing Cassandra along had been a mistake he might not get a chance to rectify.

Since tearing himself to pieces wasn't possible, he grabbed hold of every emotion raging inside him and stuffed them down deep.

No time to feel.

No time to lose.

The girls were gone, but they hadn't been for long.

"How did someone get two women out of this room, without disturbing the rubble by the door?" Lion asked no one in particular.

"They wouldn't have gone without a fight," Thunder added.

"Even if they were unconscious, he would have had to carry them over that debris," Voodoo said. "It's like they didn't leave the room through the door."

"Don't think they did," Blade called out, and Dragon looked over to see that his teammate was standing on the opposite side of the room, where it was obvious now that he looked that there was a second entrance.

"How did we not notice that before?" Steel growled.

"Because we were distracted," he said without hesitation. There was no point in making a mistake if you weren't going to admit it and learn from it. Cassandra and Rose should have stayed in the car if they'd come at all, but it wasn't just their presence that had them all on edge.

It was that they wanted this so badly.

For a decade, revenge had been all that had kept them alive. They dealt with the anger that constantly bubbled inside them all by promising it that one day it would be unleashed on the man who had played God with their lives.

Now with that revenge within smelling distance, everything was heightened, and they'd learned to rely so much on their enhanced skills over the last ten years that the bleach and the white noise generator had messed with all of them.

"Look," Lion said, holding up what appeared to be a syringe, and they all looked over to where he was kneeling, not far from the secret door they hadn't noticed when they first cleared this room. "Same as before. Whoever this was came prepared to kidnap someone."

"Then whoever was in here wasn't the person who ordered this place cleaned down, or set up the white noise generator," Thunder said.

"Could one of the mercenaries have figured out the link from the payment to this place same as we did?" Voodoo asked.

"Makes sense," Blade replied. "And it's the only reason someone would come with a vial of sedatives ready to use. Especially since we already know Dr. Gardner wants Cassandra alive."

"But there were two of them," Lion reminded them. "Two women, but only one syringe. How did he get both of them out of the room if he could only sedate one?"

"Potential signs of a struggle," Thunder replied somewhat hesitantly, his gaze darting between him and Steel.

"Rose would have fought," Blade added.

"Chances are he knocked one of them unconscious, or maybe one of them was still unconscious after the explosion," Voodoo said. "If this guy is one of the mercenaries out to collect for delivering Cassandra, then we have to acknowledge the possibility that there's a contract out on Rose as well, and we just didn't know about it."

Beside him, Steel stiffened at Voodoo's words, but there was nothing the man could say to refute them. It made sense, especially with both women missing.

"At least we know they're both alive," Lion said confidently as he pushed to his feet. "If one of them hadn't survived the explosion or had been killed in the struggle, they would have been left behind."

That at least was true, and it did offer the tiniest amount of reassurance.

For now, the fact that both Cassandra and Rose weren't in the room meant that they were both alive, both savable.

"It hasn't been that long since the explosion went off, maybe thirty minutes or so, the merc had to have been injured as well, he was in the building. If he heard something in here that's likely what drew his attention, and he figured he'd check it out. He couldn't have known at first who it was, so he had to have gotten in here, fought with the girls, then taken them. There's only one way out since we know he didn't use the main door, and he can't be that far ahead of us," Thunder said, already heading for the secret door. "Want me to run on ahead? See if I can catch up to them?"

"Can you?" Dragon asked, remembering how he'd found the man, with chunks of concrete pinning his legs. If there had been damage caused to Thunder's legs, it could either temporarily or permanently affect his ability to use his enhanced speed.

Maybe it was time they all learned to stop relying so heavily on their skills. They'd spent a decade hating that Dr. Gardner's experiments had messed with their abilities to feel emotions normally, and yet they had no trouble using the skills they'd gained with the experiments, wanting to have their cake and eat it too.

But the more time he spent with Cassandra, the more he realized he was more than a man who had been born into a violent crime family, who had joined the military to escape, and walked into an experimental program because he was cocky enough to ignore anything that could go wrong. He was more than his anger, he was more than his fears that his DNA would lead to only one possible outcome, more than a man who had to hide from everyone because he believed he was a danger to anyone who got too close.

Cassandra saw a different side of him, a man she trusted with her secrets and her body, who she was willing to be honest and open with, even when it contradicted what she knew he wanted to hear.

If she wasn't afraid of him, then maybe it was time he stopped being afraid of himself.

And that started with accepting that with or without special skills, he was a human being doing the best he could with what he had, and that made him worthy of love and affection.

Worthy of a future.

"Go," Steel ordered, and Thunder took off without a second glance.

The rest of them followed, moving fast, but not as fast. They tore through rubble, watched each other's backs, and wouldn't give up until this ended the only way it could. With Cassandra and Rose safe, and one step closer to the man who saw himself as a god.

~

January 9th
9:41 P.M.

Everything felt fuzzy.

Weird.

Like she was clouded in darkness, not just actual darkness, but like it had seeped inside her head, making everything hazy, hard to hold onto, and just out of grasp no matter how much she tried to reach for it.

Despite that, Cassandra knew she needed to focus.

Important.

That word kept shoving its way through her sluggish mind, and it was about the only thing she was able to cling to.

Close to her, something grunted.

Not something.

Someone.

The someone stumbled slightly, and all of a sudden, a flash of bright light flooded her vision, and she could make out around her piles of what looked to be rubble.

From the explosion.

A little unsure what explosion her own mind was referring to, she figured it didn't really matter. If she knew there had been an explosion, she'd just run with that.

Details could be filled in later.

Muttering a curse, the someone beside her bent, and since Cassandra moved with him, she had to assume that meant he was holding her.

Why would someone be holding her?

Who would be holding her?

Her brothers?

Had they been caught in an explosion at a family event? Had the people after them managed to strike when they were all together?

No.

That wasn't right.

They'd found the people responsible for framing her mom and stepdad as traitors. Monique. She had a sister now. Her biological dad was dead. Shot by her own hand.

Then who else would be carrying her?

Dragon?

Snippets floated through her mind. Running through the forest, someone chasing her, pinned against a tree trunk. Pain screaming through her shoulders, blood smearing her wrists. Filled to perfection, that pain had turned to pleasure, giving her the most powerful orgasm of her life. Soft words, gentle touches, tending wounds, shampooing hair, tucking her into bed. Aftercare to soothe away any lingering pain.

Everything she needed with the one person she'd always known could give it to her.

But this wasn't Dragon.

This person didn't hold her gently, and he was muttering something about more trouble than it was worth, and if he hadn't found the sister, he would have just left them all behind, but now he was going to insist on triple what the original price had been.

Sister?

Monique was there?

No, that didn't make any sense. Why would Monique be with her right now when she was ... running from someone? Hiding from someone? In danger from someone?

The someone with an arm wrapped around her waist, dragging her along with him? This someone's arm was digging painfully into her ribs. Not the good kind of pain, not the kind she craved, this just hurt, and she moaned before she could stop herself.

For some reason, it seemed important that the someone think she was unconscious.

They stopped moving, and she allowed all her body weight to drop against the arm holding her upright. Another muttered curse, but then they were moving again.

Light danced haphazardly around, and Cassandra knew that meant her eyes were open if she could see it. Without moving and alerting the person carrying her that she was awake, she tried to catch glimpses of her surroundings, but all she could see were more piles of what looked like rubble.

It wasn't until a brush of icy cold air touched her skin that everything snapped into place.

Sister didn't mean Monique, the man who had her wasn't talking about her sister, he was talking about the sister of the man responsible for the experimental drugs Dragon and his team had been given. After drugging both her and Rose, he must now be carrying them from the building.

If he got them away from there it would all be over.

Their chances of escape were virtually zero.

Pausing briefly, the mercenary dragged in several ragged breaths before moving again. He'd been in the building when the explosives went off, which meant he had to be injured too. Plus, Rose had wrestled with him, so she might have inflicted some more injuries. Enough to give her a chance at doing something?

Cassandra remembered Rose's slurred words warning her that the man had drugged her, and she remembered the prick of the needle piercing her own skin. Yet she wasn't unconscious. Not fully anyway. Rose must be though because there was no peep from her, and now that there was more light, she could just see another pair of feet being dragged along the ground as the man carried them one in each arm.

The man was carrying them across a parking lot now.

Away from the building.

Away from Dragon and the others.

When they reached a white van, he dropped both her and Rose on the ground. While her friend's body hit without rousing her, it took all of Cassandra's energy not to react as more pain assaulted her already aching body.

But somehow, she remained limp and bit back her screams.

A moment later, she watched through cracked lids as the man scooped up Rose and physically threw her into the back of the van.

She was next.

As a young woman—especially one who had six overprotective big brothers—she knew that if the man got her in the back of that van, it was all over.

Yet she didn't think she was strong enough to run.

To fight.

Her body was uncooperative, heavy, like her limbs had been encased in concrete.

So she was helpless to stop it from happening when the man reached for her, picked her up, and threw her in to join Rose.

Instead of the darkness she expected to engulf them as he locked them in, light danced across her body. A shadowy figure moved along with the light. Coming closer.

Him.

Why wasn't he driving off?

Kneeling beside her, she felt his fingers brush across her face as he moved a lock of hair off her cheek, tucking it behind her ear. If the gesture had been done by Dragon she would have thought it was sweet, and leaned into the caress.

But it wasn't Dragon.

It was a man who was going to take her to Dr. Gardner and receive a bundle of money for doing it.

His touch didn't stop there.

It dropped lower. Cold fingers trailing down her neck, then her chest, pausing to grab one breast and tweak a nipple, before sliding down her stomach and settling between her legs.

No.

He wouldn't, would he? Not here. Not now.

"I shouldn't," the man murmured. "Should get out of here. But ... the rules didn't say to leave her unharmed. Been too long. Ever since that slut of an ex decided to leave me. Won't take long."

The sound of a zipper being opened had to be the loudest one she'd ever heard.

Louder even than the explosion.

Fear and terror churned in her gut, making her nauseous.

Desperation clawed at her, and she tried to make her body move. Playing dead was only going to get her raped and then eventually killed, but it wasn't really playing if you couldn't seem to do anything else.

Blood pounding in her ears, she felt a rush of cold air on her pelvis as her pants and underwear were pulled down.

Every fear she'd ever had about her sexual tastes and what had happened to her mom played out, and she was unable to do anything to stop it.

Was this how her mom had felt?

Terrified, powerless, so very aware that her life was about to be forever altered, yet unable to stop it from happening.

Above her, the man shifted so he was positioned above her, and she could feel *it* nudging against her entrance.

You deserve it.

You wanted it rough, now you're going to get it.

Just like your mom.

Just like how you were conceived.

Punished.

You always knew you deserved to be punished.

"There's a difference between rape and consent, you know that, little rabbit. What you like is different, there's nothing you need to be punished for. You're perfect just the way you are."

Dragon's voice came out of nowhere. She knew it was just inside her head, but its power caught her by surprise.

Even though there were still lingering doubts, she knew he was right.

When a wave of nausea rushed through her, she didn't fight against it, didn't even turn her head. She allowed the contents of her stomach to empty all over herself and the man who was inching himself inside her.

He swore as vomit sprayed all over him and quickly pulled back.

Like Dragon's words in her mind had flipped a switch, Cassandra managed to get her body to somewhat cooperate, and she slammed a hand up and into the nose of the man who was trying to get away from her without touching her more than he had to.

A howl echoed through the van, and she felt something wet drip down on her.

Hopefully, she'd broken his nose, it was the least he deserved. Scrambling backward, her movements jerky and clumsy, Cassandra knew she had to run. She was pretty sure that the man would follow rather than drive off with Rose. Not only would he want the money he'd get for delivering her to Dr. Gardner, but she'd made a fool of him, hit him, thrown up on him, and he'd want to punish her for it.

Somehow, she managed to slide out the back of the van, her feet hitting the ground with a thud. Yanking up her pants, she didn't bother doing them up, she just started running. Her head was still spinning, and she wasn't really sure of where she was going. All Cassandra knew was that she had to get away, had to get help, had to find a way to survive.

CHAPTER
Twenty~One

January 9th
9:50 P.M.

"Thunder just saw them," Blade said, coming to an abrupt halt, causing Dragon to almost crash into him.

"Saw who?" Steel demanded.

Dragon held his breath as he awaited the answer. Had he seen both girls, or had he seen both of them and the man who was trying to abduct them? Or was it the man who had abducted them, and only one of the two missing women?

"Cassandra running off into the forest and a man following her," Blade replied.

Good news and bad.

It meant Cassandra was alive, relatively unharmed, at least enough to be mobile, but she was trying to make her escape, and she was being followed. Would the man after her still try to contain her or would he decide it was easier to just kill her and cut his losses?

And where was Rose?

There was no way to ask that question since Blade was with them, and Thunder didn't have the same enhanced hearing. No way to ask any of the dozen or so questions burning on the tip of his tongue.

So they all picked up the pace again, running through the secret tunnels that ran between walls and underground, jumping over debris along the way, as they searched for the way out. They knew there was one because this was the way Thunder had come, and he'd obviously found his way out.

He'd just scented fresh air, when Blade obviously heard another update from Thunder.

"Rose is in a van, parked about thirty yards from where we're going to exit, around the back of the building," Blade informed them all.

"Is she ..." Steel trailed off, no doubt unable to verbalize the question they were all wondering.

"Alive," Blade assured him, and their team leader let out a shaky breath. "Thunder is staying with her in case this guy is working with a partner."

Even though he knew it was the right call, Rose was unconscious and Cassandra was awake and trying to escape, he hated the idea of her out there alone somewhere, running for her life, with no idea they were only minutes away from coming after her.

Pushing himself harder, ignoring the thrumming pain that hadn't left him since he regained consciousness after the explosion, the others followed close on his heels as he burst out into the ice-cold night.

Above them, the sky was clear, a myriad of stars shimmering like someone had doused the atmosphere with glitter, the moon full and round, shining down upon them. If Cassandra had been safe beside him, he probably would have thought it was a beautiful night.

Now all he could think of was that he'd promised his little rabbit he'd keep her safe, and yet he'd left her alone, and she'd been kidnapped. Now that he was out there, away from the bleach, the dust hanging heavily in the air, he could smell Cassandra's fear and the acrid scent of vomit.

And blood, he could smell blood.

Steel had bolted right for where Thunder said the van was parked, the others following him, and Dragon forced himself to follow as well. Running off randomly into the forest would take longer to find

Cassandra than checking in with Thunder first, and learning which direction they'd gone in.

By the time he joined the others at the lone vehicle in the parking lot, Steel was on his knees, an unmoving Rose in his arms. Voodoo was crouched beside them, ignoring Steel's protective growl to place his fingers on the woman's neck, his own injury long since forgotten, or maybe already mostly healed.

"Pulse is strong, she's going to be fine, the drugs just need to work their way out of her system," Voodoo assured Steel as Dragon scanned the tree line not far from the van.

From the splattered blood and vomit in the van, it was clear that Cassandra had either woken up or never been entirely unconscious, then attacked her would-be abductor and made a run for it. The blood was from her attacker, he could tell by its scent, but the vomit was from her. Because of the drugs, or was she more injured than he wanted to consider?

"She went that way," Thunder told him, stepping up beside him and pointing to the closest line of trees where he would have expected Cassandra to head if she was trying to run away.

"Was she injured?" Of course, she had to have some injuries, she'd been in that building along with the rest of them, there was no way she'd walk away completely unharmed. What he was really asking, without actually asking, was whether it looked like any of those injuries were life-threatening.

"It was dark, and I only got a glimpse of her. She was weaving a little, but she was up and on her feet and running like her life depended on it," Thunder replied.

Not needing to hear anymore, Dragon took off. He knew the direction the two had headed, he didn't need to be able to see, although his night vision goggles afforded him that. All he had to do was follow his nose to find them.

"Thunder, Blade, go with him," Steel ordered behind him, and Dragon could hear the others following him, but he didn't slow down.

The three of them ran, the other two following his lead, although he was sure Blade could hear where Cassandra and the man chasing her were without having to follow him. The closer they got, the stronger the scent of Cassandra's fear became. She knew her life was over if she was caught.

"Wait," Blade suddenly ordered.

No way in hell.

When he kept running, both Blade and Thunder grabbed him, shoving him up against a tree. He fought against them like a wild animal. Cassandra wasn't far away, and he had to get to her.

"He got her," Blade hissed in his ear. "You go running in like a maniac, and there's nothing to stop him from killing her."

Much as he hated to admit it, the growing scent of Cassandra's fear confirmed his teammate's words.

Worse than that, he could smell something else.

Something that made him want to throw up.

"He's going to rape her," he growled.

"Like hell he is," Blade shot back.

"We'll get to her before he does it," Thunder quickly added.

"Thunder will go in first as a distraction," Blade said. "Then we'll follow. You get Cassandra, and I'll take care of her attacker."

"No," Dragon quickly refuted. "I'm killing the man for daring to lay a finger on what's mine." The moment Cassandra had shared with him her secrets, what she liked when it came to sex, and the fears she had, the guilt she'd heaped on her own shoulders, about how that related to her own conception, she'd sealed her fate.

She had handed herself—mind, body, and soul—over to him, and while he wasn't the best person to treat them with the tender care they deserved, nobody would defend her more fiercely than he would.

After exchanging a nod, his friends backed up, slowly releasing their holds on him. Knowing they didn't have time to discuss their plan in any more detail than they already had, Dragon jerked his head at Thunder, who quickly took off, he and Blade following.

A mere two hundred yards or so away, Dragon heard them.

"Don't," Cassandra cried out. "He'll kill you for touching me."

"He's dead, sweetheart," another voice sneered. "Don't you get it? The others all died in the explosion. No one is coming to save you. No one is going to stop this from happening."

Another fifty yards and he saw them.

Cassandra, on the ground, lying on her stomach, the man above her pressing his hands into her back to pin her in place. Despite the position she was trapped in, his little rabbit did what she always did, she fought back. She was fighting with a desperation that filled him with pride, broke his heart, and ignited his rage.

"What the hell?" the man shouted as Thunder streaked toward him.

Caught off-guard, he shifted off Cassandra as he reached for his weapon, and trusting Blade to do whatever it took to protect his girl, Dragon launched himself at the man who dared to think he could touch what didn't belong to him.

Every emotion he'd ever suppressed, every single drop of anger he'd ever felt toward his family and Dr. Gardner, all exploded out of him as he took Cassandra's attacker to the ground, and finally, at thirty-three years old, allowed the red haze of fury to consume him.

January 9th
10:01 P.M.

One second, her foot was catching on something, and Cassandra was landing hard on her hands and knees on the unforgiving forest ground. The next, her assailant was on her, shoving her further down, telling her what he was going to do to her.

And then ... he was just ... gone.

A scuffle behind her had her attempting to drag herself back up onto her feet. She had to take advantage of this opportunity to run. There might not be another.

While she prayed like she'd never prayed before that the man was wrong, and that Dragon and the others weren't dead, just trapped in the building and trying to make their way out, she couldn't rely on anyone to come swooping in to save her.

If she wanted to live, she had to keep fighting.

Stopping even for a second could literally mean the difference between life and death.

So Cassandra summoned strength she didn't have, did her best to ignore the drugs still in her system, and got to her feet.

She took no more than two steps forward before she collided with a wall of solid muscle.

Muscle, not a tree, she could tell by the heat emanating from it, and she'd certainly crashed into enough trees on her run through the forest.

A whimper escaped as hands closed around her biceps. He had a partner. Of course he did. The man who had broken into her home did too. She should have known there would be another one of them out there. Should have been more careful, not lost her footing, not fallen, not taken so long to get back up.

"Shh, Cassandra," a voice soothed when she began to fight against the hands gripping her.

Couldn't stop.

Had to fight.

Survive.

She wasn't just fighting to live but to have the future she craved, one that had seemed permanently out of reach this last year. Now it was within her grasp, and she wasn't letting go of it without knowing she'd done everything in her power to get to it.

"Boo."

The barked word caught her by surprise. She expected the mercenaries who wanted the money for delivering her to Dr. Gardner to know her name. But how would they know of a nickname she'd had since she was a toddler that no one other than her family ever called her?

"There you go," the voice encouraged. It wasn't one of her brothers, but it was familiar.

Hardly daring to hope, Cassandra brushed a lock of hair out of her eyes and tilted her head back. Standing before her was Blade. His expression was concerned, but steady, and she choked on a sob as she realized not only had the guys come for her, but they were alive and unharmed.

"You good?" Blade asked, and when she nodded, he quickly scooped her up into his arms.

"I'm all disgusting and filthy," she offered as a weak protest, but honestly, the presence of anyone she knew and trusted was too good not to soak up.

Making a sound of dismissal, Blade kept his hold on her, and she turned her head to see that her almost rapist was now the one on the ground. Dragon was above him, his fists slamming into the unmoving man over and over again while Thunder stood and watched.

Neither Thunder nor Blade made any move to stop Dragon, as if they understood that his sanity depended on this. But they were wrong, Dragon might need an outlet for the rage that had been simmering inside him since his childhood, but he didn't need to keep beating on what even she could tell was an already dead man to let it out.

"Dragon," she called. As much as she was reassured by Blade's presence and knew she was safe with him and he wouldn't let anyone hurt her, he wasn't who she needed holding her right now.

Immediately, Dragon's head snapped up, his fist paused in the air above the man's head. There was an emptiness in his expression that scared her. He'd succumb to the anger, and if he let it, it would consume him and he might never be able to fight his way free of its hold.

"Please," she whispered, allowing her emotions to seep into her words. "I need you."

Like a switch had been flipped, he shoved to his feet. His chest was heaving with each breath he took, but she knew it wasn't from the exertion of beating her assailant to death. It was finally allowing his tightly controlled anger out of its box.

"I need you," Cassandra repeated.

Still in somewhat of a haze, Dragon closed the short distance between them. For a long moment, he just stood there and stared, not reaching for her, and she forced herself to stay still, to meet his gaze, to let him find whatever he needed to see in it.

Then he grabbed her, yanked her against him, his face buried in her neck as he held her clutched tightly against him. Pain throbbed through her body, but it had shifted once again to the good kind. The kind that said she was alive, Dragon was alive, and for now, they were safe. That was all that mattered.

"I hear sirens," Blade suddenly announced.

With another ragged breath, Dragon pulled back a little. "How badly are you hurt?"

"I have no idea," she answered honestly. There was still too much adrenaline and drugs in her system for her to identify the sources of her pain.

"Did he ...?"

"Started in the van, but I threw up all over him, then I think I broke his nose and ran," she replied. There would be time to process that later, but it wasn't now. Not when they were still out there and vulnerable.

"I wish I could kill him again," Dragon said with such seriousness that she almost smiled.

"Dead is dead," she reminded him. "Is Rose okay? He drugged us both, but I think maybe he only had the one syringe since he was after me, so he didn't have enough for both of us, and she got more. She was unconscious when I ran. I didn't want to leave her behind, but I needed to get help. I should have run to the building, tried to find you all, but I wasn't thinking clearly, and I didn't know if you were all alive."

"You did the right thing," Dragon assured her.

"And Rose is fine, just sedated," Thunder added.

"Someone else is out here," Blade said, his head cocked to the side as he stared off into the distance in the direction she'd been running.

"You think whoever set the explosives and had the place cleaned out?" Thunder asked.

"Either that or a partner," Blade replied.

"If he had a partner, they would have been waiting at the van," she reminded the guys.

"She's right," Dragon agreed.

"Then it has to be the mystery woman, someone working for her, or someone working for Dr. Gardner," Blade said. "Regardless, we can't let them get away."

The man was already moving when Thunder stopped him. "Wait, I'll come with you."

"No. You need to go with them just in case there is another threat out there," Blade insisted. "Get back to the van, get Steel and the others, and get out of here. We don't want to be here when the cops show up. We can't let this opportunity pass by. Whoever is out there, I'll find, no way they can escape me. Once I have them contained, I'll let you guys know."

"You want us to find somewhere to hide out while we wait?" Thunder asked.

"No, get Cassandra and Rose home. I'll call when I know something," Blade answered before taking off into the forest, which quickly seemed to swallow him whole.

"Will he be okay on his own?" she asked, exhaustion crashing at the corners of her mind now that she knew she was safe.

"Don't worry about Blade, he'll be fine," Dragon assured her as he began walking with her tucked safely in his arms. "Rest now, little rabbit, you did good, but you can consider yourself off duty. I'm here, and I won't let anything happen to you. When you wake up, you'll be back home."

Home.

To her, it had always been people and not a place. Her mom and the dad she barely remembered, her brothers, her grandparents, and now Dragon. Maybe the reason she'd been struggling so much these last couple of months was because she'd been sequestering herself in her house instead of surrounding herself with home.

She didn't care that there were a million logistics to work out before they could make anything permanent. Cassandra was ready to embrace the life she wanted with the man who made her feel safe, desirable, strong, capable, and protected.

The rise and fall of Dragon's chest beneath her cheek, and the feel of his strong arms cradling her, quickly lulled her to sleep, feeling more sure about who she was and what she wanted than she had since she learned the truth about how she was conceived.

CHAPTER

Twenty-Two

January 10th
11:18 A.M.

Stepping out of his bathroom and into his bedroom, Dragon stopped dead in his tracks.

The sight before him was everything he'd been positive he could never have, and yet everything that had fallen into his lap.

Lying spreadeagled and tied to his bed was Cassandra. She was naked, the cuts and bruises from the explosion clearly visible, along with the wounds from the attack in her home a week ago. As much as he hated seeing those marks on her beautiful body, they were reminders that she was a fierce warrior, stronger than everyone—herself included —gave her credit for.

Last night, she had fought for her life and won, and while he would never be able to erase the image of her pressed into the forest floor with that man on top of her, preparing to rape her, she was there, safe with him, and proving once again that she could handle anything.

The flight back there had been quiet, and Cassandra and Rose had both slept through most of it. He'd stripped her out of her ruined clothes the second they got into their vehicle and dressed her in one of his spare shirts instead. Seeing her in his clothes had filled him with a possessiveness that had made it difficult to let Voodoo examine her.

Once they were finally back home, he'd bathed her slowly, attentively, caressing every inch of her body as though he could erase the pain she suffered. They'd spoken more about what had happened in that van, and she'd told him in broken whispers how the man had started raping her, penetrating her, although not all the way, before she'd thrown up then broken his nose and run.

Holding his little rabbit while she cried had been easier than he would have thought. That instinct to protect, but in a different way, was one he was sure he hadn't possessed, yet the moment tears began to shimmer in Cassandra's eyes, she was in his arms.

Neither of them had spoken, there hadn't been a need for words. Nothing he could say would erase what had happened, and they both knew that. All Cassandra needed was support, to know she wasn't alone, to know he would do his best to slay the monsters that lived inside her head as well as the physical ones.

When she started shivering as the water in the bath cooled, he'd scooped her up, carried her to his bed, and held her as they slept.

If it were up to him, he wouldn't have initiated anything sexual until Cassandra had had plenty of time to heal. Especially knowing her fears about there being something wrong with her because she liked rough sex, and her mom had been raped. While he knew in her head she understood the difference, when she was vulnerable, it was hard for her to remember it.

But he'd been woken by Cassandra's hands stroking him, a sultry smile on her face, a plea on her lips that she needed him to wipe away the memories, not let that man take something important from her.

Because he never wanted to be someone Cassandra doubted, he needed her to know that he was always there for her one hundred percent, that she only needed to ask and he would do anything she wanted, he'd given in.

So now he had her tied up, thick bandages around her wrists because while he knew she liked to see her blood flowing, he wasn't going to reopen the wounds on her wrists after she'd just survived an explosion. She'd given into the compromise, and once he had her restrained he'd grabbed one of the toys he'd bought to use on her, turned it on, put it inside her, and then left her there, squirming in his bed, while he took a shower.

Now he stood, leaning his shoulder against the wall, one of his hands absently stroking himself as he watched Cassandra writhe on the bed. Her skin was flushed, dotted with sweat, as her hips rocked, seeking more stimulation than the toy he'd left set on low could offer.

Her green gaze moved to meet his as she realized he was watching her, and she whimpered through the gag.

Stalking toward the bed, Dragon stood beside it, staring down at his pretty little captive. Grabbing one of her breasts, he kneaded it roughly, then took the hardened peak of the nipple between his thumb and forefinger and tweaked it hard.

Moaning, Cassandra thrust her chest up, seeking more, but he withdrew his hand, drawing another whimper from her.

"You ready to beg yet, little rabbit?" he asked, trailing his fingers down her stomach and between her legs. Holding the end of the toy, he pulled it out slowly, then shoved it back in, making her back arch and a moan tumble from her lips. "Well?"

Defiance sparked in her green eyes, and she gave a sharp shake of her head.

Chuckling, he reached for the remote to the toy and turned the setting up a couple, enough to torment her, keep her hovering on the peak of an orgasm, but not allowing her to fall into it.

"Okay then, little rabbit, your choice. I told you, you wouldn't be coming until you begged for it. If you're not ready, I certainly am."

Climbing onto the bed, Dragon placed his knees on either side of Cassandra's head, removed the gag, and then positioned his already achingly hard tip against her lips. Before he went any further, he paused to check her gaze, to confirm this was still what she wanted. She had a safe word and a signal in case her mouth was otherwise occupied, but that didn't mean he wasn't going to check in constantly to make sure she was okay.

When he saw nothing but hunger and desire flaming in her green depths, he tangled his fingers in her long locks and pressed into the warmth of her mouth. Since he knew she didn't want gentle, that she wanted to be used and controlled, Dragon let himself fall into a rhythm, taking her mouth hard and fast, while maintaining enough cognizance to ensure that he didn't hurt her.

Tears streamed down her cheeks, her skin reddened further as she couldn't draw in as much air, and her hips buckled wildly behind him as she sought a release that wasn't coming yet. But throughout it all, he saw the arousal in her eyes and knew she was as into this as he was.

More so.

As he came down her throat, he kept himself there until he was sure she had swallowed every last drop before slowly pulling out.

"Ready to beg yet, little rabbit?" he asked as he moved down her body until he was kneeling between her spread legs.

"I need ... I need to come," she whimpered.

Flicking his fingertips against her swollen bundle of nerves, Dragon shook his head. "That's not begging, little rabbit, and you know it. If you want to come, you have to beg for it, that was our deal."

"Your deal." She huffed.

"You were the one who woke up wanting to play," he reminded her as he pinched her bud hard enough to make her squeak, her hips instinctively attempting to draw away, but he maintained his hold and began to roll her bud between his fingers.

"Please," she moaned.

"Please what?" he taunted, pressing the palm of his hand against the bottom of the toy and shifting it inside her, making Cassandra's eyes roll back.

"Please let me come."

"Are you begging me, little rabbit?"

"Y-yes. Please, I'm begging, I need to come, I want to come, please, Dragon, let me come," she pleaded, and the scent of her arousal hung so heavily in the air that he was powerless to do anything other than give her what she needed.

Easing the toy out, he shut it off and tossed it aside, then pressed his nose to her center and dragged in a deep breath. This scent right here, this complete and utter trust Cassandra was offering him, was what he wanted to cement in his mind. Any time he doubted himself, that he could be what she wanted, needed, he wanted to remember this moment.

At the first swipe of his tongue, her hips flew off the bed, and he pressed a hand to her stomach, holding her in place as he feasted. Keeping his touch light and slow, he worked her higher and higher. On the pillow, her head began to thrash, her fingers were curled into fists, her hips would have rocked if she were able to, and rambled pleas fell from her lips, growing increasingly desperate as he took his time.

Licking, sucking, nipping, Dragon devoured what was his, and when he was ready, he scraped his teeth against her bud, and she exploded as a powerful orgasm rushed through her. Even without Blade in the house, he was pretty sure everybody else had heard her scream as her release tore through her.

Suckling her gently through the aftershocks, when she went limp on the mattress, Dragon moved, untying the ropes, inspecting her wrists for any signs of damage to her skin beneath the bandages, and then gathering her into his arms to carry her to the bathroom so he could clean her up.

"Thank you," she whispered, touching a kiss to his cheek as he cradled her in his arms.

"For what?"

"Giving me exactly what I need and want. For being more than I could ever hope for."

Her words, so honest and true, sank deep into his soul, smoothing out all the hardness he'd had to learn to create in order to survive. Cassandra thought he was the one who had given her what she needed and wanted, but she was the one who had given him everything.

She had saved him from himself.

～

January 10th
4:55 P.M.

. . .

Standing at the tree line, Cassandra watched the house.

Sooner or later, Dragon would notice she wasn't in it, and as soon as he did, she planned on running.

Nothing and no one was going to steal her newfound joy of sex. She'd only just reclaimed that side of herself, and she wasn't going to let her would-be abductor steal that from her.

No way.

She wanted to live freely.

After playing in the bedroom with Dragon this morning, they'd gone downstairs and eaten with the rest of his team, and then she'd called her family. She'd asked them all to gather together, and she'd explained to all of them that she had been struggling more than she had been letting on.

Seeing the hurt on their faces, the guilt she knew they felt because they'd allowed her to fool them, their regret that they had prioritized themselves over her, had almost made her quickly brush everything aside again, but with Dragon beside her, she'd stood firm. Assuring them there was no need for guilt or regret, that she'd wanted them to focus on themselves, it was why she'd kept her mouth shut, she'd promised to be more open, to allow them to be there for her rather than shut them out.

Of course, she had absolutely not mentioned the sex thing and her issues with embracing who she was and what she liked, that was something for her to work through with Dragon, not her brothers.

Major eww.

But it felt good to be honest and open, like setting down a huge weight she had been voluntarily dragging around with her when there was no reason for her to.

Despite her good phone call with her family, and the excitement of her brand-new relationship, Cassandra could feel the tension hanging heavily in the air. Certainly wasn't immune to it. Blade was still out there, and while he'd checked in once, they were all anxiously awaiting hearing more from him.

She and Dragon might be getting their personal happy ever after, but this entire mess was far from over. After what had gone down with Rose and her brother, then adding the mystery woman and her warning into the mix, she knew that the guys were in more danger now than they ever had been since they escaped Dr. Gardner's clutches.

All of them were, because she was part of this now, too.

Movement near a window had her grinning, and she waved, knowing without being able to see that it was Dragon, and he'd realized she had slipped out.

Confirmation came less than two minutes later when the front door was flung open.

"You want to play, little rabbit?" Dragon's voice came to her clearly despite the distance between them. "Then run, and you'd better hope I don't catch you."

Turning on her heel, she took off into the trees. She would do her best to remain uncaught for as long as possible, but the fun of the chase was the inevitable capture.

Barely noticing the cold, she ran, dodging between trees, changing directions often to try to make it harder for Dragon to track her, and pushing herself beyond what she'd thought she was capable of giving. Adding running to her morning workout routine was a given, she loved her yoga, it helped center her for the day, but she needed something to train her body for endurance so she could drag out their fun.

She had no idea how long had passed when she heard his voice. "I can smell you, little rabbit, and when I catch you, I'm going to punish you for running from me."

A delightful shiver rocketed through her that had absolutely nothing to do with the cold.

Punishment was exactly what she wanted.

Refusing to give in and beg Dragon for an orgasm had been fun this morning, and she'd held out a whole lot longer than she thought she would have. Again, begging had been inevitable, especially when he'd tied her up, slipped that toy inside her, then left her there while he took the world's longest shower.

But holding out had resulted in the most powerful orgasm of her life. After came more tender aftercare as Dragon checked her already cut up wrists for more damage, then carried her to the bathroom, ran her a bath, and cleaned her down with careful attention.

Whatever happened out there when Dragon caught her, Cassandra already knew would end with more gentle care, and it made the thrill of the coming pain all the better. She was in her element, and Dragon was giving her everything her body craved. She knew their games were giving him what he needed, too. An outlet for his anger, which would always be a part of him, a way to take her the way he needed to, and know that she was getting as much pleasure out of it.

Even though she knew he was coming for her, knew he was close, she was caught off-guard when something suddenly flew at her, tackling her to the ground. Despite knowing this was a game she wanted, Dragon couldn't completely stamp down his protective instincts.

Right before their bodies hit the ground, he turned them slightly, so his took the brunt of the impact. That was the only concession he gave her, though. Her body was roughly shoved into the dirt, and his weight settled above her, pinning her in place.

The position was eerily similar to what had happened to her last night, and for a second there was panic. As badly as she wanted to ruthlessly shove away the memories of what the mercenary had done one game of sex at a time, it wasn't until she felt Dragon's nose trail along her throat and heard him inhale her scent that she felt grounded to the present.

"We don't have to do this if you don't want to," he whispered. "You can change your mind at any time. Say stop, and I'll pick you up and carry you back to the house. There's no pressure, no need to push yourself."

Yet she wanted to push herself.

Wanted to reclaim herself.

Didn't want anything to steal her newfound freedom.

"I want this. Want you. Want you to make me forget," she whispered back.

Her permission was all he needed. His nose left her throat, and he grabbed the hem of her coat, shoving it up over her head enough that it tangled in her arms, effectively pinning them together, and covered her head, blanketing her in darkness.

Rough hands unzipped her pants, shoving them down enough to bare her backside to the cold.

There was no time to feel it, though. Her blood felt like it was on fire, and heat seeped into her from where Dragon's large hands gripped her hips, holding her still as he shoved into her in a single thrust.

Sharp, stinging pain almost stole her breath as her mostly unprepared body accommodated his size, but it was the most perfect of pain. It reminded her that she belonged to this man who would always prioritize her needs and wants above his own. Dragon might think that between his DNA, the way he was raised, and the experiments done on him, he no longer possessed the ability to care for others, but at every turn he showed how wrong he had been about himself.

"Say you're mine, little rabbit," he ordered as he held her hips tighter, pumping in and out of her with a brutal speed that was going to make her sore and bruised tomorrow.

Just the way she wanted. That way, the memories of their game would seep deep inside her, eradicating anything else, including her own insecurities and doubts.

"Say it," Dragon commanded, and the tone of his voice had her internal muscles begin to flutter as an orgasm tore toward her.

"Yours," she cried out as the next thrust brushed against that amazing spot inside her.

"Forever."

"Forever," she quickly agreed.

With a roar, Dragon came, emptying himself inside her and marking her in a different way. The combination of his weight against her back, his tight grip on her hips, and his pleasure set off her own release, and she screamed out Dragon's name into the otherwise quiet forest.

When she finally floated back down from her high, she was lying limp and spent against the cold ground, Dragon's body settled against hers. His nose was at her neck, nuzzling her, and she knew he was inhaling her scent and committing it to memory so he didn't forget this moment.

Knowing that with his declaration of possession and promise of forever that they had a lifetime to go of moments just like this one, Cassandra gave a contented sigh, and arched her hips up a little, taking Dragon, who was still inside her, deeper.

A mere week ago she was consumed by guilt, loneliness, and a sense that something was deeply wrong with her. Now she might be covered in cuts and bruises, had faced death several times over, but she couldn't be happier.

She'd found her new home, her place to belong and be accepted for who she was, and it was with the man touching a kiss to her neck, then scraping his teeth along her sensitive skin.

"Home," she murmured happily.

CHAPTER

Twenty-Three

January 10th
   5:39 P.M.

"Not yet," Cassandra whispered when he went to move.

"It's cold out," Dragon reminded her. And he had her coat tangled around her head and arms, plus her pants pulled down enough that he'd been able to bury himself inside her.

"Don't care," she murmured, her tone all content and sleepy. "Like feeling you against me."

Nuzzling her neck, he slid his arms beneath her body, lifting her slightly off the hard forest floor and pressing a little more of his weight on her. If he could keep her like this forever, safe and in his arms, then he would be more than happy to.

Even as his now softened length was still inside her, reality began to creep back in. His little rabbit wasn't safe. So long as the mystery woman and Dr. Gardner were out there, she never would be. They were all lucky they'd survived that explosion, but what happened next time?

As badly as he wanted to say there would never be a next time, he knew that the world was full of evil people. Once this threat was erased —and he refused to believe that they wouldn't wipe Ridge Gardner and everyone who worked with him off the face of the Earth—there was always the chance there could be another.

While his protective instincts screamed vehemently at him, he knew the best way to keep her safe wasn't to lock Cassandra away, wasn't to restrict her ability to live her life, wasn't even to stay glued to her side.

The best way to keep her safe was to train her.

"Starting tomorrow, I want you working out with the guys and me. Rose too," he announced.

"Working out with you? You have to know there is zero percent chance I can keep up with you guys."

"We'll work something out. But I want to work on your skills. Shooting, self-defense, using a knife, other weapons, I want you ready to face anything that might come your way. As badly as I want to lock you away from the rest of the world, I know I can't. I want you to be happy, free, and at peace, so I need to make sure that you are as trained as I can get you."

"Okay. And moving silently like you can do," she added.

Her ready agreement surprised him. Dragon had expected a little resistance. He knew that she'd killed to protect herself and her sister before, and her brothers had made sure she knew the basics, but at heart, Cassandra Charleston wasn't a fighter.

"Yeah?" he asked as he sat them both up and pulled out of her so he could turn her on his lap and tug her coat back down.

"Of course," she said when her green eyes met his. "We both know I'm never going to be able to match even what you could do before the drugs you were given, but I want to learn more. I want to feel more confident if I'm ever in a situation like I was yesterday. I want to help you in this fight, Dragon. I don't want to sit on the sidelines anymore and let other people fight my battles for me. This was your fight, but I became part of it when that woman approached me, I want to stand by your side until we win this war."

"And then?" He slipped a hand between her legs and found her swollen bundle of nerves.

Cassandra gasped as he pressed his thumb against the sensitive bud. "And then I want to stand at your side in a different way."

"Forever," he reminded her as he roughly worked her until she was panting and writhing against him.

"Forever," she agreed, just like she had before. Maybe it was wrong, but Dragon was pretty sure he was going to need to hear it a whole lot more before it finally sank in.

"Come," he ordered as he pressed hard against her bud, and she flew apart for him, his name falling from her lips as he drank in the sight of her face flushed with pleasure, eyes bright with arousal.

"Hmm, two orgasms should not wear me out that much," she said as she snuggled down to rest against him.

"Because your body is still recovering from yesterday," he reminded her as he brought his fingers, coated with her arousal, to his lips and licked them clean. After being knocked unconscious, drugged, and almost assaulted the day before, she should be resting today, but they'd already played this morning, and again now.

Fixing her clothes, Dragon stood with Cassandra in his arms and began to walk back to the house. With his girl snuggled safely against him, he felt almost normal for the first time in his entire life. All the things he thought about himself, all the reasons he never believed he would be safe enough to be this close to another person seemed to fly out the window when it came to this woman.

The right woman for him.

There was no one else who would give him the perfect mix of sweet, sunshiny, and light to counter the anger and darkness that had been born and bred inside him, and the outlet for that anger in the form of rough sex where he could take what he needed, secure in the knowledge that she was enjoying it too.

Cassandra Charleston was quite literally made for him.

"Dinner, bath, and bed," he told her as he walked up the porch steps.

"It's six o'clock," she reminded him with a giggle. "Way too early to go to bed."

"Not after yesterday." His tone brooked no arguments, because

Cassandra had already told him that as much as she loved pain and roughness when it came to sex, she also loved aftercare, and this was part of taking care of his girl.

"And if I'm bad, will I get a punishment?" Her hand shifted between his legs, and she stroked him through his jeans. Didn't matter that he'd come only minutes ago, when it came to this woman, he was ready to go, anytime, anyplace.

"Ugh, I did not need to hear that," Lion muttered as Dragon carried Cassandra inside at the same time the other man was walking through the foyer. But he saw Lion's lips twitch and knew that his friend was happy for them and just teasing.

"Oops. Didn't see you there," Cassandra said, her cheeks, already pink from the cold and arousal, reddening even further.

"Maybe we need a new house rule. All couples must lock themselves in their room before engaging in any sexual activity or discussion, because I just walked in on Steel and Rose going at it in the kitchen," Lion said and gave an exaggerated shudder.

"Not on any counter or the table," Steel yelled out from nearby, making them all laugh.

"Living room now," Thunder called as he came streaking down the stairs, his enhanced speed making him look like a blur.

"What's up?" Voodoo asked as they all hurried to the main living room.

"Don't you guys have your phones on you?" Thunder asked, his own in his hand.

"Left mine in the kitchen," Steel said, a little sheepishly.

"Ditto," Rose added.

"Didn't take mine with me when I realized Cassandra was outside," he replied.

"Mine's charging," Lion said with a shrug.

"Got mine, and Blade just texted us all," Voodoo said as he pulled his own phone from his pocket and scanned a message.

"What did he say?" Steel asked, tone all business, even as he kept Rose tucked against his side, his hand absently stroking her arm.

"Said he's sure that the woman he followed is her," Thunder replied, also reading a message on his phone. "The one who contacted Cassandra."

"Here." Voodoo held out his phone to Cassandra, who glanced up at him before reaching out and taking it.

One glance at the picture and she nodded. "That's her. She's the one who warned me that Dr. Garnder had an antidote to undo what he did to you all so he could do it again and try to figure out why you all survived and none of the others did."

"She warned us, but then she tried to kill us," Lion said. "Makes no sense, but if she was there when the place exploded, she has to be the one who set the explosives. No other reason to do that than to wipe us all out. If she really wanted to save our lives, she could have warned us, or gotten us out before they went off."

"Why would she do that?" Cassandra asked, handing Voodoo his phone back.

"No idea," Dragon replied. But they were going to find out.

As though sensing what was about to happen but needing clarification, Cassandra leaned further into him. "What's Blade going to do?"

"Whatever it takes to get answers," he replied honestly.

"Torture her?"

"If that's what it takes," again he answered truthfully. They'd been in this place before, when she found out what they had planned for Rose, and he waited to see if her response would be the same. As far as he was concerned, this was different. Rose was an innocent, and he knew going after her had been wrong, even if it had all worked out okay. But this woman wasn't innocent, she was up to her neck in this, and whatever happened next was on her own shoulders, a consequence of her choices.

Looking around at all of them, Cassandra nodded slowly. "I still don't like it, but our family comes first. We have to protect each other, and I understand why Blade needs to do whatever he does."

Grasping her chin, Dragon tilted her head up and crushed his lips to hers, relief hitting him hard for everything Cassandra was offering with her acceptance. "Thank you."

Blade will do whatever it takes to get answers from his pretty captive in the third book in the action packed and emotionally charged Prey Security: Delta Team series!

Sinful Revenge (Prey Security: Delta Team #3)

Also by Jane Blythe

Detective Parker Bell Series

A SECRET TO THE GRAVE

WINTER WONDERLAND

DEAD OR ALIVE

LITTLE GIRL LOST

FORGOTTEN

Count to Ten Series

ONE

TWO

THREE

FOUR

FIVE

SIX

BURNING SECRETS

SEVEN

EIGHT

NINE

TEN

Broken Gems Series

CRACKED SAPPHIRE

CRUSHED RUBY

FRACTURED DIAMOND

SHATTERED AMETHYST

SPLINTERED EMERALD

SALVAGING MARIGOLD

River's End Rescues Series

SOME SAVIORS CAN BREAK YOU

SOME REGRETS ARE FOREVER

SOME FEARS CAN CONTROL YOU

SOME LIES WILL HAUNT YOU

SOME QUESTIONS HAVE NO ANSWERS

SOME TRUTH CAN BE DISTORTED

SOME TRUST CAN BE REBUILT

SOME MISTAKES ARE UNFORGIVABLE

Candella Sisters' Heroes Series

LITTLE DOLLS

LITTLE HEARTS

LITTLE BALLERINA

Storybook Murders Series

NURSERY RHYME KILLER

FAIRYTALE KILLER

FABLE KILLER

IVORY'S FIGHT

PEARL'S FIGHT

LACEY'S FIGHT

OPAL'S FIGHT

Prey Security: Bravo Team Series

VICIOUS SCARS

RUTHLESS SCARS

BRUTAL SCARS

CRUEL SCARS

BURIED SCARS

WICKED SCARS

Prey Security: Athena Team Series

FIGHTING FOR SCARLETT

FIGHTING FOR LUCY

FIGHTING FOR CASSIDY

FIGHTING FOR ELLA

Prey Security: Charlie Team Series

DECEPTIVE LIES

SHADOWED LIES

TACTICAL LIES

VENGEFUL LIES

CORRUPTED LIES

TRAITOROUS LIES

Prey Security: Cyber Team Series

RESCUING NATHANIEL

RESCUING TOBIAS

RESCUING MICAH

RESCUING JOSIAH

Prey Security: Delta Team Series

PERFECT REVENGE

FATEFUL REVENGE

SINFUL REVENGE

Christmas Romantic Suspense Series

THE DIAMOND STAR

CHRISTMAS HOSTAGE

CHRISTMAS CAPTIVE

CHRISTMAS VICTIM

YULETIDE PROTECTOR

YULETIDE GUARD

YULETIDE HERO

HOLIDAY GRIEF

HOLIDAY LOSS

HOLIDAY SORROW

Conquering Fear Series (Co-written with Amanda Siegrist)

DROWNING IN YOU

OUT OF THE DARKNESS

CLOSING IN

About the Author

USA Today bestselling author Jane Blythe writes action-packed romantic suspense and military romance featuring protective heroes and heroines who are survivors. One of Jane's most popular series includes Prey Security, part of Susan Stoker's OPERATION ALPHA world! Writing in that world alongside authors such as Janie Crouch and Riley Edwards has been a blast, and she looks forward to bringing more books to this genre, both within and outside of Stoker's world. When Jane isn't binge-reading she's counting down to Christmas and adding to her 200+ teddy bear collection!

To connect and keep up to date please visit any of the following

www.ingramcontent.com/pod-product-compliance
Lightning Source LLC
Chambersburg PA
CBHW050418260626
47156CB00003B/1055